Pilots
Die
Faster

C. W. Morton

Pilots Die Faster

St. Martin's Press
New York

A Thomas Dunne Book.
An imprint of St. Martin's Press.

Design by Ellen R. Sasahara

Library of Congress Cataloging-in-Publication Data

Morton, C. W.
     Pilots die faster   /   by C. W. Morton.—1st. ed.
          p.   cm.
     "A Thomas Dunne book."
     ISBN 0-312-15624-3 (hardcover)
     I. Title.
PS3563.O244P55 1997
813'.54—dc21   97-6271
                                          CIP

First Edition: July 1997

10 9 8 7 6 5 4 3 2 1

You write a book, you think that's the end of it. It's not. Meet the rest of the team:

George Wieser and Jake Elwell, the best agents in the world.

Neal Bascomb, overworked and underappreciated editor.

Tom Dunne, the publisher that believed.

Lisa Vecchione, production editor, and Heath Lynn Silberfeld, copy editor, who saved me from some silly mistakes and made the story stronger.

James Wang, for astounding cover art.

Harry Arnston and Digby Diehl, who taught me how to write and encouraged me.

Lynette Spratley and Virginia Parker, and the rest of the superb writers on the Prodigy Writing Techniques bulletin board.

Captain Bud Weeks, former Commanding Officer of USS *Jouett* (CG 29), who taught me what going to sea is all about.

Finally, my friends Ron Morton and Cyndy Mobley, and all the other sailors that have been and will go into harm's way.

Pilots
Die
Faster

PILOTS DIE when they run out of luck and air space at the same time. Stalled engines, hydraulic failure, frozen ailerons, or the ass end of the aircraft carrier coming through the canopy are occupational hazards, but all are survivable when luck runs hot, true, and righteous. When it doesn't, the aircrew dies fast and young. A last, frustrated "Oh, shit" echoing on the airwaves says it all.

I knelt down beside the body and touched the wet flight suit. One second I saw a pilot in a flight suit, the next a young woman. The first you expect might die young. In a righteous world, the other never would.

When a pilot buys it, there's usually damned little evidence of what went wrong first. Carrier-based aircraft aren't equipped with a telltale black box in-flight recorder. The sea hides crumpled airframes and bodies under fathoms of black water, rotting both metal and flesh with corrosive salt water and crushing pressure. Unless the pilot and crew eject before cold sea water on incandescent engines causes an explosion, there aren't any bodies to recover.

One exception. Big exception. Three hundred aviators who'd experienced some form of luck failure over small, nasty Eastern Asian countries. The largest collection of surviving crash victims in captivity, each in his own individual display cage. We would have called the *Guinness Book of Records,* but the phone service in the Hanoi Hilton was damned unreliable.

I only spent two years there, and I still hadn't decided whether that was the result of some residual bit of pilot luck or not. Many of the men in our small community were there longer than I was. But if my luck really was holding, why was I there at all? Ten more miles, and I would have been back over the ocean. A few hours in the water, maybe, then the helo would have pulled me out.

Lots of sharks in those waters, though. Who's to know if I would have survived the ejection only to get eaten by one? So maybe ending up as a POW *was* lucky, compared to getting eaten by a shark.

This case wasn't as hard to decide. The body was stretched out on a narrow metal crosswalk. Her flight suit was ripped in seven places, exposing ragged-edged gashes in her skin. Seeping blood barely darkened the wet fabric. Water beaded on her pale face and black smudges ringed her eyes from either mascara—I doubted it—or lack of sleep and trauma.

Sailors two decks above me leaned on the shaky guardrails and peered down through the lattices of iron grating. Walkways crisscrossed the entire engineering compartment, snaking at acute angles between massive machinery and pumps. Steam leaks and heat from the pumps brought the air temperature up to well over 95 degrees, with humidity about the same.

Alive, before political correctness became the watchword in the Navy, Gina Worthington would have been called a babe. Her sandy brown hair was cropped short to fit under her helmet, and she had deer eyes—huge, almost black, deeper than dark should be. The last time I'd seen her, her face had been lit with the unholy glee you see on a pilot's face when he's just wrestled his F-14 onto the deck in nasty weather.

She, I mean. *Her* F-14. Women'd been in the fighter squadrons for a year, but I still suffered from pronoun ambiguity.

Back when I was flying A-4 Skyhawks off aircraft carriers, it was strictly a men's club. We were all invulnerable in the air, arrogant on the ground, and irresistible to women. In the public spaces of the carrier, the squadron ready room, and on the flight deck we were godlike creatures who strapped aircraft on our asses and slipped the surly bonds of earth.

Even when we talked about the fear, it was with a hard smile, maybe a frown. But alone in our staterooms at night, sometimes it hit us.

Flying a two-seater aircraft was tougher than the single-seat Skyhawk in some ways. Those pilots had the responsibility for more than just their own lives. Then again, they also had someone else to talk to besides the ship on the cold, rainy approaches back to the carrier. Still, I'd always preferred the A-4 way of doing business, alone and unafraid, like the Hornet pilots today.

"How long ago?" I asked the flight surgeon.

Doc glanced up at me and then turned her gaze back to the body. She was crouched down on the other side of the body, one hand resting on Worthington's shoulder and the other splayed flat on the metal grating. Sweat beaded her upper lip, and her dark blue eyes had gone squinty. Female flight surgeons took as much getting used to as female fighter jocks. Annoy them, and they let their fingernails grow longer. Makes for a hell of an interesting flight physical.

"The roving patrol found her maybe ten minutes ago, floating face down in the bilges. He pulled her out and called the corpsman, who called me. I just got here," she said.

"How long ago did she die?" It was the same question, and Doc knew it.

"I can't tell for sure."

"Guess."

"No. There are complicating factors, Bud," she said. "I'm sure you can understand, under the circumstances."

Yeah. A hotshot female F-14 pilot murdered on the ship. Lieutenant Worthington had been the most senior of her peculiar breed, and a lot of people were going to be interested in those stab wounds.

Doc sighed and touched Worthington's face, smoothing the damp hair back. She leaned over to examine a gash on the pilot's forehead. "The autopsy's not going to be the worst part," she said, not looking up.

"It's a murder, Carol," I said, trying to be gentle. "You expect to lose some in the air. It's part of the deal. This breaks the rules. We should be discussing an aircraft fatality mishap board, not a homicide investigation."

Doc's eyes went shiny, and her mouth twitched down at the corners. "I hate what's coming. I work for Captain Charles, and he works for Admiral Fairchild," she said finally.

"I don't."

"I know."

"And that's a problem right now," I said. "For you. Not for her anymore."

She nodded. I tried to feel sympathy for Doc's difficult political position. She knew I had jurisdiction over the murder, just as she knew it was more than a murder. Worthington's death could end several promising careers, starting with the Admiral's. I glanced down at the dead, battered pilot again. Sympathy for the living was slow in coming.

"Rigor mortis? Lividity? Those aren't exactly classified details." I touched the zipper on Worthington's flight suit. "If you turn around for a couple of minutes, I can puzzle it out myself."

Doc Benning clamped her hand over mine and glanced at the herd of engineers and machinist mates clustered fifteen feet away. I could feel her fingers trembling just a little. I gently removed her hand. She winced a little, looked away.

"No rigor mortis," she said. "But she was floating in the water. You know what that means."

"Engineering getting sloppy?" I glanced down at the bilges. Dark, oil-slicked water eddied gently under the grating. A lot of water, even for a big ship like an aircraft carrier.

"You'd have to ask them." She jerked her head toward the engineers, who had given up trying to pretend they were working and had settled for just staring.

I reached down and dipped my hand in the water. "Cold. Looks like about ten inches down there."

"Wouldn't be warm. Not this far below the waterline."

She was right. Nature's most efficient heat sink was only a few inches away from my hand. "Any idea why there's so much water?"

"No. The machinist's mate said something about it. I didn't

catch the details." They'd probably told her in excruciating detail the source of the water, as well as the intricacies of the engineering malfunction that'd caused it. Too much detail for someone who could name every nerve in the human body to worry about.

"I count seven wounds. That about right?"

She nodded. I removed my hand from the zipper as a reward.

"Anything else I ought to know about?"

She shook her head.

"I'll take some pictures, check out the area. Then you can move her. Tox screens. Full postmortem," I said.

"You'll have to ask the Admiral about that."

"It wasn't a question."

She shook her head, unwilling to acknowledge the inevitable. I stood up and felt my knees crack. Doc Benning stood as well. She moved closer to me and spoke directly into my left ear.

"Bud? How well did you know her?" Doc asked.

"I knew her."

"She was the first, you know," Doc said, looking away. "*Our* first. I've lost pilots before and it's not that the others don't matter. It's never easy. But this one—it's a different hurt."

"I've lost them too, Carol. And I knew her well enough to care that it's her. That enough?"

She nodded, a clipped bob of her head. "It will be. Tomorrow, if not right now."

"You're the closest thing I've got to a forensics expert right now. Can you do the honors?" I gestured vaguely back toward Worthington's body.

To her credit, Doc Benning paled only slightly. For her, that was a strong reaction. As the chief pathologist onboard *Lincoln,* she'd seen a lot more dead bodies than I had. Still, it had to be different when it was someone you knew. One of your own.

She moved away and started giving curt instructions to the corpsmen. Two of them left hurriedly on some errand. Doc Benning sat down on the grate next to Worthington's body to wait.

I had my own tasks to finish. I gathered the Masters-at-Arms around me and explained what we were going to do. They looked at me doubtfully. "Wouldn't it be easier to just have the engineers drain the bilges?" Chief Barker asked.

"Good point, but do you know how coarse the filters are in the system?" I asked.

He considered the question for a moment. "Not fine enough, I guess," he concluded reluctantly. "Something could get through—something we might want to look at."

I nodded. "I saw the ESWS insignia on your shirt," I said. The ESWS—Enlisted Surface Warfare Specialist—told me that he knew more about the guts and machinery on this ship than most sailors. While as a Master-at-Arms his primary job was serving as an onboard cop, the ESWS qualification was a grueling process that paid no attention to traditional rating fields.

"So we go diving," I said. Resignation settled on their faces.

I set the example, lowering myself stiffly onto the grating and dangling my feet over the edge. I was wearing boots, Navy-issue type, and the water lapped up to the first shoelace. There was no point in waiting. I shifted my weight to my hands, and lowered myself carefully down into the bilges.

Standing on the bottom of the hull, the metal catwalk came up to my chest. The water swirled around my knees, thick, oily, and black. I tapped around on the bottom carefully, wary of the myriad fuel lines and other pipes that ran along the bottom of the compartment. Satisfied that the area around me was clear of obstructions, I squatted down, letting the water come up almost to my shoulders, and started feeling around on the deck.

Above me, the Chief MAA quickly outlined a sector search and put the rest of the team to work. Within moments, we were all chest high in dirty water, groping around on the hull.

Only a few inches of steel hull separated my hands from the dark, black water below the ship. The metal pulsed and throbbed under my fingertips, an acoustic sump for every piece of machinery that rotated, rattled, or vibrated on the ship. The strongest pulse came from the propeller shafts, a gentle, insistent beat, fuzzy at the edges as other sounds modulated its fundamental frequency. A healthy sound—the voice of a ship that could take you into harm's way and get you back out in one piece.

While the Chief didn't know it, I was probably almost as familiar with engineering as he was. Not by choice.

During our two years in the Hanoi Hilton, we'd resorted to a lot of tactics to stay sane. One of those was teaching each other everything we knew about some abstract subject we knew well. For me, that meant lecturing other POWs via tap code on the joys of flying and the outer limits of the Skyhawk performance envelope.

Brinker McCauley had been a naval engineer by training, a graduate of the California Maritime Institute. After listening to me for hours rhapsodizing over the sheer joy of flying, Brinker would take his revenge with a lecture on shipboard engineering. By the time we were released, he could recite the Skyhawk stall parameters from memory and I could trace the path of a drop of water through an engineering plant. Brinker had always claimed he could tell his own ship's speed from touching the bulkheads in engineering.

Back then, I thought the information might come in handy someday, maybe give me a head start on qualifying for command of an aircraft carrier. Brinker and I both thought we still had careers in the Navy. When I returned to the States, I found out just how wrong I was. The Navy thanked me, made me into a hero, and moved me quietly out of the mainstream of tactical aviation and into a support job.

Now, feeling the steel and ooze slide through my fingers, I could almost hear the delicate tap-tap of Brinker's fingers on the wall. And, even though I'd never spent much time in shipboard engineering plants, I figured I could damned well build one from memory.

Thirty minutes later, we concluded the search. No convenient murder weapon, no wallet complete with driver's license dropped in the bilges, and no clues. We did turn up a number of soiled rags, paper cups, three screwdrivers, and two used condoms. At least I thought they'd been used—it made me wonder.

By the time we'd finished, Doc Benning had had a privacy screen erected around Worthington's body. With the help of a corpsman, she'd made a preliminary examination and was just zipping up Worthington's flight suit when we finished.

She stood, put her hands at the small of her back, and leaned backward slightly to work out a muscle cramp. "The gross examination reveals nothing particularly enlightening. At this point, I'd call the cause of death heart failure due to loss of blood as a result of the seven wounds to the body." Her voice was cool and professional.

I nodded, not sure what to say. I settled for "Thank you."

"I can move her now?"

I nodded again.

I finished a preliminary examination of the scene and then let the Masters-at-Arms, or MAAs, secure the area. The *Lincoln* had four power plants. Having immediate access to every square inch of this particular engineering space wasn't critical, and the snipes who owned the spaces would just have to live with a few detours. The corpsmen finally moved the body, strapping her into a metal Stryker frame and manhandling the iron-mesh transport basket up four decks to Medical. She'd wait there until I could get through to the Resident Office on SATCOM and make arrangements for her body to be airlifted back to Alameda Naval Hospital.

Lincoln isn't much different from any other aircraft carrier of her class. Roomier than the older *Ticonderoga* I used to fly off, with wider passageways. The overhead piping and electrical wires concealed behind acoustic tile. Utility conduits that couldn't be hidden were painted white to blend in with the bulkheads, except for certain critical functions. Fire-fighting pipes were painted red, and CHT a putrid gold. Fitting, since CHT tubes were the sewer system. You got used to the idea of walking down a passageway next to a sewer pipe, but it still made me a little nervous when I saw one overhead.

I followed the corpsmen up the ladders to Medical and made sure security arrangements were in place. While Navy medicine can be a rough and tumble affair, the corpsmen were peculiarly gentle with their burden. I'd seen them the same way with sailors fatally injured on the flight deck, and when we'd flown back from Vietnam on a C130 transport. It'd seemed strange then, unnervingly so. After years of never knowing when one will get one's face kicked in, kindness from a stranger felt damned dangerous. It'd taken most of us half the flying time back to the Philippines just to quit flinching.

Gina wouldn't have known about the Philippines. By the time she'd gotten to her first carrier, the new government there had ejected us from the Navy's finest liberty port in the world. We replaced the known dangers of the PI with new ones in Singapore and Hong Kong.

That caused problems. Before, we could count on the older sailors to brief the virgins on what bars were safe, which ones weren't, where they could get laid without getting rolled, and how to stay out of Shore Patrol's clutches.

I'd been assigned to the *Kitty Hawk* at the time, my first tour as an NCIS special agent. The Admiral tapped me to give security briefings on the new liberty ports to the squadrons. Gina Worthington had been at one of them, a Lieutenant nugget on her first deployment. I kept finding myself staring at her, the tone of my little "be safe ashore and don't get VD" lecture drifting into a lecture from an overprotective parent. She caught it and shot me a pointedly bored look.

We'd talked a couple of times after that, gradually melting the ice. Gina couldn't afford any signs of weakness in front of her peers, not with the women newly assigned to the squadrons and still proving themselves. I guess she thought I might understand. She was right. The North Vietnamese had done a good job of teaching me about human frailty.

While liberty ports and in-port engineering configurations might change, a few things were absolute constants onboard a ship. Even moored, one man had absolute authority over everyone and everything on his ship.

Everybody, that is, except me. While I was certain that the news had already reached him, there would be no substitute for a personal briefing from NCIS to the Admiral.

I hauled myself up another five decks to Flag Spaces, wondering whether I should have spent more time warning sailors about engineering instead of bars.

"THE TIMING SUCKS, Wilson." Rear Admiral Fairchild peered at me over his stubby glasses. The old-fashioned black-framed reading glasses went with his faded flight suit. "You don't know how bad it is."

As the Commander of Carrier Group Three, Fairchild rated the best accommodations on the ship. Ashore, his cabin would have qualified as a mediocre hotel suite. Memorabilia from prior commands plastered the walls, and the deck was carpeted in cheap shag.

I envied him the flight suit more than the cabin. Old ones get worn down to chamois softness by the ship's mangling laundry. His was covered with Velcro-backed "been there, done that" patches.

Velcro issued in a whole new era of naval aviation fashion. Finally, aviators didn't have to keep sanitized flight suits, ones with no patches or identifying insignia, for those nasty little high-probability kill missions. Put patches on for daily wear, take them off for the mission. Easy, with modern technology.

"We're going to have to run east to get back inside COD range," he continued. "It's not something I want to be doing right now."

"Worthington probably thought it fairly inconvenient, too," I answered.

"There's going to be a lot of attention on this one. I want this handled carefully but routinely. Whatever that means for a murder investigation."

"Murder's never routine."

"But dying is. You know that."

All Admirals ought to look like Admiral Fairchild. Like eagles temporarily grounded, on deck just long enough to eat what they killed.

His hair was darker than mine, shaded symmetrically at the temples with silver. Piercing dark eyes, solid jaw, perfect posture—the whole nine yards, majestic and deadly. Think of recruiting posters and you've got him.

I hadn't aged as gracefully. Random patches of gray sprouted out of scars on my head, and I had crow's-feet and lines in places the

Admiral didn't even have skin. My deep baby-blues with gold around the iris, the ones that used to be surefire pogie bait, had faded to dull icewater. Even worse, most of my aging had to do with joints and organs.

"Any leads?" he asked.

"I've got it narrowed down to five thousand sailors and Marines. Plus or minus two hundred contractors authorized access to the ship."

He sighed. "You're a lot of help."

"Admiral, it's been less than an hour since she was found. It's going to take a little longer to unravel it."

"How long?"

"Depends."

"You're a wordy bastard, you know that? If I didn't know you as well as I do, I'd have fired you months ago."

"You can't."

"I could try."

"But you won't. Because I'm so useful to the Admiral in keeping good order and discipline onboard the Admiral's ship. And off the ship, too."

The last time we were in Hong Kong, Admiral Fairchild hadn't listened to my liberty briefing. He'd made several critical errors in judgment. Too much wine, too little sleep, and a misunderstanding about the cultural mores of his favorite port of call. Hell being that senior and getting rolled instead of laid. Worse when you're tossed out of a very nice limousine in your skivvies minus your wallet and pants.

He could have resolved the problem himself, being an Admiral. But not quietly, not without his military ID card, and probably not without Shore Patrol finding out. He'd called me, and I'd managed to get him sprung from local custody without anyone else knowing about it.

In some men, that would have inspired gratitude. With Fairchild, it convinced him I'd use what I knew to keep my spot on his staff. Eight months had mitigated his paranoia to reflexive suspicion.

He frowned and leaned back in his high-backed chair. The black leatherette and chrome struts clashed with the flight suit and ancient glasses.

"Because of that," he admitted, surprising me slightly.

I tried to look please. "Didn't think you'd noticed."

"There's something about you that makes people cooperate, whether they want to or not. I don't like you, Wilson—but I think I need you. Especially now. This one has to be closed, and someone's got to take the fall for it. Before—"

"Before what?" I asked when he stopped.

His eyes flickered over toward a message on the side of his desk. I tried to read the subject line upside down. He caught that and slid a brown folder over it. "You're not cleared for this anymore."

"If it has any bearing on why someone would want to kill Lieutenant Worthington, I'm cleared for it."

"It doesn't. Trust me on this one." He put one hand on the folder, drummed his fingers lightly on it.

I stared at his hand, frustrated. For the last three weeks, *Lincoln* had been steaming in circles, running round-the-clock surveillance operations in the middle of the Pacific Ocean 1,500 miles from the nearest land. While tactical considerations were outside of my ken these days, it bothered me that I was no longer privy to everything that went on inside this giant gray office building we called home for six months out of the year.

An unworthy thought occurred to me. "A message from the summer promotion boards?" I asked, immediately regretting my perpetual tendency to engage mouth before brain.

His face turned colder than a metaphor we used to use back in the dark ages before women were assigned to the ship. "No. And fuck you," he said. "It has to do with why Third Fleet deployed the ready carrier—us, in case you've forgotten—last month on such short notice. And why we're cutting doughnuts in this part of the ocean. None of it's any of your business. You just have to find out who killed my pilot."

"She was your pilot, Admiral. Now she's mine."

He sighed. "Just find out who did it, Wilson. That's all. And do it fast."

2

I DIDN'T need the Admiral to tell me that the Worthington case was my top priority. Not only was it the most serious crime that had been committed aboard *Lincoln* during my tour there, but it hit me hard personally. On the way back to my office, I had the visceral feeling that around the next corner, somewhere on a ladder just above, I'd catch a glimpse of Gina Worthington. For a few seconds, I entertained the possibility that I was asleep, that I'd wake up in a few hours and know it was all a bad dream.

But it wasn't. And, regardless of how much it pissed me off, I had a few other cases to take care of as well.

The resident NCIS agent on a big ship has the same range of cases as any normal cop. Deaths, assaults, the occasional spicy hint of counterintelligence operations—all that and more, since some serious offenses in the military weren't even crimes in civilian life.

Like sex. I had two cases sitting on my desk right then that involved what the Navy delicately called "inappropriate contact" between young sailors. In my day, that would have meant homosexuality, still a crime in the Navy then. Today, it was more likely to be a couple of lusty eighteen-year-olds who couldn't keep their hands off each other.

I triaged my case folders, shoving aside everything that could wait for a couple of weeks. At least I optimistically hoped I could find the son of a bitch that had killed her in that short a time.

There were only two cases that really needed my attention, and those only because they involved safety of personnel. A delicate way of saying that I had snitches to protect.

The first case dealt with a small gang of Crips onboard the ship. Over the last five years, the gangs had infiltrated the Navy. Not nearly to the degree that they were evident in civilian society, but still enough to cause problems. The latest incident pitted them squarely against the other case folder on my desk—the white supremacists. Again, a tiny proportion of the population, probably no more than four or five people. Still, in the enclosed confines of a ship, even a large one like the carrier, aberrant groups like the neo-Nazis and the Crips could do more than make you uneasy walking down the street at night. They destroyed team unity and the instinctive trust every sailor had to feel in his shipmates.

According to my snitch, the neo-Nazis would be meeting later today to plan their next mission. That was what they called it, "a mission." As though it had anything in common with those honorable callings that the Navy traditionally refers to as missions.

My snitch was going to be there. I glanced at my watch—two hours. Since I'd already rigged electronic equipment in the space they would be meeting in, I had a little time.

I decided to track down Worthington's Commanding Officer. While he damned sure wouldn't know who killed her, it was a place to start.

"SOMETIMES I WISH they'd just recruit lesbians." Commander Henry Blues, Jazzman to his fellow aviators, glanced at the tape recorder. The reels still weren't moving. "I signed up to fly fighters, not become an expert on the Navy's day care policy."

He wore shipboard-wash khakis with his rank insignia on his collar, pilot's wings, and small command insignia gleaming against the soft, faded cotton shirt. Blonde hair, blue eyes, clean, sharp bones. His reputation as a pilot was golden, and he'd been selected early for his last two promotions. I thought I remembered what that felt like.

"And no, before you ask—I don't know why anyone would kill

her. Jesus, Wilson, no one in the squadron could have done it. She was one of ours, damn it!" He leaned back in his chair, and his face softened. "I'm going to call her parents on SATCOM. Today, at fourteen hundred."

"And the media after that."

"Screw them. Let the Admiral handle it. I don't give a shit about the reporters. They hounded her from the second she graduated from Basic at Pensacola and started the Tomcat pipeline. It wasn't any easier on her than it was on us. Not since Tailhook, anyway." He glanced up at me. "You ought to understand that."

I did. Back then, my organization had been called the Naval Investigative Service, or simply NIS. It'd been attached to, and part of, the military chain of command, with a Navy Admiral heading it up. Hadn't worked too well, but we'd made do with the foxes guarding the chickens.

During the Tailhook investigation, one of our agents had acted like an idiot with Lieutenant Coughlin, the victim. He'd asked her out, made lewd remarks, and generally made a fool of himself. And us.

The press had a field day with NIS. Congress finally took action. We no longer reported to admirals but to the civilian Secretary of the Navy. He changed the name to the Naval Criminal Investigative Service, brought in a team of professional, retired Secret Service agents, and turned us into a real law-enforcement agency.

Not everyone in the Navy was happy about that. Especially not the commands we worked with. Their old Academy roommates were no longer our bosses, and investigations and prosecutions got a hell of a lot tougher to influence.

"Tailhook changed a lot of things for a lot of people. Lieutenant Worthington was one of them," I said.

"And look where it got her. Don't get me wrong. She was a damned fine pilot. I'd fly with her any day. And, for the record, I fully support the Navy's integration of women into combat squadrons."

I reached over and tapped the tape recorder. "It's still off, Skipper."

"I know, I know. But you never know. This whole gender thing— see? I'm even trained to say gender instead of sex. Damn. First the Soviet Union breaks up, then we get women on the combatants." Something that looked like a mixture of anger and nostalgia crossed his face. I wasn't sure which bothered him more.

"Co-ed's not working?" I asked.

"I didn't say that. Maybe it is, maybe it isn't."

"I see all the incident reports, remember?"

"Yeah. There've been a few fraternization problems, I know. Not to mention the whole pregnancy thing."

"How about Lieutenant Worthington? Any problems with her in those categories?"

The tape recorder bothered him. He looked at it again. I picked it up and slid it into my drawer. Thumbed it on in the process. He relaxed.

"I don't know. I don't think so—I never heard anything," he said.

"Would you?"

"What do you think?"

"I think if I were in command, I'd know. One way or another, I would," I said. It wasn't as much opinion as clear, cold certainty.

Jazzman's eyes finally met mine. He was looking for something. I tried to look like I had whatever amorphous quality it was he wanted.

"You never know. She was a damned good-looking woman. She could have been sleeping with someone in the squadron. If she was, she was discreet," Jazzman said finally.

"Who would be your first guess?"

He stared at me for a moment longer, then looked away. The distance between us couldn't be measured in feet anymore.

"You were one of us," he said. "Tell me, what would you have done if someone had asked you that about one of your pilots?"

"Same thing you're doing, probably. Dance around the questions, send someone down to clear out her personal safe before anyone else could get into it. I leave anything out?"

He shook his head, not denying it but protesting the statement.

"You have our full cooperation, Special Agent Wilson."

"I've got more than that, Commander. I've got a Master-at-Arms in her stateroom preserving evidence. Your XO's probably looking for you right now to tell you BM1 Fullworth won't let him in her safe."

"And you were in command of a tactical squadron," he said softly. "Jesus, I hope I don't have that short a memory." Anger flashed across his face. "You do what you have to, Wilson. And so will I."

"Sometimes a short memory is a blessing," I said.

FOUR HOURS LATER, I started remembering how much power a Commanding Officer had. Jazzman had been busy since we'd talked.

A wonderful job of detecting, I told myself. Truly superlative results. I could not remember a time since I'd joined NCIS that I'd managed to so skillfully ensure that almost everyone who knew the victim would bullshit me. The squadron had closed ranks on the outsider.

I walked forward along the 0-3 starboard passageway that ran the entire length of the ship. Up here in flag country, the bulkheads were freshly painted. Marines buffed the dark-blue deck tile to a high gloss every morning.

My office was down two knee-torturing ladders, on the 0-1 level. Not as spiffy a neighborhood. Even worse, my office was in the forward part of the ship. In rough weather, the deck pitched and pencils rolled off my desk.

A bottle of generic military ibuprofen was calling my name. Bad case, bad leg. The latter I could usually live with. The Vietnamese had always been better at breaking bones than setting them.

I took out my small green wheelbook and stared at the notes. Lieutenant Worthington, according to every officer I'd talked to, had been a fine upstanding pilot. Skilled in every way, a perfect shipmate. Inspirational leader, strong on motivating her troops. I felt like I was reading her last fitness report. It told me only one thing—that their skipper had gotten to the people who knew her before I could.

I tossed the notebook aside and took out the press release the squadron Public Affairs Officer had given me. It contained the usual bio information, followed by her assignments so far. A short list, one that wouldn't get any longer.

I looked at the release again. Unlike the Air Force, the Navy assigned its pilots and flight officers to real billets along with their flying duties. Lieutenant Worthington had been the Avionics/Weapons Division Officer, an assignment she'd picked up just the week before she was killed. Since each squadron division is composed of several smaller workcenters called branches, AVWEAPS DIVO usually went to a senior lieutenant, one who'd done more than one Fleet tour. For a relatively junior Fleet officer like Lieutenant Worthington, it would have been a plum—and a tough assignment. I wondered what she'd done to rate it.

And hoped she'd done more to deserve that than she had to deserve winding up dead in the bilges of an aircraft carrier.

3

THE NEO-NAZIS started without me. By the time I made it back to my office, picked up the gear I needed, and headed back down toward the auxiliary machinery spaces they were supposed to be meeting in, it was fifteen minutes past the appointed hour. I swore quietly, knowing there was no way I could make it to my covert surveillance point without getting spotted.

I glanced up and down the passageway, looking for an observation point. Next to the hatch leading to the machinery spaces was one of the ubiquitous communal heads—bathrooms, in civilian lingo. It looked like it shared a common wall with the compartment I was interested in. I turned the knob, shoved the door open, and walked in.

A honeycomb of urinals and stalls took up the bulkhead to my right. They all looked to be unoccupied. I walked over to the wall, examining it for any way of gaining access to the next compartment over. No such luck. About what I'd expected from a watertight compartment, anyway.

I sat down on one of the toilets for a moment, and tried to decide whether I had enough evidence to break the meeting up immediately and charge them.

I didn't. My sole snitch was a scared young sailor who would undoubtedly recant every bit of his statement at the slightest intimidation. The most I could hope for at this point was maybe one tiny building block in an eventual case, my own personal observation of the four suspects meeting in out-of-the-way places.

I sighed, flushed the toilet in case anyone was listening, and headed out of the bathroom. Give it some time, develop some more leads, and do the basic, methodical sort of solid investigation that they'd taught us in school. Build a case the right way, and don't even think of talking to the suspects until you've got them nailed cold and hard to the wall.

Just as I stepped out into the passageway, I saw a figure leaving the engineering compartment. One of my suspects.

"Hey!" I shouted, throwing my carefully laid plan of surveillance out the window. "Hey, asshole."

The figure took off running. I gave chase, against my better judgment. He hadn't even bothered to look back, so all I knew was that he was white, had short, dark hair, and stood a little bit shorter than I did.

And he was fast. Jesus, was he fast.

Normal shipboard reflexes made the other sailors in the passageway crowd up against the bulkhead, moving out of our path. My guy darted down the passageway, leaping kneeknockers and obstructions with the ease of a triathlon winner. I followed, careening off the occasional bulkhead, slowing down at the kneeknockers.

He cut hard to the left, heading down a cross passageway. I swore, followed, and wished I'd gotten close enough to see the stencil over his left rear pocket.

I seemed to be moving in slow motion, barely moving faster than a walk. By the time I got to the intersection of the two corridors, my quarry was long out of sight.

I knew at the other end of the fore and aft passageway was the enlisted dining facility, what we used to call the mess decks back in the days before we grew a kinder, gentler Navy. Once he made it there, he'd quickly be lost in a sea of blue chambray shirts, dungarees, and short haircuts. He'd look like any other sailor queued up and trying to decide between veal and stir-fry. All sailors look alike when they're hungry.

Except for the women, I amended. That much I was relatively certain about—it was a male, all right.

I leaned against the wall, trying to catch my breath, wondering just who in the hell I thought I was.

Another thought occurred to me. I'd made the assumption that he'd been the last one out of the machinery space. But what if he hadn't? A stupid move, I decided, chasing someone who might be no more than a snipe with a serious paranoia complex without even bothering to check and see if there was anyone else left in the space.

"Are you okay, sir?" a sailor asked. "I can call a corpsman, if you want." He looked me up and down doubtfully, as though wondering whether I'd last long enough for that.

"Fine, thanks," I muttered. I shoved myself away from the wall. At least I'd had the foresight to plant a tape recorder in the light fixture of their meeting room.

I walked slowly back down to the compartment and shoved the hatch open. No one home. Big surprise. I pulled over a chair, climbed up, and felt around for the tape recorder.

It was gone. What, they were getting smart enough to check for that kind of stuff? That worried me a little. I didn't have any real fancy gear onboard. Anything more exotic than a voice-activated recorder, I'd have to request from the Regional Office.

If I couldn't do any better than this against a gang of punks, the prospect of solving Worthington's case within the next two weeks looked doubtful. Maybe the next person on my list would have a little more insight into her than Jazzman had. The Maintenance Officer, her immediate supervisor.

I FINALLY CAUGHT up with Commander William Burroughs at Maintenance Control, the cubbyhole jammed with multipart Maintenance Action Forms (MAFs), flip boards, and grease-penciled status boards. A Senior Chief Petty Officer sat behind the battered Navy desk scowling at a stack of yellow MAFs clutched in a junior technician's hand.

Commander Burroughs was the Maintenance Officer for VF-95,

the F-14 Black Knights squadron. I'd never met him, but one look at him told me enough to know he'd be a pain in the ass. Imagine Napoleon's runt brother just getting over adolescent acne. Add big ears and a little power in his own corner of the world. Europe wasn't in any danger from him, but I suspected his Maintenance Department would know how the French aristocrats had felt.

He was on the telephone, his hand partially covering the handset as he whispered urgently into the mouthpiece. He glanced up at me, frowned, and pretended not to have seen me.

The Senior Chief broke off swearing long enough to look up at me. He put his hands flat on the desk, a pro forma preliminary to standing up that took the place of actual movement. "Help you?" he asked.

I pointed at the maintenance officer.

"MO be with you in a minute." He thought for a second, then added, "Sir."

I nodded. Tough to know exactly where I fit into the pecking order of the ship. The Senior Chief had made the safety plays. I didn't eat in the Chief's Mess, so I had to be the civilian equivalent of either junior or senior to him. Since I was looking for the MO, probably the latter, I rated a "sir," at least until he saw how the MO treated me.

The Senior Chief tapped the MO lightly on the elbow and pointed at me. The MO acknowledged it with a brief bob of his head and then returned to ignoring me. The Senior Chief took that as a cue and ignored me as well.

I was supposed to be impressed with how busy he was. It wasn't working.

I'd done my junior officer tours in the Maintenance Department of an A-4 squadron, and I could gauge exactly how busy both of them were. Glancing at the status board, I saw the maintenance schedule was busy but hardly impossible.

I leaned again the enameled wall, painted hard shiny white. Dried splatters of coffee and black scuffs marred the lower part of the wall, evidence of the thousands of bodies that trod down these narrow passageways each day. Too little sleep and too heavy loads made sailors clumsy. White paint never lasted long in its pristine condition, but it was better for morale than the puke-green alternative.

The MO finished his semiwhispered conversation and replaced the handset with a little more force than was really necessary. I hadn't found that telephones tended to come unseated quickly. He flipped through a couple of the charts on the wall, discussed an engine change-out with the Senior Chief, and then deigned to acknowledge my presence.

"You're Wilson," he said abruptly.

"Jazzman filled you in, I take it?" I wasn't certain that that was who he'd been talking to, but his expression confirmed my suspicions.

"The *Captain* told me you would want to talk to me, yes," he said. The Senior Chief glanced at the MO, then back at me. Pecking order incongruity. I felt free to refer to his skipper by his call sign, and the MO was taking offense. Wardroom business, and too complicated for him to bother with. I saw the Senior Chief give a mental shrug as he returned to scowling at the enlisted technician.

"Got a few minutes to chat?" I asked.

The MO sighed heavily and glanced at his watch. "Will this take long?"

"Faster we get started, the faster we're done."

"My office. But I'll warn you—we're busy today."

I followed him forward, through the Dirty Shirt Mess, and into the honeycomb of offices crammed into the ship between the mess and the forecastle. His office was slightly smaller than mine and ten frames forward.

Small is relative on an aircraft carrier. Imagine packing an entire town of five thousand people, with all the administrative, supply, and infrastructure services, into an eighteen-story building. Then add five acres of airfield, 85,000 tons of aviation fuel, over one hundred aircraft, a hangar, and 2,520 tons of ordnance to the same building. Pack it all into a hull 1,101 feet long and 133 feet wide. Space for the actual human bodies gets tight.

The MO gestured abruptly at a battered chair in front of his desk. His own chair looked slightly less comfortable than the Admiral's, but not by much. In the narrow confines of the ship, status symbols are what they are. It wasn't like he could insist on a window office.

"This is about Lieutenant Worthington, I assume," he said, settling back into the chair. "Naturally. The memos on pilferage I've sent you never warranted personal attention. Ten seven-day clocks missing in the last month, five sets of—" He finally noticed the look on my face. "Tragic—Worthington, I mean." He folded his hands across his stomach and waited.

"She worked for you," I said, reining in the impulse to reach across the desk and throttle him.

"As much as any of the pilots work for me," he answered. "Their maintenance jobs aren't their top priority. They're more interested in flying them than fixing them."

"How about Lieutenant Worthington?"

"About like the others. She did a decent-enough job, but her Division Chief did most of the real work."

"I notice she was a Division Officer, not a Branch Officer. Wasn't she relatively junior for that billet?"

He shrugged. "Maybe."

"Why was she in the billet, then?"

"Ask the Captain. He tells me who I get for a billet."

"He ask your advice?"

"Sometimes."

"Not often, though?"

"Often enough."

I'd had easier conversations with airplanes. "You know, I've been thinking about a career change," I said casually. "Maybe you can give me some advice. Be a reference for me, even."

"Pardon?"

"I figure I'll quit NCIS and go into dentistry. By the time I finish talking to you, I oughta be fairly good at pulling teeth. Whaddya think? This has been fairly painless so far, hasn't it?"

"I don't know what—"

"Oh, come on. You know what I'm talking about. Every one of

you is backing and filling so fast that it's a miracle this boat is still floating."

"Listen, I don't have to take this from a damned sand crab! It's bad enough—"

"—to take it from the pilots," I finished for him. "You started off in the pipeline, didn't you?"

He nodded, barely moving his head.

"And just what accident of nature or act of God washed you out?" For a moment, I thought he might not answer. To ask a man why he washed out of pilot training was considered the height of rudeness. If he hadn't irritated me so much, I wouldn't have.

Not that I needed an answer from him. I had access to every service record on the boat. Furthermore, the reasons for failure are rarely hushed up. It's common knowledge, a community thing. Pilots want to know whether the care and feeding of their birds is entrusted to a maintenance officer who can't fly or has a physical weakness. Wing envy—an ugly personality disorder, incurable and chronic.

"Vertigo," he said finally. "Inner ear problems. Didn't show up in primary. I was already at the A-6 RAG before I found out."

"So high-G ops make you dizzy. Why didn't you go fixed wing?"

He shot me a bitter look. "Like P-3s or transport? Right."

For a man socialized into tactical air, flying one of the land-based aircraft was a serious loss of status. It meant propeller aircraft instead of jets or hauling cargo instead of strapping weapons onto the wing. In the hierarchy of naval aviation, even the lowly carrier-based helicopters ranked above them.

Fallen angels, we called them. Men who started out as pilots and couldn't hack it for some reason. If it showed up late enough in the pipeline, sometimes they were transitioned to fixed-wing shore aircraft. Most of them either resigned their commissions, transferred to surface warfare, or went into the Aviation Maintenance career path.

Personally, I'd always thought resigning was preferable. Being around aircraft all day, fixing them and watching them launch, knowing you would never take to the air again made men bitter.

Going into the Surface Warfare Officer—SWO—pipeline wasn't much better for them. They eat their young. Your first tour on a ship was likely to include a couple of shotgun blasts to the face, public castrations, and generalized suffering at the hands of the senior SWOs. Instead of night-formation flights at Mach 1 so close to another aircraft you could touch it, screaming through heavy night air under stars so close they almost hurt your eyes, you experience the sheer thrill of being within two miles of another ship at speeds of up to thirty knots.

As the saying went, no one ever flunked out of the surface pipeline and got sent to pilot training.

So the MO had been one of those who chose Aviation Maintenance. That told me one thing about the man—he was willing to settle for second best.

"None of your business anyway," the MO said finally. "Has nothing to do with Worthington."

I nodded. "Many things aren't my business. I still ask the questions."

"Look, you want to know how she was as a Division Officer? She was OK. You want to trace out my career path? Then go bother someone else. I got work to do." He shoved himself back from the desk and made those small preparatory motions that small men make when they're trying to look powerful.

"Maybe it was her degree," I suggested, not moving from where I was planted.

"What?"

"Her undergraduate degree." I waved the Public Affairs bio sheet at him. "Aeronautical engineering, from University of California at San Diego. Must have given her a leg up on the competition, at least as far as understanding aviation maintenance goes."

"We don't design aircraft, we fix them. The Division Officers are more concerned with bailing sailors out of jail than laminar flow theories."

"Sounds like that's something you know a little about."

"Same degree, different university. That's why I know an AE degree has damned little to do with a squadron."

"Bet that was news to you. Four years of engineering, only to find out it doesn't really matter."

He stared at me coldly. "It's a different situation for me, mister. In my career path, we deal with things like that."

"Just not the flying part. Like kissing your sister. Always the bridesmaid, never the bride."

The temperature in the room plummeted.

"I think I'm through answering your questions, mister," he said, shoving his chair back from the desk. "If there's anything else you need to know, put it in a memo."

I stood up as he came around the desk, which was jammed against the wall next to the door. To reach the hatch, he had to either shove me out of the way or edge past me. Given the disparities in our sizes, the former wasn't an option. Not unless he expected the bow wave generated in front of him by his own elevated sense of importance to shove me.

"Move," he said finally. I revised my initial opinion of him. Usually short guys don't have the balls to make demands on me. I gave up, moved out of his way, and followed him out of his office. He locked the door behind him.

ALONE IN MY office, I tried to summon up a sense of regret over the interview with the MO. Didn't have much luck. Since he didn't know that I'd been in carrier aviation myself, he couldn't have realized that I could read the subtext behind his answers.

Fallen-angel syndrome, certainly. There was more to it than that, though. It was the women.

It must have eaten at him, seeing all those sweet young things swaggering up and down the passageways like pilots do. I'd seen them—they'd picked up the culture and mannerisms so fast that I sometimes wondered how long it would be until they started bragging about their dicks. Certainly, they'd have known the MO had bilged out of the flight program.

Would some sweet little feminine character trait have made them go easy on him? Some instinct for mothering the crippled and less fortunate?

Not a chance. Male or female, the kind of person who succeeds in carrier aviation isn't noted as a caring nurturer. They're competitors, the kind of only-child-captain-of-the-team individuals who play for one reason—to win.

It's not that the system raises them like that, but it does select them out. You figure that to make it into even the basic training program, the prospective pilot has to have good eyesight, meet some tough mental and physical requirements, and have the kind of temperament that thinks going Mach 2 in a steel tube sounds like a damned good definition of fun. Take that basic population and put them under the tender care of United States Marine Corps sergeants for sixteen weeks of Aviation Officer Candidate School. Surviving their gentle ministrations alone weeds out the 20 percent of nonhackers.

Then toss them into an intensive basic flight training program on a generic training aircraft. Tell them that they can pick which airplane they'll fly after Basic based on their class standing. Give them airplanes, instructors, classroom lessons, and ground school. Stir briskly, and wait to see which ones float to the top.

Cream rises. So do fighter pilots.

So if the young ladies now manhandling those Tomcats in the air were just a trifle bit arrogant, a little bit aggressive, and tended to stomp nonaviators like the MO into the ground like dead cats, it wasn't particularly surprising. We didn't make them that way— they came prepackaged.

If I read him right, the MO was more than a little put out. Lots, maybe. Bad enough to suffer at the hands of pilots, but from female pilots—for a short guy, there's nothing like a little humiliation from the opposite sex to bring Napoleon out of the closet.

How bad had it been? Bad enough that he'd taken a knife to a female pilot?

It was a long reach from wing envy to murder. The practical problems were considerable as well. How would he have talked her into meeting him down in the engineering plant? Or, if she hadn't been killed there—which the lividity pattern seemed to support anyway—how did a strapping 120-pound shrimp like the MO lug a woman the size of Gina Worthington down into the bilges? And wouldn't somebody have noticed him dragging her body around the ship? It would have been a tad conspicuous, even for a carrier in port in the Philippines.

I had my own prejudices about believing another officer could be a murderer. Strange preconception about men and women whose jobs basically involve killing people and machines in the air and on the ground, but there it was. It was one thing to blow some gomers to hell and back in ground-attack mode or to snake through the sky trying to get killing position on another aircraft—another entirely to kill one of your own.

For two years I'd lived in the tightest community of men that ever existed. We were in individual cells, but we found ways to communicate. Tap code, messages scratched on bark, tiny notations hidden in the toilet paper—when there was any. We'd done almost anything, risk our own death, just to make contact with another POW. The bonds there were the only things that kept me alive sometimes. To kill another officer—no, that was the job of the Vietnamese. Murdering your own went beyond criminal and into sacrilege.

Maybe that's why I joined NCIS after I retired from the Navy. Less a job than a conviction. More a lifestyle choice than a job.

The MO had made his choices, just like I'd made mine. Somehow, I thought mine might be easier to live with.

4

A FTER INTERVIEWING Lieutenant Worthington's boss and peers, I still had no clearer picture of her than I'd had before. My own recollections of her in the passageways, the times I'd run into her coming on or off the ship, and those few peculiarly intimate conversations I'd had with her many years ago were more vivid than the words of the men and women she saw every day.

Aviators understand about death. Every one of us lost classmates in the training pipeline and on cruise. If you're going to keep climbing into the cockpit, you develop ways to cope with it. A compelling belief in your own immortality works, as does an abiding conviction in your own skills. You wouldn't have made those mistakes that killed your squadronmate, you would have caught the hydraulics leak on preflight, and you would have been smarter, faster, quicker to catch the first signs of a problem in flight. Barring all that, you would have punched out in time. It always happens to someone else.

Even with the denial, dying in flight you understand. Gina Worthington's death was something different, and I could tell that some of the officers were more shook up than they would have been over a ramp strike or a midair.

The Assistant Maintenance Officer—the AMO, Lieutenant Commander Brian Gerrity—fell into the more category. He was one of the last officers on my list to interview.

Given enough time, Gerrity would grow into that look that Admiral Fairchild had in a way that Jazzman never would. Jazzman would always be the golden boy, aging imperceptibly until he finally retired with either stars or a permanent streak of bitterness.

Gerrity, on the other hand, had the right starting ingredients. The gray had just started to touch at the temples. It might not have been there yesterday, judging from the haggard look on his face. Pale, far too pale for someone who spent any time on the flight deck or in the cockpit like a pheasant under glass. Dark hair, dark eyes, all the darker for being framed in pallor. He looked crumpled in the chair, although I could tell when he'd walked in that he was almost my height. His eyes were fixed in the distance, the sclera touched with red and the pupils vaguely unfocused.

"Have you found out who did it? Are there any clues?" His voice sounded steady enough, unless you've heard a lot of men trying to pretend that they're all right. I heard the barely detectable waver in the harmonics, the signal that pressure was piling up.

I shook my head. "Just getting started, talking to the squadron. You knew her pretty well, I take it."

He nodded. "We were good friends. She didn't have a lot of them, you know. A lot of the men—well, it was them or their wives. The other women in the squadron were all a lot junior. I know she wasn't close to many of them."

"Four other female aviators, right?"

"That's right. Two pilots, three radar-intercept officers. RIOs, we call them." He finally looked at me and saw something he recognized. "You already knew that. That they're RIOs."

My turn to nod. Sometimes it's worthwhile to explain. "I spent some time in A-4s, years ago."

"Good aircraft," he said reflexively. "Never been in one, but the only thing bad I've ever heard is they could have used a little more power under the hood. Single engine, though—don't know that I'd like that."

"It makes you careful about flameouts," I agreed. We spent a few more minutes discussing the relative merits of aircraft, something any two pilots in the world can spend hours doing with no more provocation than a simple question. When he started to relax, I worked the conversation back around to the women.

"That's one thing that worried me, when I first heard women were coming to TACAIR," I said. "Hydraulics problems. You have to manually wrestle that airframe around, you want some serious muscle onboard."

"Would have been a problem back in your day"—I let him live anyway—"but not so much anymore. Too many redundancies, and with fly by wire even a big guy's in trouble if the computer goes tits up."

"Lieutenant Worthington could have handled it?" I asked.

He lost the little color that had crept back into his face, and his eyes locked on mine. "Yeah," he said finally. "She could have handled that."

"I suspect you ought to know." I didn't, but instinct suggested I should. "This is hitting you pretty hard. I'd like to know why."

"We were good friends. Period."

"I'll find out if you weren't," I said softly. "If you weren't just friends, I mean. This is a murder investigation, son, and sooner or later someone is going to talk. It'll be better if I hear it from you first."

He stood up. "Anything else?"

"Not unless you want to start with the truth."

"You've got the truth, Mr. Wilson. You may not like it because it doesn't give you any instant solutions. You might just have to work a little harder to find who really did this without trashing Gina's reputation. And if you start making any accusations, you better be prepared to back them up with facts."

He was out of the office before I could come up with a snappy retort. Several occurred to me immediately after he left, but I thought it would be bad form to make him come back just to hear them, for several reasons. First, good comebacks get stale too fast. And second, unless I were way out of the pattern, it would be cruel to taunt someone whose lover had just been murdered.

Unless he'd done it.

THERE WERE PLENTY of reasons for Gerrity to lie to me. In the wake of Tailhook and the other Navy sex scandals, a special cult of paranoia now surrounded that most basic of human drives. Sexual-harassment cases, the policy on allowing homosexuals into the military, and the Navy's decision to resume prosecuting charges of adultery had the effect of criminalizing about any kind of sexual behavior that might occur. Sex on a ship was one major sin, the felony kind. So was sex with someone in the same command. Given enough time, the Navy would get around to prosecuting married couples for sodomy, which the Navy defines as any sexual conduct not involving straight missionary intercourse. So much for the proud traditions of the sea service that had always smiled warmly on a decent blow job.

If Gerrity and Worthington had been lovers, he'd probably face more than just murder charges. If he were lying, I might not approve, but I wasn't certain I blamed him. In his shoes—or rather, his sheets—I'd be tempted to do the same thing. Hell, if I were his CO, I'd probably have encouraged him to.

But I wasn't his CO, and Gina Worthington's death was more than a little personal to me. There were over five thousand men and women on the ship, but she was one of the ones I knew. I have a thing about people stabbing people I know.

Until I had some facts, Gerrity's involvement with Worthington was going to remain my own little hypothesis. One career had already ended in a particularly ugly way. I had no desire to kill someone else's. Yet.

FIRST PRECEPT OF naval leadership—shit rolls downhill. Admiral Fairchild was fielding a fair load coming downhill from Washington, Hawaii, and all points in between. Not to mention the feces incoming from sideways, the yammering hordes of media pilot fish latching onto the tragedy like it was fresh kill dripping off a shark's teeth. Pilot, female, murder. Blood chum in the water.

The Admiral left me alone for almost four hours. About 1300, his Chief of Staff summoned me to the great man's office.

"You need to keep me updated, Wilson," the Admiral said. "You ought to be able to figure out what's going on outside of this ship. Unless you can show me some significant progress—and I mean fast—I'm going to be requesting some outside assistance."

"You already have that, Admiral," I pointed out. "The NCIS Regional office is ready to send over two investigators and a secretary if I want them. Alameda is doing the forensics and the autopsy. I don't know that that will provide any surprises, but we won't have the complete results for a couple of days. Anything we need, the Regional Office has got."

"Well, that certainly reassures me," he said. Call me paranoid, but for some reason I didn't think he meant it. "NCIS is on the ball again. And, just so I've got this straight, this is the NCIS that claimed a homosexual love spat was responsible for the *Iowa* gun mishap. And that investigated when the Commanding Officer of the USS *Vincennees* got his van blown up after the airbus incident? And that drove its car into the middle of the bombing scene, parked its car in the middle of the debris, and then locked its keys in the car. That NCIS?"

"They didn't lock their keys in the car."

"Oh, well. That reassures me. I guess it's OK for me to entrust the rest of my career to this fine group of professionals that doesn't lock its keys in its car, then. I feel good about this now. Just forget I ever mentioned that your organization has got the biggest collection of buffoons that has ever had the audacity to flash badges, OK?"

"Find any buffoons in Hong Kong, Admiral?"

For years, I'd wondered about the phrase "if looks could kill." Nothing like a live example to make you understand colloquial English.

Twenty years ago, his stare would have induced a reflexive sort of fawning as I tried to undo the damage. Hell, twenty-five years ago, I wouldn't even have said it. That was when the silver stars were still in view, not a certainty but a definite possibility that could happen if I kept my nose clean and continued the career that was not just a job but an adventure.

"I want answers before we get back into COD range, and I want to be in the loop every step of the way. Keep in mind that we're not going to be so far out that I can't fly in someone to relieve you the second I feel it's necessary. And if I think you're jerking me around on this, what you did in Hong Kong isn't going to stop me from doing that. Washington's antsy enough about this to give me anything I want. You got that?"

I stood up and locked eyes with him. "I got it. In more ways than one."

5

WORTHINGTON LEFT the ship for the last time later that night, right after *Lincoln* inched into the maximum safe range for a C-2. I watched the aircraft launch, lose altitude as it left the end of the carrier, then struggle back up into the air, its two Allison turboprop engines huffing and chugging like the Little Engine that Could. All my physical evidence went with it.

I walked back down to my stateroom, depressed. The passageway was dark, splotched with pools of red lights designed to preserve night vision. The arcs didn't overlap, leaving stretches where I could barely see the kneeknockers. It didn't matter. They were five paces apart, just like they'd always been. I counted steps without thinking about it, mulling over with a sinking feeling the Worthington case.

I saw someone moving toward me. Someone else up late—nothing unusual about that. At night, the duty section ran the ship, manning a wide range of functions from the consoles in Combat to the bakery. People strolled around at all hours, headed back to their spartan accommodations after a late night in one of the three weight rooms or on a Lifecycle, just getting off watch, or simply unable to sleep. Only the creature comforts shut down at night—the Exchange, the small store on board, some supply centers. The dim red lights were mostly a concession to the aviators that might have to be up and airborne before their eyes had time to adjust to the night.

The other person veered slightly away from me, hugging the other side of the passageway. A little strange but not that unusual in the rabbit warrens of the berthing areas on the ship. Just as he drew even with me, he slammed into me, knocking me up against the bulkhead.

His fist drove deep into my gut. I doubled over, gasped, struggled to draw in air, then felt the panic that starts with getting your breath knocked out of you. He grabbed my hair with one hand, and jerked, and shoved me back against the bulkhead, quickly shifting his grip to my throat. Something cold and sharp bit into the front of my neck. I felt the skin part, then a thin trickle of blood well up around the cut.

Despite the agonized spasms in my guts and diaphragm and the urgent need for air, I tried not to move. A knife at your throat goes a long way toward helping you control autonomic reflexes.

"You're a traitor to your race," the man hissed. His features were smashed and distorted under a stocking, and a black watch cap was pulled down low over his forehead. Tinted glasses partially obscured his eyes, but they looked light. Green, blue—hell, I couldn't tell. And right then, I damned well didn't care.

"Don't move," he said. He seemed satisfied with my response, which was to continue doing exactly what I'd been doing— nothing. "Not so tough now, are you? Big bad Fed just about to shit his pants." He sneered, increased the pressure on the knife a little. "I could kill you right now and nobody'd ever know who did it."

Worthington. One part of my mind detached. It was a more foolish part that didn't seem to understand exactly how important personal survival was, that even in the worst agonies insisted on staying conscious, anchoring me into a reality I neither wanted to experience nor expected to survive. Vietnam had taught me nothing if not just how complicated the human mind is.

"This is a warning. You keep your nose out of our business. Next time, you're going to get hurt real bad. You got that?"

He drew the knife back from my throat a little, then nailed me in the balls with his knee. The pain finally overcame the paralysis in my gut, and I sucked down a deep breath. For all the good it did me. The world dissolved into red brighter than the dim night lights and nothing existed except the agony in my crotch, nausea, and hate.

I slid down the wall, banged my head on the water pipe running along the bulkhead, and collapsed into a small heap on the deck. I curled up, trying to be smaller than I was so there'd be less of me to hurt.

I know pain, and it knows me. It gets familiar but never any easier. The only thing you learn is to wait—to narrow your universe down to a series of tiny pearls on a string, each one discrete, and to let them slip easily through your mind. It's something you understand when you're in it, but never after the fact.

I held onto the fact that I was alive and waited.

I WAS JUST starting to breathe regularly again when I heard footsteps pounding on the linoleum. Someone crouched down beside me, shook my shoulder. "Hey, mister? You OK? What's—aw, shit." Disgust at the pool of vomit, I supposed.

"Help me up," I managed.

"No." Surprising firmness in the voice. My gut clenched—my attacker, come back for another shot? "You need medical help. Don't move."

I heard him move off, pound on a door demanding that the occupants wake up. A few obscene words, then worried, urgent conversation. The world faded away again, leaving me alone with the pain.

IT COULDN'T HAVE taken more than ten minutes or so, but it seemed like days. More people crouched around me, talking. I came to more quickly this time, managed to focus on the faces.

"Can you talk?" Doc Benning asked. Something tight and urgent underlaid her normal professional tone. "Come on, Bud, talk to me." I felt her hands on my shirt, unbuttoning it, then sliding down to undo my belt.

"I'm OK," I wheezed, reached for her hand. "Just—I'm OK." For some reason, I didn't feel like discussing the pain in my groin with her. Or having her examine it. Call me an old-fashioned kind of boy.

They got me down to Medical, made me hang around for a couple of hours, then let me loose after they were sure my dick wouldn't fall off. A herd of MAAs clustered around me, taking notes and trying to get me to make a statement. I brushed them off. I needed some time to think before I started making statements.

Victim or not, this was going to be my bust. For Gina.

EVERYONE SEEMED TO be convinced that whoever assaulted me was also responsible for killing Worthington. I wanted to believe that, too—tried to. Was *willing* to. But, while it was a distinct possibility, there wasn't anything to firmly nail the two crimes together. If they'd said something about her, anything at all, I'd have been just about convinced. But they hadn't.

Call it a weakness, but I have this thing about physical evidence. Maybe I'm good or maybe I just got burned too many times during Vietnam by relying on Intelligence estimates that turned out to be no more than sheer imagination. The last time I'd made that mistake, it'd gotten me shot down.

I was fairly well convinced it was the skinheads, although I'd never thought they'd have the balls to actually attempt anything. A gang whose idea of real violent behavior is passing out hate literature wasn't particularly threatening. I'd known guards in Vietnam that could scare me more by just breathing heavy.

Still, they were the only group on the ship that had advertised a predilection for violence, and the man who'd been carving on my throat sure as hell hadn't been black. If nothing else, I needed to see if there was any connection to the Worthington case. Maybe they'd branched out from racism to chauvinism and killed Gina because she'd had the audacity to fly.

Criminals aren't smart. Killing me wouldn't make any difference, not in the long run. I had the skinhead case thoroughly documented. Ever since they'd slipped the first homicidal note under my door, I'd kept a duplicate copy in the Security Manager's vault. Off me, and the next NCIS agent would pick up where I'd left off.

My snitch? I gave the idea a few minutes thought, then dismissed it. The last person I felt like dealing with was a weasel. At least I had enough to pull every one of them in for questioning, but I'd be a hell of a lot happier with some physical evidence. It was time to trot down to their little lair and take a look.

The skinheads operated with either brazen impunity or criminal stupidity. I was betting on the latter. They'd found a small, empty compartment down on the seventh deck and appropriated it for their own. It was less a room than a closet, but a small group doesn't need much space. There was enough floor in it for five people to stand in the compartment if they were on relatively good terms.

I'd taken a quick look through the room several times and never found anything incriminating enough to bust them. Hid a tape recorder in the light fixture once, but it'd fuzzed out halfway through. I'd been meaning to try it again, had even ordered a fancy new one, but hadn't received it yet.

No more. They'd made it personal.

The chain was draped around the handle, the lock looped through the links. I touched it, careful to keep the chain from rattling. The shaft of the lock pulled out of the hole, rotated easily away from the body of the lock. It was supposed to look like it was secured. They were in there.

I listened by the door, trying to hear voices or noises. Nothing. They'd be keeping their voices down, glorying in the feeling that they were some sort of powerful, dangerous force on the ship, gleefully going over the details of the attack again and again, savoring the one time they'd actually done something besides talk big.

Thinking about it, I started to get annoyed. More than that— seriously, seriously pissed. Bust them now? Why not—they hadn't bothered to wait for warrants, evidence, or any sort of justification for threatening to skewer me. Why the hell should the good guys play by the rules and get screwed?

I reached for the handle, started to turn it. Common sense kicked in. Barge in there now and blow a potential murder case. I could screw it up just like I'd blown the earlier surveillance on their meeting.

That'd go over real well with the Regional Office. I could let the Navy cut a second career real short.

I stood out in the passageway, feeling the ache in my groin and from the cut on my neck, and staring at the door. It took five minutes for brains to veto testosterone. I let them live for now, just like they'd done for me last night.

6

THE PRELIMINARY autopsy report arrived the next evening on the COD, the sturdy C-2 transport aircraft that shuttled people, repair parts, and mail between land and ships. Along with the criminal history reports I'd requested on Lieutenant Worthington, the autopsy results were packaged in a large, double-wrapped brown envelope.

I read the autopsy report first, scanning the protocol report quickly and skipping the big words. The information I was really interested in was located midway through the typed report.

The vaginal samples were positive for sperm. My balls ached as I read the word. They were still swollen and painful from my late-night encounter.

Whomever she'd slept with was a secretor, which included 45 percent of the average male population and meant that we could identify the blood type from the sperm sample. Type O-positive, which narrowed the population of suspects down to 30 percent. The report indicated that the sample was relatively fresh, deposited within the last twenty-four hours.

The ship had been at sea for almost five weeks before her murder. Whatever else it told me, the report meant that Lieutenant Worthington was not as squeaky clean as the public story said. My guess was that one of her squadronmates was equally as guilty of "inappropriate contact."

Was it relevant to her death? Maybe, maybe not. She'd been put in the bilges after she was dead, and the report contained no indication that any force had been used during the sexual contact. Aside from the abrasions Doc Benning had noted at the scene, there were no scratch marks and no ligature bindings. The only bruises on her body were the multiple purple lumps that we all accumulated on our shins from misjudging the height of the kneeknockers at the bottoms of hatches. I'd have been surprised if she hadn't had a couple of those.

Carol's observation was confirmed by the report that noted a straight-line abrasion on her right side, up under the armpit. The report called it post mortem. Except for the presence of sperm, the autopsy report was singularly unrevealing.

There was little doubt in my mind that Admiral Fairchild would want to see the autopsy results. There was even less doubt that I wasn't going to show them to him, not until I decided how relevant the results were.

By keeping the results secret, I was violating the second great precept of naval leadership: Never let the boss get ambushed. Despite the bold-print warning on the top of each page of the report—"Confidential, Privileged Material, Not Releasable"—dynamite like this had a way of surfacing in the press. A junior hospital corpsman tasked to photocopy the results and willing to earn a couple of extra bucks, a disgruntled assistant or nurse, or even a pathologist with a taste for indiscretion—the possibilities were limitless. Nevertheless, I wasn't going to make the media's job any easier by adding potential sources for leaks to the loop.

Admiral Fairchild would figure it out quickly enough, though. Someone in Medical would tell him that I was looking through medical records, and it wouldn't take one of the nuclear engineers we carried onboard to figure out why.

Would he pressure me to tell him what the report said? Does an F-14 have to reach 130 knots off the end of the ship to get airborne?

I slipped the reports into my pants pocket, washed down a preventative dose of ibuprofen with cold coffee, and headed for the nearest ladder down to Medical.

DOC BENNING HAD never been stupid. She knew immediately why I wanted to look at the medical records I requested, and she offered me a private examining room, partially to preserve some semblance of confidentiality but just as importantly so she could interrogate me in private. She told the corpsman to bring in all of the VF-54 medical records, then turned an appraising eye on me.

She made me tip my head back so she could check out the scratch on my neck. "You know what this will do," she said quietly as she poked gently at the skin around the cut.

"I do. But there're only two people right now who know what I'm looking for—me and you. I'm not telling anyone, and you don't know for certain."

"Won't work. Captain will know you were down here. Even if I didn't tell him, someone would." She tapped on the side of my neck lightly. "A scratch. Bad one, but it'll heal up nicely." She looked down pointedly at my crotch.

I felt my face go red. "So? Tell him my knee was bothering me again and I wanted you to take a look at it. Tell him I had pneumonia, hot flashes, or the crabs. Up to you. And no, you're not checking the rest of it out. It's fine."

"I know you're not going to tell him. But before I can decide how I feel about this, I need to know one thing. Was it rape?"

I handed her the report and shook my head. "Read it for yourself. No evidence of force, no defensive wounds or ligature marks. No vaginal abrasions or evidence that she was anything other than a willing participant. I'm not ruling it out completely—could have had a knife or a gun to her throat—but I'm not calling it a rape-murder."

"So she gets trashed for being a victim and a slut."

"You'd rather she were raped?"

"No, of course not. But this won't have any context to it. You know it won't."

"Carol, just because it doesn't look like rape, that doesn't mean the man involved didn't kill her. Could have been consensual sex, followed by a lover's spat. I'm not looking for a perpetrator right now. I'm looking for witnesses. With the caveat that one of them might turn out to be the perp. You understand the difference?"

"I see, but I don't like it. Her sex life wasn't anyone's business."

"Not until she committed a crime by screwing around on the ship. And not until she ended up dead. The more I know about her, the better chance I have of figuring out who did this."

"Who are you going to tell?"

"Nobody right now. Not unless I have to."

She thought about that for a moment. "I won't either. Admiral Fairchild's not going to like it, though."

"You think that's news? Why don't you do something constructive and help me with these files?"

"OK. What blood type are you looking for?"

"Good try, but forget it. Just divide them into the four standard groups for me. You know where to find the stuff faster than I do."

Doc and I spent the next fifteen minutes sorting the medical records into five stacks. A, B, AB, and O, all positives. The Rh-negatives I lumped in one stack, partly because there were so few of them and partly in hopes it would mislead her into thinking the sample came from someone who was Rh-negative.

"Thanks," I said, as she tossed the last record onto the B-positive stack.

She made no move to leave.

"Go away, Carol. I'll tell you what I can when I can, but not now."

"We could have done this faster using the computer," she said, still staring at the stacks as though one of them contained a snake.

"Right, and have everyone watching me ask for a printout, as well as relying on your corpsmen not to have made any mistakes. No thanks. Call me old-fashioned, but I like to see paper in hand and be just a tiny bit discreet."

Finally she stood up. "There's not a damned thing that's discreet about this case, Bud. Not a damned thing. If you need me, I'll be in one of the other rooms."

I waited until the cloth curtain was pulled shut behind her before I reached for a stack. On the off possibility that she might find some way to peer through the gap between the curtain and the bulkhead, I reached for the Rh-negative stack first, almost hoping she was watching and interpreting that as a sign of special interest. I wouldn't put it past her to run through the records herself, just to see if anything interesting jumped out at her.

As I went through each pile, doublechecking the blood types and marking them next to the names on the VF-54 squadron roster, I thought about Doc Benning's reaction. As a senior Commander almost certain to be selected to Captain soon, she'd grown up in a Navy where women stayed ashore. By the time they'd started opening up the flight surgeon program to women, she was a Lieutenant Commander and had earned a solid reputation in pathology. She'd thought about going Flight, she'd told me, but making the career change at that point would have put her behind the power curve for the rest of her career. She hadn't been happy with the restrictions that the Navy put on women serving on ships and had been one of the first to volunteer when the Navy opened up carriers to women.

Hard to pin down exactly what her attitude was toward the other women. I'd seen her run the gamut from fiercely protective to harshly vindictive. She cut the other women damned little slack but was one of their fiercest advocates onboard the ship. I'd heard she was called the head bitch by more than just the men.

The women seemed to treat her with an odd mixture of deference, fear, and admiration. If they needed medical help, they looked for her. If they wanted the day off because of cramps, they tried to see one of the male docs. Even those didn't often countenance shirkers, because if Carol Benning found out she'd make them pay for it.

I hadn't been surprised to find Doc Benning down in the bilges beside Gina Worthington's body. It'd have been more of a shock if she hadn't been there. Up until now, I'd had the feeling that Doc considered this at least as much her case as mine. But if Gina had been screwing around on the ship, it wouldn't matter to Doc that some male member of the crew was also at fault. Gina had been one of hers, which meant she damned well better be just a little bit smarter, faster, and better than any of her male counterparts.

I paused to glance at the curtain. No sight of any peekers. Gerrity's record was the second one down on the stack, and I wanted to leaf through it for more than the blood test results without Doc unexpectedly appearing over my shoulder.

I pulled his record out, checked the blood type, and shook my head. A match, but only one of fifty-three others in the squadron. A quick scan of his last physical and the medical history pages revealed nothing interesting. No lengthy history of VD, or any other particularly enlightening diseases. A few colds, one incident of a strained tendon in the knee, reportedly caused by playing tennis. Not a conclusive clean bill of health, though. There was no rule against a sailor seeing a civilian doctor for medical problems, and if Gerrity had anything in his background that he didn't want the Navy to know about, he'd probably have seen someone outside the military medical system. Unless it turned up on a routine flight physical, there wasn't much chance of the Navy knowing about it.

Still, I had the information I wanted. Gerrity and fifty-three other men in the squadron were possible matches for the sperm sample. If I could convince them all to submit blood samples, DNA testing could either exclude them or provide damning evidence.

DNA testing takes several weeks, and only goes that fast if the Navy is willing to spring for some fairly sophisticated outside testing. Running it through the Navy labs would take at least six weeks, and that was assuming that I could get the CO to order every member of the squadron to submit a sample. Every male member, I corrected myself. No point in having the women submit samples to match the blood type found in a sperm sample.

I doubted that the Navy would be willing to wait six weeks for results. Even two weeks would be a damned unattractive figure for them with the press baying and yapping at their heels, especially when there was no guarantee that someone in the squadron had killed her.

OLD RULE IN investigations, one I'd learned from the MAA on my first ship, and heard again at NCIS: Talk to the suspect last. It made

47

sense, since I needed a little more evidence to confront Gerrity than simply a matching blood sample.

One of the advantages of having been in the Navy—and in a squadron in particular—was that I had a pretty good sense of who knew what secrets. I might not know exactly what the secret was, but I could take a guess at who did. Without that experience, I probably would have started by talking to the aviators again, on the theory that if Gerrity was screwing Worthington, they would be the ones who'd know.

They'd also be the ones who wouldn't talk. Aviators go deaf, dumb, and blind when a shipmate fucks up.

Even the man sharing his stateroom wouldn't have anything to say. Nope, never got locked out or asked to stay gone. Never smelled anything suspicious in the room. Never seen Gina come there for anything other than squadron business, and never seen his roommate alone with the woman.

I knew who might know, though. Someone who might be willing to talk.

If he hadn't joined the Navy, Airman Fernandez might have been a *chollo,* a member of a group of other tough young men who identified themselves with cryptic block initials, secret hand signs, and just the right color of Nikes. I would lay odds he had an L.A. Raiders cap stuck somewhere back in his locker.

Can't shake me, man, his expression said. I been there, I done that, and you ain't shit. The Navy had added enough polish to him that he probably would have said you ain't shit, *sir.* Wonder what his *'manos* would say if they knew what his job was in the Navy?

AN Fernandez was a compartment cleaner. Swabbing, waxing, and buffing decks, picking up and returning laundry, providing clean linen and a cursory vacuuming once a week to the officers of the squadron had replaced tagging and gang-banging as his daily routine. Fernandez might not appreciate it now, but being a maid on an aircraft carrier might be the only thing that let him survive growing up in Los Angeles.

Or perhaps he did know it. Another one of those misconceptions born of serving with the hordes of young draftees during the Vietnam conflict. Fernandez had volunteered, I reminded myself. He hadn't been forced to join the Navy by a judge or signed up to avoid the Army.

"Airman Fernandez," I said politely. "Thank you for coming here."

He seemed slightly taken aback. Politeness from a geezer as old as I was probably something he wasn't used to.

"No problem. Chief said to. Gets me out of field day for a while." He trotted out a blasé look and studied my deck. "You need some buffing in here, man. Ought notta let them get away with this shit."

"You think? Where?" I stood up and walked around my desk to stare at the spot on the deck.

"Over there, man," he said, pointing at the corner. "They ain't stripped in here for long time, I guess. You got shit built up bad."

"Maybe I ought to get the Chief to send you down later. Get the regular crew in here, let you supervise them for a while."

"You clear it with the Chief, I help you out," he said.

"You might be able to help me with something else first."

Guarded. He'd been through the buddy-buddy prologue to interrogations before. "Don't know nothing."

"You know what I want to ask you about?"

He shook his head.

"Then how do you know whether or not you know anything about it? What if I was doing an investigation on dirty decks?"

"Yeah, right. You're the NIS guy, and you're wonderin' about decks."

"NCIS, now. We changed the name."

"What for?"

"Bad rep with the old one. New people, new name."

He nodded, as though that were a perfectly reasonable thing to do. "Have to do that sometimes."

"So things are a little different these days. You know what I'm working on now?"

"Got a good idea. That dead lady."

"Right. You heard what happened to her?"

Of course he had. Every detail of Lieutenant Worthington's murder would have made the rounds on the ship within hours. MDI, we used to call it. Mess Decks Intelligence, the fastest, hottest gossip circuit in the world. You want to get the latest dirt on anything, hang out on the mess decks for a few hours. Better yet, ask one of the cooks.

"She got stabbed. Down in the bilges," he said.

"You're right. Seven times."

"Didn't have nothing to do with it, man," he said. Not worried, probably had proof he was somewhere else that night.

"I didn't think that you did. There's someone else I wanted to ask you about. Lieutenant Commander Gerrity—you know him, right?"

"Yes, sir." The sudden reversion to courtesy worried me for a moment.

"How well do you know him?"

"Pick up his laundry, do his stateroom. That's it. I just know who he is."

"You ever talk to him?"

"Coupla times."

"How about Lieutenant Worthington? You knew who she was, didn't you?"

"Everybody knew who she was. So what?"

I could beat around the bush for a few more minutes and trot out some standard interrogation techniques, but I had the uneasy suspicion that AN Fernandez was probably better at this than I was.

"Was Gerrity sleeping with her?"

A flash of disdain. What kind of way was that to do an interrogation, he seemed to say.

"Fernandez, you're a smart guy, you've been around. You realize what's going to happen with this, don't you? If there's any way possible, the Navy's going to nail an enlisted man for this. You think an officer's going to take the fall?"

"Hey, I didn't do anything!"

"No, but I think you might know better than anyone just exactly what the relationship between those two was."

"You saying Mr. Gerrity did it?" He shook his head. "Don't want to tell you how to do your job, but I don't think so. Man's not the type."

"But maybe somebody who had the hots for her is the type. He sees her shacking with him, goes a little crazy, she disses him—you see how it could be, right? I agree with you about Gerrity, but I got to know if he was screwing her so I can find out who *is* the type to kill her."

He nodded judiciously. "But Gerrity gets his ass busted for screwing her, then."

"Maybe, maybe not. They'll cover that up if they can. Was he?"

"Was he what?"

I was getting tired of playing games with him, so I let his question hang in the air.

"Maybe I know something, maybe I don't," he said finally. His Hispanic accent had partially disappeared. "But who wants to be snitching on an officer?"

"Tell me what you might know. Hypothetically, you understand. If you did know anything, what would it be?"

"I might know about something smelling funny in the compartment. Maybe about a pair of underwear that got left somewhere. That's about all I'd know."

"Smelled like sex? Perfume? How many times?"

"Couple of times. Maybe. I ain't saying I smelled it at all."

"Understood. If you did, was one time last week?"

He thought about the question for a moment, making sure it was still firmly on hypothetical ground. "Yeah, probably."

"You tell anybody about it?"

His face shut down. "Wasn't nothing to tell. Like you said, this is just hypothetical." The word came easily to his lips—he'd heard it before today, probably from his lawyer.

"Would you hypothetically like to take a guess at who the woman was?"

"Naw, man. Didn't see anybody coming in or out." He smirked a little at the pun, but the words had a ring of truth to them.

A few other sundry pieces of information surfaced. According to

MDI, Lieutenant Commander Gerrity never bitched about his compartment cleaners, usually hung his clothes up instead of throwing them over a chair, and kept an iron in his stateroom to touch up his uniforms, not relying on the laundry's efforts. He remembered laundry days and didn't have to be prompted to leave the sack out on the designated days, nor did he leave his collar devices on his shirts. Overall grade, from a compartment cleaner's viewpoint: a good guy, for an officer. On such small virtues a reputation often turns.

AN Fernandez gradually relaxed as we talked and occasionally slipped into standard English. Finally, when it appeared we'd exhausted his knowledge of Gerrity, I asked, "Why did you join the Navy?"

He shrugged, and something flickered across his face. "Don't know, man. Something to do, I guess."

"Lots of things to do in L.A. Too many, sometimes."

"Like you say. There was—" he stopped, and glanced up at me. "You the guy that was a POW, right?"

MDI at work again. Gerrity may not have known about my history, but at least one story had made the rounds.

I nodded. "Two years."

"Bad shit. Lotsa guys died there, right?"

I nodded again, and a glimmering of where he was headed dawned.

"You just get tired, sometimes," he said finally.

"Two years is shorter than eighteen," I said.

He nodded. It might have been a smile if it hadn't been so bleak. "Sometimes they come and get you out. Sometimes you gotta escape on your own."

I digested the analogy.

"Thanks for talking to me," I said finally. "You ever need any help, you know where to find me."

"Not likely I'll be needing it."

"You never know. One POW to another." I held my hand out. He stared at it for a moment, then took it as though the gesture was unfamiliar. His grip tightened around my hand for a moment, and then he pulled back hurriedly. The tough young *chollo* resurfaced and settled on his face before he slipped out the door.

Maybe it wouldn't be admissible in court, but it was enough confirmation for me. There was more to the relationship between Gerrity and Worthington than he'd let on. He might not be a murderer, but now I knew that he was a liar.

I CALLED THE ready room looking for Gerrity. He was up in CVIC at a planning conference, the Duty Officer informed me, and was expected back around 1500.

I decided to go through Lieutenant Worthington's personal effects, to see if anything might provide more insights into her personal life. A diary would be nice. An unmailed Dear John letter to Gerrity would be even better. Barring either of those classical clues, I'd settle for getting a better idea of what made her tick. Know the victim, know the perpetrator, the old saw went.

BM1 and one of his compadres had carefully inventoried the contents of her locker and safe. The classified material had been turned over to the squadron security office. I glanced at the list. A NATOPS manual, the comprehensive checklist of guidelines and safety instructions for flying the Tomcat, a few pages of notes from a conference labeled "Working Papers," and a couple of classified messages having to do with aircraft mishaps had been signed for by the security officer. Nothing above my security clearance, and nothing out of the ordinary.

The unclassified material was also inventoried and bundled together with a rubber band. Personal letters, some photographs, division records of performance, her last couple of fitness reports, and a folder of notes and rough drafts. I leafed through the folder. "JAG INVESTIGATION" the header on each page said.

Nothing unusual about that, either. Every day, a multitude of Judge Advocate General investigations are in progress on a ship this size. Every time a sailor loses three days of work due to an injury, a pair of binoculars turns up missing, or some complicated offense under the Uniform Code of Military Justice—the UCMJ—is committed, someone gets assigned to investigate it. Most of the investigations are farmed out to junior officers as SLJs—shitty little jobs.

I glanced at the first page. The first paragraph was enough to make me sit up straight.

Lieutenant Worthington had garnered a more sensitive assignment than a routine accident. She'd been assigned to look into the circumstances surrounding a maintenance problem. I skimmed the background paragraph.

Two weeks ago, when we'd been on training ops off the coast, one of the VF-54 catapult officers had noticed a control surface problem on one of the aircraft. One of the last things a pilot does before launching is cycle the surfaces by taking the stick forward, back, and to each side as far it will go. It's called wiping the surfaces, and it's a last check before you get shot off the pointy end of the ship to make sure that you have control of the ailerons and rudder.

Tomcat 301 had bobbled when the pilot cycled the stick to the right. The rudder had refused to travel the full distance. The technicians took a quick look, found a roll of duct tape impeding the travel of the mechanism, and pulled the aircraft off the catapult for a complete check. Nothing else had been found, so the Tomcat had been cleared for launch.

Leaving something in an aircraft after performing maintenance is somewhat like a surgeon forgetting to take out a sponge during an appendectomy. It might not cause problems immediately, but sooner or later anything not tied down within the skin of the aircraft will break free from where it's left, ricochet around the compartment while the aircraft's in flight, and may cause problems. Murphy's Law being what it is, loose objects always cause problems. In this case, the roll of duct tape might have prevented the pilot from leveling off after takeoff, causing him to continue the steep initial angle of ascent until he looped over backward and came down headfirst.

An uncontrolled climb is just one of the many things that can go wrong off the catapult. The amazing thing is not that people die during carrier operations but that so many live. A soft cat—insufficient steam pressure to the piston that drives the catapult shuttle forward—can dribble you off the end of the carrier like a basketball. If the pin holding the aircraft's nose wheel to the catapult breaks prematurely, same result. In heavy seas, the catapult officer can misjudge the launch, which has to occur as the bow of the carrier rises up on a wave, not as it's plunging down. I'd seen movies of the COD surviving a catapult through the waves that brought my admiration for that sturdy little workhorse aircraft to new levels. The COD had simply smashed through the wave and struggled along barely above the water until the pilot gained sufficient air speed to pull back on the stick and lift the aircraft out of reach of the sea. A tactical jet probably could not have survived a similar incident. Cold seawater on hot turbine engines usually results in a nasty explosion.

Tomcat 301 had checked clean, been preflighted again a little more thoroughly, and launched with the original crew. Jazzman had ordered a JAG investigation to determine which maintenance practices had let the dangerous situation develop.

Squadrons have a strong paranoia about tools and maintenance. Every set of tools is carefully inventoried and checked out by a technician assigned to the job. At the end of the day, the tools are counted again to make sure nothing is left in the aircraft.

The problem with Tomcat 301 was that duct tape and other supplies that technicians use to hold wiring harnesses in place while tinkering with them were not accountable. In addition, for some reason, Quality Assurance—QA—hadn't conducted a post-maintenance inspection of the repairs, something that's required on any maintenance on control surface or anything else on the "safe for flight" list.

I thumbed through the pages, now intrigued by a mystery smaller than the investigating officer's death. Why had QA not been called to check the repairs? And why had the Maintenance Control chief who reviewed the completed MAF not caught the omission?

The same question had been bothering Worthington, according to her notes. She found some ambiguity in the maintenance instructions that failed to define the repair action as one requiring QA's signoff. The actual repair required disconnecting a rudder strut to reach a wiring harness and reconnecting it once the harness had been visually examined and tested. By some arcane indexing system,

NAVAIR had failed to include that particular action in the list requiring QA's signature.

Worthington's handwritten recommendations included a note addressing that and recommended an immediate safety message to the other squadrons to alert them to the potential danger. A good suggestion, and one that I would have taken if I'd been Jazzman. I'd have to check and see if he knew Worthington had found the problem and whether or not the other F-14 squadrons had been notified.

I put the folder aside and reached for the stack of letters. A few from her parents, one to her sister. Glancing through the photos, I matched faces with names on the letters. Standard letters from home, with no hint that her family knew anything was bothering her or anything about her relationship with Gerrity.

Who would she have told about Gerrity? Anyone? Maybe nobody on the ship. If what I suspected was true, she'd hesitate to confess to anyone, since that would have made them an accomplice. Her sister, maybe? I studied the picture for a moment, and then dismissed the idea. Gloria looked to be about my kid's age. I doubted that older sister would be discussing her affairs with a fifteen-year-old who might have more enthusiasm than discretion.

If anyone on the ship knew, it was probably either her roommate or her compartment cleaner. I made a mental note to talk to Airman Fernandez's female counterpart first.

7

Y OU MIGHT have told me she was working on a JAG report,"
I said.

Jazzman looked annoyed. "Why? It wasn't any big deal, and she
didn't have a chance to finish it."

"She finished a first draft." I handed him a photocopy of Worthington's notes. "Thought you might want to see it, since she uncovered an unsafe maintenance practice."

He took the pages and tossed them on the corner of his desk
without looking at them. "I'll have to assign someone else to finish
it. They'll probably want to start all over."

"Maybe not. She's got all her findings documented. It looks like
it was just a matter of polishing the language on it."

"I can't very well get her to sign, though, can I?" he snapped.

"Not since she's dead, no. It'd look suspicious."

A trace of something that might have been embarrassment
flashed across his face. That and something else I couldn't put a
name to.

"Sorry. That was uncalled for," he said. "It's not her fault that all
this is happening, not at all."

"All what?"

"You remember. The paperwork drill. Every damned department
in the Navy has a different requirement. And the funeral—oh, shit."
He rubbed his hands up his face and rubbed at his temples with the

fingers. "You lose one, it's bad enough. Especially like this. There're so many details to sort out, so much bullshit, that sometimes you end up getting mad at the victim. Really sick."

"It happens," I said. "There was a time when I wrote at least one letter a week back to somebody's next of kin. Never easy. That's why they talk about the burden of command."

Aviation squadrons do a better job of getting their people ready for command than the surface-ship side of the Navy. Prospective Commanding Officers get selected—screened, it's called—for command when they're midgrade Lieutenant Commanders. They report to their commands after they're selected for full Commander and spend eighteen months as Executive Officer before fleeting up to take command. By the time they're in the driver's seat, they know the people, the aircraft, and the culture of the squadron and have been under the gentle tutelage of the person they're going to relieve.

Surface ships and shore commands are different. Surface Warfare Officers, or SWOs, do their Executive Officer tours of fifteen months on a ship, then get transferred to some other billet, usually a shore or a staff job. A year later, longer in some cases, they finally get back to sea, spend a week or so getting the skinny from their predecessor, and then are on the spot. It's a brutal process, with both the Executive Officer and Commanding Officer jobs preceded by six months to a year in a training pipeline that wastes a lot of time. The training pipeline is designed to accommodate aviators who've been picked for command of a ship as a preliminary to taking command of an aircraft carrier. By law, the Commanding Officer of an aircraft carrier is always an aviator—and usually a pilot. Since most carriers are nuclear powered, the aviator is also sent to nuclear propulsion school with the bubbleheads, the submariners. By the time they get to command, they've been to almost every highly technical school the Navy has to offer.

Like they say, no one ever flunks out of the surface track and gets sent to aviation.

"You don't think this had anything to do with her being killed, do you?" Jazzman asked. He'd picked up the report and was flipping through it. "I mean, it's not like there was a crime or a lot of money missing or something. Who'd get excited enough about unsafe maintenance practices to kill her?"

"I doubt it's related. It's just something I found in her safe, that's all. Figured you might need the information."

"But you kept the original."

"As I said, it was in her safe. That means something in a murder investigation."

"Not unusual, you know. Plenty of us keep work in our safes."

"And other things. Things that might turn up missing in a case like this."

"Yeah, well." He looked at me thoughtfully.

We both knew what safes were for, and what provisions carrier pilots made for the material in them. Security regulations required that only the officer concerned and the squadron CO have the combination to a safe. In practice, officers who made their living executing controlled crashes onto the deck of an aircraft carrier and trusting their fate on the other end to a good cat made arrangements. In a combat squadron like this one, a trusted friend would have the combination as well. In the event that "something happened," the friend would get to the safe first and clean out anything that was too personal to be packed out to the next of kin. It would be unkind to let a grieving spouse find a pack of condoms in the personal effects sent home after a death at sea, particularly if the dead spouse already had a vasectomy. Squadrons take care of their own, and the trusted friend was just part of the culture.

"Did you get there before the MAA?"

"Not that I know of," Jazzman said frankly. "I would have liked to. But judging from what you've found, it wasn't really necessary."

"You'll have to trust me this time. This, and other times, if it comes to that."

"Hard to know which side of the fence you're on," he admitted. "I know who you were—a lot of the guys do. But who are you now? Your new employer doesn't exactly inspire confidence and warm feelings in most of us."

"There're reasons for that," I acknowledged. "But like most organizations, this one has individuals in it. You go with what you know and understand, not with the preconceptions."

"Would you have?"

That took me a moment longer to answer. "Don't know. It would depend on the person, I think. And whether or not I had a choice."

"I guess I don't this time. Can you tell me this, at least? Anything you found going to embarrass her parents? I mean, it's bad enough they lost her, and the media reaction's going to make it worse. No point in adding unnecessary pain to it."

"You got lucky this time, skipper. Nothing in her safe that you wouldn't want to go home. So you don't have to decide whether or not to trust me this time."

"This time. There might be others, God forbid."

"Not like this, I think. But if it ever comes up, we'll talk then. My word on it," I promised.

"That's all I ask." For a moment I could see the commander behind the pretty face. They hadn't made a mistake on this man, not if the hard responsibility of being responsible for his people wore on him like this. It was good to know. I wondered if Lieutenant Worthington's parents would see it, too.

Trust works both ways and is easier to win when it's already been given. "I'm concerned about Gerrity."

"He sleeping with her?" he asked bluntly. Jazzman didn't miss much.

"Do you think he was?" I countered.

He thought about it for a moment. "I don't know. It's possible, I suppose. They were always tight, but they never gave me a reason to suspect it was something more. Discretion or good sense, who knows? Have you got something on him?"

I told him about the blood type match and the bare outlines of what Fernandez had told me, without mentioning the compartment cleaner's name. If he were really inclined, Jazzman would figure it out. If he were starting to trust me, he wouldn't try.

He nodded as I talked and then spiked a small smile. "I'm not inclined to put all my faith in just blood types. After all, I know who else is O-positive."

"I noticed that. Anything you want to get off your chest?" I said it with just enough bluntness to tell him it was a crude joke.

"Nope, not me. I may be crazy, but I'm not stupid. Sleeping with one of my officers would be about the fastest way I can think of to earn a COD ride off of here."

"So much for that theory," I said. "And here I was going to have this wrapped up before noon."

His expression grew sober. "It's a damned shame, Wilson. That girl was a damned fine pilot, and she sure as hell didn't deserve to die like that."

"You know anyone who does?"

"Not since a Marine Corps drill sergeant smacked me around in AOCS. You find who did this, Wilson. That'll go a long way toward proving who you are now. And do it the right way."

"My intention, skipper." I found myself liking the man that I'd thought of as a peacock politician. Whatever shortcomings he might have, I could tell he gave a shit about something besides the next promotion board and screening for a major shore command.

He stood up, and I took the cue to stand as well. "I'll send Gerrity down to see you when he gets back. And this conversation was just between us. Will you tell me what you find, when you can?"

I nodded. "When I can." And I would.

After i left Jazzman's office, I hunted down Worthington's compartment cleaner. Unlike Fernandez, she knew nothing useful. It would have been too much to ask her to have photographs or tape recordings of her late officer engaged in some sort of misconduct, but it had been worth hoping for.

Gerrity showed up in my office two hours later. He still looked haggard but not as hard-down as he had the day before. He sat down in my chair hard, as though he had some right to it.

"Have you found out anything?" he demanded.

"Is there a reason I should tell you?" I asked.

He seemed taken aback. "Is there some reason you shouldn't?"

"There might be. I think you know what those reasons would be."

Gerrity was the second person in as many days to find the deck of my office compellingly fascinating. But for an expert opinion, I'd stick with Fernandez.

"I told you in the beginning to be up front with me about it," I said finally.

He mumbled something I didn't quite catch. Too many years listening to engines spooling up and aircraft turning in enclosed spaces had sanded off the high-frequency end of my hearing. I didn't like being reminded of that.

"Speak up," I ordered. The tone of voice came back to me naturally.

"The skipper talked to me," he repeated.

"And?"

"He said I was to give you my full cooperation. That he didn't need to know what I told you, but that it damned well better be the truth. I didn't know about Vietnam—I'm sorry, sir."

"That was a long time ago."

"Not too long ago for the skipper. I guess that's good enough for me." He took a deep breath and looked me in the face. "We were lovers. Aren't you supposed to read me my rights or something now?"

"Why? Did you kill her?"

He stood up and started to reach across the desk and then caught himself. He slumped back down in the chair. "No. Jesus, no. I couldn't—" His face twisted up ugly. He took a deep breath and made a visible effort to control himself. I could tell what that cost him.

"I would never have hurt her. Ever. She could have threatened to tell the skipper, and I wouldn't have said so much as a harsh word to her. We were going to get married when we got transferred. If one of us had got caught, we would figure it out. One resign, both resign—we even talked about that."

"You slept with her on the ship."

"Yeah. Stupid, but we did it. We weren't the—well, that doesn't matter. So what happens now?"

"I try to find out who killed her, knowing that I'm investigating a straight murder instead of a rape-murder. We do some DNA typing to make sure you were the only one, just to rule rape out, but I think it will be."

"Do you have any clues or anything?" Gerrity suddenly looked like exactly what he was—a junior officer whose lover was murdered two days before, and one that might just be in a hell of a lot of trouble. "Is there anything you can tell me? Anything at all?"

"Just that I'm sorry as hell for you, son. Because if you're not guilty," I saw him go pale on me again, "then this is going to be rough for you. Let's talk about where you were the night she was murdered."

8

ERRITY HESITATED for a moment. An odd thing to do—it wasn't a tough question. Not unless you're making sure your answers fit together neatly.

"I had duty that night," he said.

"You were on watch all night?"

"No. I was Command Duty Officer. Tower Flower during flight ops, just checking in with the ready room the rest of the time."

"You held musters, that sort of thing?"

For the first time, he ruffled. "The Squadron Duty Officer isn't required to. The section's got a strong Chief—she handles it. Why? Are you implying I was derelict in some way?"

"That worse than being accused of murder?"

He slumped back in his chair. "I didn't kill her."

"I don't think so, either. Which is why I find it so very curious that you're lying."

He started to deny it, but he wasn't any better at righteous indignation. Finally, he gave up.

"Worthington was on watch that night, too."

He nodded.

"Convenient." I let it be a question.

"It was a stupid thing to do," he muttered. "Stupid."

I could pretend to misunderstand and make him tell me explicitly, or I could continue the conversation we were not having. "But understandable. You're both stuck on the ship with some time on your hands. A little cooperation from your roommate is all it takes."

He looked up, and I saw shame on his face. "I know better, though. *We* knew better. We'd been talking about it, agreed that we wouldn't—you get caught, you're out with a bad discharge. Maybe a court-martial. These days—hell, we *knew.*"

"Wouldn't be the first time a man let his small head do his thinking for him. It's a crime under the UCMJ. But it's not the one I'm investigating." That much was true, at least. "She talk about anything special that night? A fight with somebody or something?"

He nodded slowly, his eyes growing dark. "One of the reasons it—we—she was upset. Angry more than anything. The MO was on her case again."

"About what?"

"Anything, everything. He didn't like her, but there wasn't much he could do about it. Not now."

"Not with the politically correct agenda, you mean."

"That's right. It's one thing to dress a guy down for something—harass him, even." He shrugged. "Harassment's a normal part of being a lieutenant. You live with it, you outgrow it. But with the women, everybody's still on thin ice. You don't know how it will come out in public. The women that work for me—I think twice about it, sure."

"Any particular reason he didn't like her?"

"He doesn't need one. She's a pilot. That's enough."

"So what was it this time?"

"FMC rates—Full Mission Capable statistics. You know the paperwork drill. We have to report Mission Capable and FMC rates every day to CAG, telling him how many of our birds can fly and how many are fully functional. It's important to the skipper. Even more so to the MO."

"She was Av/Weaps. Was he pressuring her to fudge the gripes? Swap parts out for a day so she could count both birds as up?"

"Something like that. There're a million ways to make yourself look better than you really are. Some are riskier than others. Gina did some of the obvious ones, but she didn't go in for the real complicated fudging. The MO does. FMC is sacred to him."

"So she was upset that night?"

"Real understatement. Royally pissed would be more accurate." He tried on a smile, found it didn't fit. "Gina never just got upset. The Italian blood, I guess."

"I know." That I remembered about her. The hard edge lurking at the edge of her coolness, the chin thrust out, head tilted back to stare you in the eyes. It was a look that made you want to get something solid between her and your balls. I saw it once, maybe twice. That was enough.

"Look, could we do this some other time?" he asked. I saw him starting to crack around the edges, slivers of his public persona eroding away. Talking about Worthington was getting to him. The voice would go next. It was already pitching up three notes higher than when we'd started.

I nodded. "Tomorrow?"

"Thanks." He made a small motion as though he were going to hold out his hand, then didn't. "A little time—listen, maybe even later today," he said. "I'm on the flight schedule for an afternoon hop, but I think I'm going to snivel out of it. My concentration's shot, and you don't want to be flying the Tomcat if you're distracted."

"I think that'd be a damned good idea. If anybody hassles you, tell them I have to talk to you. I can make it an order, if you need it."

"It won't be a problem. Lots of lieutenants itching for stick time. Maybe later—I'll find you, OK?"

I watched him leave. It's never a sure thing, figuring people out. They're both more complicated and less than you'd figure. But judging from his reactions, he hadn't been the one that ended Lieutenant Worthington's career with a knife.

Not intentionally, anyway. I paused, and tried to figure out what that meant.

THERE WAS SOMEBODY else I should have talked to before Gerrity, but he hadn't given me a chance. The compartment cleaners were one source of information, and so were Gerrity and Worthington's roommates. I decided to start with Worthington's, based on some obscure table-manners idea of alternating male and female.

I found Lieutenant Berkshire in her stateroom. Yesterday's flight schedule had her down for five night traps, so I figured she'd be sleeping in.

When she answered the door, it was clear that she hadn't been awake that long. Her hair still showed signs of sleep rumple and a rack burn creased one cheek, the standard result of sleeping on Navy pillows.

I introduced myself, asked if we could talk. She waited a moment before answering, as though she were considering pointing out to me that she wasn't too damned awake yet. Finally, she opened the door wider and motioned me in.

She sat back down on the lower bunk, her back against the steel tubing at the head. She was wearing sweatpants and a sweatshirt. She yawned.

I glanced around the stateroom, trying not to look at the implements of female occupancy that were scattered about. Parts of the room looked oddly vacant. The squadron had already inventoried Worthington's gear and personal possessions, a preliminary to sending it to her next of kin.

The few available spots on the wall were covered with some superb aviation photos. A Tomcat streaking off the cat, two others flying close formation. Not Worthington's, since they were still in the room.

"Good pictures," I said, by way of an opening remark.

"Thanks." She yawned, but something in her voice told me it was more than a simple acknowledgment of fact.

"You took them?"

She nodded. "Last cruise."

We exchanged a few more preliminary comments. She was starting to look more alert by the time we got to her current assignment. She was Aviation Ordnance Branch Officer and had worked for Lieutenant Worthington.

Chelsea Berkshire wasn't a talker. I got short or one-word answers to most of my questions, sometimes just a nod or a shake of her head. Almost as tough as talking to the MO, but a good deal more pleasant to look at. Finally, when I could see her eyes starting to track together, I moved into the meat of the interview.

"You and Worthington get along OK?"

Berkshire nodded.

"You probably had a lot in common. Both ROTC for commissioning, both flying the same aircraft."

For some reason, that seemed to bother her. "We weren't all that alike," she said finally, the longest sentence I'd gotten out of her so far.

"Were you friends?"

"Not really."

"That seems odd. When I was in the Navy," I saw her eyes start to glaze over as though dreading a spate of ancient sea stories, "I spent a lot of time on liberty with my roommate. You live together in close quarters, you get to know each other pretty well."

"I guess."

"Did you know Lieutenant Worthington well?"

"Look, she was my roommate for three months. We were in port or in workups the first two months, so we both pretty much lived ashore. And we've been flying our asses off out here. If you were asking me these questions after cruise, I'd have different answers. All I can tell you now is that I knew her, she was an OK officer and a good stick and seemed to have her shit together. Hey, it sucks that she got killed, but I don't know who would do it."

"You're in the Av/Weaps Division, aren't you?" I asked, ignoring the hint that I ought to get the hell out of her stateroom and let her go back to sleep.

She nodded. "Ordnance Officer."

"You know anything about how she got along with the MO?"

"I heard it wasn't great. The MO's a pain in the ass—Gina could be, too."

"How so?"

She shrugged. "Little stuff, mostly. We're supposed to let the Chiefs and the senior enlisted handle the production. We're there for evals, recommendations for advancement, some career counseling. That's how it's supposed to work. She didn't see it that way."

And that, I surmised, made her a pain in the ass as a Division Officer. At least from Lieutenant Berkshire's point of view.

Some things about the Navy never change, and this was one constant difference between the surface warfare officers and the aviators. You ask a black shoe—an SWO—what's wrong with some piece of equipment his people own and he can damned near recite every detail there is: how long it's been since the last scheduled maintenance, when the fireproof lagging was last replaced, whether the pump likes high-speed ops or craps out when it's warm outside. They do all that in addition to standing combat, bridge, or engineering watches every twelve hours. That's probably why they never sleep. You'd sure never catch one in his rack this late in the morning.

The aviators—brown shoes—are a different case. They leave the technical stuff up to the people who understand it best: the senior enlisted men and women in their shops. Being tired when you're supposed to be ready to fly is dangerous.

Berkshire's attitude bothered me. I knew these women were tough, but Jesus, even if she hadn't liked Worthington, it ought to have bothered her more. I opened my mouth, hoping a piercingly intelligent question would come out. She spoke before it happened.

"Listen, could we talk about this some other time?" She gestured vaguely around the stateroom. "I need to take a shower, get something to eat. If there's anything else you need, you can call me."

I agreed. I certainly could call her. And would, when I found out why she never even bothered to ask me if I had any leads or evidence.

I TRIED TO track down Gerrity's roommate, Lieutenant Commander Paul Franklin. Franklin was the Safety Officer, so I planned on pumping him for some information on Berkshire as well.

Franklin, however, had been flying that morning and had since disappeared somewhere into the bowels of the ship after lunch. I could have had him paged, but decided not to. It wasn't like he was going anywhere too far away without landing.

I decided to stop by the security office and check out the results of Worthington's background investigation. All tactical pilots hold top-secret clearances and undergo background investigations while they're in the training pipeline. Every five years—more often if they're involved with SCI, Specially Compartmented Information—they get what's called a "bring-up," an investigation that covers the time since their last one. Sort of rule of thumbing it, Worthington would have been due for another one either last year or the year before. The DIS—Defense Investigative Service—might not have uncovered anything she'd really want to keep hidden, but it was somewhere to start.

Everybody's got secrets. Some people have more than others. Some are better hidden. If I knew what Worthington's secrets were, I might have a better line on who wanted her dead. A secret's safe only when no one else knows it.

The Security Office was buried down on the third deck. Lieutenant Commander Jim Beam was conflicted about whether or not he was really glad to see me. We're on the same side, sort of, but everything I do causes more work for him. Security clearances get yanked, investigations lead into discrepancies—however much you might personally like a guy, you gotta wince when he doubles your workload.

Jim pulled Worthington's file for me. Before he handed it over, he leafed through it. I didn't mind. If there were something off-kilter in her file, he'd find it faster than I would. It wouldn't be too bad—or too obvious—or she wouldn't be flying.

"Nothing pops out," he said after a few minutes. He closed the file, tapped it lightly against his palm, then slid it across the desk at me reluctantly.

"Worried I'll find something you missed?" I asked.

"It's easier to see something out of order after a person's been killed," he said reflectively. "Murder elevates minor sins and bad habits to motives."

"Hindsight," I agreed. "I find anything, I'll tell you. Did she have access to any other safes? Other than the one in her stateroom?"

"I don't think so. Hold on, I'll check." He stood up and disappeared into an adjoining office. "Nope. Or at least not officially."

I looked through the file, noting the date of the last Investigative Summary. As I'd thought, her last bring-up was last year. According to the report, Lieutenant Gina Worthington was as clean as Jazzman thought she was. At least for the last five years.

Below the current slew of biographical data forms and clearance requests was the stuff from her original background investigation. I took my time, reading the background information forms carefully.

At age twenty-two, Worthington had been a typical college graduate. A few store credit cards and student loans, professors listed self-consciously as references, two traffic tickets. Kappa Delta sorority, some other campus organizations. I started getting bored and flipped back to the Investigative Summary.

Well, well.

Prospective Ensign Worthington had neglected to list a few other matters. Nothing significant, but the mere failure to answer the questions completely told me something else about her. The one that caused DIS to hiccup was a drunk driving conviction in her sophomore year at New York City College. Paid a fine, went to alcohol school, and spent a weekend picking up trash off the highways—normal sentence for a first conviction. That alone wouldn't disqualify her from pilot training—but lying about it almost had. The follow-up noted that she stated she simply forgot to list it. There were no other criminal offenses listed.

Beam was watching me read the summary, alternating between watching my face for a reaction and reading it himself upside down. I finished, closed the folder, and handed it back to him.

"That DWI—worth anything?" he asked.

"Don't think so. It was a long time ago, and she hasn't had any other offenses since then. They chalked it up to youth. I do, too."

"She didn't disclose it," he persisted.

I nodded. "There's that. Again, a long time ago, before she maybe really understood they were serious about all that crap."

He picked the folder up, two-blocking the front and back cover neatly, reassured that he hadn't missed anything. I started to ask him if he still had her original fingerprint card, but thought better of it. If I really wanted to run her prints again, Alameda could get me a fresh set. And if I asked Jim for them, I risked putting it into the MDI network. There's not much that stays secret on a carrier.

"Long shot, but worth checking. Thanks." I walked over to the hatch, contemplated the eighteen-inch-high kneeknocker, and stepped carefully out into the passageway. As I turned to pull the hatch shut, I saw Jim standing behind the service counter, staring at me.

9

I climbed up one ladder to the deck my office was on and stepped into the main fore-and-aft passageway. Ten frames forward, I could see an open doorway, the metal door out of view inside the office. Just about where mine should be.

I moved quickly down the passageway, ignoring the complaints in my knees. No one except the Damage Control people had the keys to my office—no one. As I approached, a sailor started backing out of my office. He was hunched over slightly, his arms extended in front of him, ropy muscles standing out along the bone.

"Hey!" The sailor ignored my shouted objection and took another step backward into the passageway. One end of my desk appeared. He sidestepped, twisting the desk to pull it out while holding it up to clear the metal rim to the door.

"What the hell are you—" I started. Fernandez's face popped out from the door frame.

"Hey," he said. A greeting. "Chief said I give you a hand down here. Brought my crew. Man, this deck real bad." He shook his head, pursed his lips, then motioned to me. "Lemme show you what you been living on, man."

I took a deep breath and tried to remember whether or not I'd left anything of importance lying out on my desk. Doubtful. Old habits—I lock everything up every time I leave the office, even for head calls.

"How did you get into my office?" I asked finally.

"Good thing I did. Look at this shit in the corner here." He crouched down and ran his hand over the deck.

"Fernandez, forget about the deck for a minute. Tell me how you got into my office."

He glanced up at me, faintly disappointed that I wasn't interested enough in the condition of my own deck to examine it more closely. "Key. I got master keys for everything."

"Everything on the ship? Not just for the staterooms you do?"

He nodded, moved closer. "Not everything. But we like—swap, you know. Each other's rooms, sometimes. You do yours and another guy's one day, he does yours the next. Get a whole day off, 'cept for the Chief. And you know when he's gonna check, you head him off. Go see him in the Mess first before he comes looking for you."

"Nobody's supposed to have keys to my office," I said.

"You empty your trash yourself?"

"I usually take it back to my stateroom. Or shred it."

"Don't have to do that. Leave it for the compartment cleaner."

I stopped and considered the matter. "I've never seen anyone come in here."

"That's the problem. He don't. See this shit?"

"But—" I gave up, crouched down, and looked at the floor. Old dust and dirt embedded in diluted wax filled the corners and spread out across the tiles. My last meaningful experience with floors had been in AOCS, but I recognized a poor job of field day when I saw it.

"Some shit," I agreed. Fernandez nodded, mildly pleased I recognized the seriousness of the situation.

"We fix it. You clear out for a coupla hours. Come back after lunch maybe."

"I appreciate that. But Fernandez, you can't be coming into the office without telling me ahead of time. I've got some stuff in here I don't want anybody to see. What if I'd left evidence laying out, something that proved who killed Lieutenant Commander Worthington? As long as I'm the only one with a key, I have control of the chain of custody. I'm the only one who can get to the file, and

I'm sure as hell not going to tamper with evidence. But if you can get in whenever you want—"

"All fucked," he finished. "The defense lawyer'll get that shit suppressed." He glanced sideways at me, assessing whether I understood that the words were not new to him.

"You got it," I agreed. It was perfectly normal for me to be crouched down on a dirty deck discussing floor wax and evidentiary matters with a young sailor, I reassured myself. There was no incongruity—none.

"Then you just lock it up," Fernandez said. "Bet you do anyway."

"You'd be right about that. I try to. But what if I forget someday? You want this guy to get off just because I can't empty my own trash?"

He appeared to contemplate it for a moment. Had I used a lesser crime as an example, I wouldn't have been so sure of his response. Finally, he said, "Naw, man. You ought to get that guy. We'll work something out."

After some negotiation, we agreed that Fernandez and his crew would clean my office twice a week, Tuesdays and Fridays. I let him keep the key, fairly confident that my habit of locking everything up would prevent any problems. Besides, you trust a *chollo,* they remember it.

Evicted from my office, I headed topside. As I climbed the ladder, I heard the sound of freedom—the deep, menacing scream of a jet engine turning at military power. I could picture it exactly.

By the sound of it, it was an F-14 on the bow catapult. The aircraft would be shivering slightly on the shuttle, straining against the tieback that held her motionless until the steam piston below the deck reached the proper pressure. The Catapult Officer would be just forward of her, only his head visible through the plastic bubble that protruded above the flight deck. A yellow-shirted handler would be on the deck, running the pilot through cycling the stick, checking for any last-minute mechanical problems, flashing a plastic grease-penciled board with takeoff weight on it up at the pilot.

When everything in the delicate ballet came together, the pilot would salute the handler, signifying he—or she, damn it, when would I get that down?—was accepting responsibility for the aircraft. The handler would return the salute, then drop to the deck in a crouch, his arm pointing forward. Seconds later, the deceptively gentle rumble of the piston slamming forward, tossing the Tomcat off the pointy end of the boat at 130 knots. After that, it was up to the pilot.

There's something about carrier aviation that never lets go of you. I hadn't been tactical in six years, but I could still feel the pounding adrenaline that coursed through you when the afterburners kicked in and the feeling of skin pulling back from your face during the cat shot. It's sheer terror and beats any ride at Disney, no contest.

I decided to risk the knees and headed for the tower. Primary Flight, or Pri-Fly, was located on the 0-10 level, putting it thirteen ladders above my office. Twenty-four, if you counted the fact that I'd have to get back down eventually. Not a lot of room for lookie-loos, but the Air Boss didn't mind if I wandered up occasionally for a nostalgia trip.

Besides, I rationalized, everyone I need to talk to is either flying, getting ready to fly, debriefing from flying, or working on the aircraft. Or cleaning my office.

AIR BOSS GIL Shaughnessy was good. A Tomcat pilot himself, he had a way of keeping the pattern moving and the deck clear without ever seeming to become unduly ruffled. Sure, he screamed sometimes— Air Bosses always do when some dumb fucker wanders onto the deck and disrupts the coordinated efforts of one hundred other people trying to get 40,000-odd pounds of aircraft back on deck in a controlled crash.

Tonight, he seemed a damned sight more tetchy than usual. I heard him snap at the OOD, complaining about the wind across the deck instead of just telling the bridge what he needed. The crew in Pri-Fly was quieter than usual, not that there's usually a lot of banter during flight ops. I could see faces shut down and carefully neutral, hear an extra edge of formality in the routine reports. The Mini-Boss, seated to the left of the Air Boss in a matching elevated chair overlooking the flight deck, kept glancing nervously at the cof-feepot as though going into caffeine withdrawal.

"God DAMN it," Gil screamed. Everyone froze. "Why the fuck can't those fucking pilots learn to fucking read fucking gas gauges? You think I want to launch two tankers tonight? FUCK NO!"

I edged away from the door, prepared to head back down the way I'd come. My knees wouldn't like it, but it looked like a bad time to be invoking my squatter's rights.

Gil caught the movement out of the corner of his eye and mo-tioned abruptly at me. I stopped, walked over, and stood in the space between the two elevated chairs.

"You making any progress?" he asked abruptly. "Worthington, I mean."

I thought over the request for a moment. Gil wasn't in any chain of command that pertained to me, yet from the looks of Pri-Fly, he was damned upset about something. "Nothing I can tell you about," I said finally. "You know her well?"

His head snapped aft to follow the incoming track of a Tomcat looking covetously at the deck. As the aircraft snagged the three-wire and pitched its nose down, he turned back to me.

"She did her first tour in my squadron," he said in a quieter voice, the anger leaking away in two seconds. "You remember."

That I did, although it hadn't occurred to me earlier.

"She was a good kid," I said carefully.

He snorted. "Kid—not hardly. A good stick, even with all the bullshit she had to put up with to get into this flying club." He looked up at me, assessing my face. "You find who did this, Bud. After all the time and work I put in on her, some asshole goes and wastes her. I'm taking this one damned personally."

"Everybody is, Gil."

"Sure, sure. Underwear in knots all over this damned boat, every-body worried about whether their careers are on the line because of it." He stared out at the flight deck and suddenly looked a lot older. "You send them out there time and time again, Bud. They walk across your flight deck like they own the whole damned world. Their mommies love them and they've got the biggest damned toy in the world—ninety-eight thousand pounds of hot airframe that they treat like their own personal hot rod. Sometimes they don't come back."

"I remember."

He glanced over at me. "I guess you do. You ever get used to losing them?"

"No. Sometimes it's a little easier at first if you didn't know them as well, but then you feel guilty about that. You write the letters to the next of kin and try to convince them it matters to you. It does, but not as much as it does to them. The wives you know—even worse."

"Husbands now, too. How the hell is that going to be?"

I shook my head. "Don't know. Gina wasn't married, so Jazzman won't find out—this time."

"Jazzman." Something got very still around Gil. "You come see me later—we'll talk, OK?"

"Do you know something?"

He shook his head. "No. I wish I did, because then I'd know whether or not it was important."

"Tomcat 201, call the ball."

"Roger, ball."

I squinted aft. A tiny black speck in the air, getting bigger every second. An F-14, on final to *Lincoln*. Gil quit talking and started Air Bossing, grumbling about deck multiples and elevators. He'd already forgotten I was there.

I backed away from the Air Boss area that protruded out from Pri-Fly and took station in the small observation area located back and to his left. With the last set of F-14s now starting their passes at the deck, Gil was going to have too much on his mind to talk. Besides, he'd made it clear that whatever was on his mind wasn't for public consumption.

The rhythm of launch and recover, trap and cat, is hypnotic. Soothing, even, to those of us who used to do it for a living. I watched the deck while the last birds from that cycle landed, remembering.

———

By the time I'd finished my flight deck fix, the afternoon was almost gone. I put off leaving, waiting for that moment when the line between sea and sky blurs into dark gray-purple. Until the stars come out, you feel suspended in some different medium that's not air or sea, but a mixture of both.

Gil had cooled off. The first cycle of night traps was spinning up on the deck, and from the way he looked there was a good chance a public castration would not be held to set an example for the others. Not this time at least.

I spun out my excuses for being up there long enough to watch the first night-trap launch. Afterburner fire spat out of the ass end of the Tomcats, splaying across the scorched metal JBDs. At night— or early evening, in this case—you really understand the need for the JBDs, the jet blast deflectors that pop up from the flight deck to shield people and planes from the exhaust.

This was my job once, playing Tower Flower and watching my squadron fly, but not anymore. Younger eyes, quicker reflexes would keep them safe in the air. I had something else to do—find out who killed them on the ground.

Thirteen ladders later, I was standing in front of my office. I tried the doorknob. Good, locked. I'd expected Fernandez to make sure of that, and it was nice to see my trust hadn't been misplaced.

I used my own key and shoved the door open. The pungent smell of fresh wax wafted out and the light reflecting off the deck damn near blinded me. Just so I could tell him later that I did it, I walked over to a corner and inspected the deck.

No shit. Good deal.

One of the good things about being the resident agent on a carrier is that you have easy access to all your witnesses and perpetrators. Sure, they fly aircraft, clean decks, and cook meals, along with a hundred other essential jobs in this small town, but they're always around somewhere. Even the aviators had to land eventually, and once we were in blue water ops, it'd have to be on the carrier.

Blue water ops. A term of art, one that adds an extra pucker factor to each cat shot and trap. The phrase means you're out of bingo room. You run low on gas, have a mechanical failure, or simply suffer one of those infamous luck failures, and you've got nowhere to go. You're too far out to divert from the carrier and make it to a bingo field, your usual backup ground base, not without some heavy-duty tanking support from the Air Force. And try getting one of their KC-10s or KC-135s to fly out and save your ass on less than forty-eight hours notice. The Air Force combat doctrine is nothing if not orderly.

For carrier aviators, blue water ops means no room for mistakes. You get aboard, one way or the other, even if it means CAG launches ten tankers to pass you gas while you get over the shaking and sweating from a bad pass.

I checked my notes and got Gerrity's stateroom telephone number. I wasn't after him, but his roommate I needed to see.

The phone rang five times, which is how long it can take to spit out a mouthful of toothpaste or wake up enough to figure out what the damned noise was. No answer. Probably at chow or hanging out in the squadron ready room, munching popcorn and waiting for the juniormost officer in the squadron to rack up the evening movie.

Might as well go find out. I hauled myself up, hating the realization that my knees were screaming at the prospect of climbing ladders again. The squadron ready rooms were on the 0-3 level, three decks above me.

"Aerobic exercise," I announced. "Doc Benning said I should do more of it. It's either ladders or the exercise cycle down in Bike Alley."

The knees quit complaining. I smiled. Nice to be able to blackmail your own body parts.

THE SMELL OF popcorn eddied and drifted through the passageway. Each squadron had its own industrial-size popper and secret recipe for perfect popcorn. Two reasons for that. First, it was a tradition. Second, it was traditional.

The noises coming from Jazzman's ready room weren't. Boisterous you expect. But not loud, screaming anger. That was more normal in the passageway where the Executive Officers for the squadrons lived.

I pushed open the door and stepped into the middle of a fight. A body hit me and slammed me back into the rear row of padded chairs. I caught myself with one hand on the back of the chairs, shoved myself back to my feet, and was ready to retaliate when I noticed the dead quiet spilling across the room.

Trying to simultaneously face each other and me, Gerrity and Berkshire stood taut. Gerrity was in a boxer's stance, his hands that had been up, covering his face, now pinned behind him by two other officers. Berkshire was standing almost casually, part sideways to Gerrity. I noticed the careful distribution of her weight, the cocked, ready look in her muscles, all 125 pounds of her poised and tense. Her forward foot rested lightly on the ball. Martial arts training, it screamed. Whatever she was feeling, it wasn't fear.

I tried to think of something to say. No one moved. Finally, an aviator in the middle of the pack shifted his weight and coughed. That small movement broke the spell. Gerrity shucked off the people holding him back angrily, gave a shoulder-loosening shake that ended with his chin jutting out. I saw Berkshire assess that vulnerability carefully.

I made myself drop my own hands and unclench the fists that'd formed. "Looking for Lieutenant Commander Franklin," I announced to no one in particular.

One of the men holding Gerrity back raised his hand. "That'd be me."

"Could we talk?" I glanced around the room, saw eyes avoiding me and dislike shuttering their faces. "Just for your info, I'll be talking to most of you in the next several days. You can figure it out." A few nodded. Most of them just moved away, turning backs on me. Regardless of what Jazzman might have said to them, there was little he could do to reverse the almost reflexive dislike most aviators now have for NCIS. For shipboard agents that weren't accustomed to social isolation, the legacy of Tailhook made it tough.

Franklin regarded me with an odd mixture of irritation, caution, and uneasiness. The first two I expected. Bingo.

"My office," I added, and turned to walk toward the door without waiting to see if he followed. No footsteps followed for a few seconds, long enough to demonstrate to the rest of the squadron that he wouldn't have gone if he didn't have to. They knew they all had to cooperate—Jazzman had probably made that explicitly clear—but they didn't have to like it. Not even from someone who once could have thrown them all in hack for the scuffle I'd just witnessed.

I felt the air push against me as he followed me out the door. He let the door shut on its own, banging. He followed me five steps down the passageway before he said, "Wait."

"What?" I said, and continued walking.

"Could we—oh, hell, hold up just a minute. Sir." I stopped, waited a moment, then turned around to face the aviator standing in the middle of the passageway. Courtesy, however grudgingly rendered, deserves positive reinforcement.

The passageway was wide enough for three people to walk side by side if they were good friends. Social custom demands that if you stop walking, you move to the side of the passageway to let others get around you. Franklin had already done that, more out of reflex than thought.

"Just—sir, are you going to tell the captain about it? What happened back there?"

"Any reason I shouldn't?"

He broke eye contact and found something of interest on the opposite bulkhead. "No, sir, I guess not. Flash's under a lot of pressure, that's all. What happened—we wouldn't have let it get any farther. And Berk—she started it. I—"

"I haven't decided yet," I broke in. "Not something I want to discuss in the starboard passageway, either. No point in telling every airman that walks by about squadron business, is there?"

He nodded, looked slightly relieved. Not much. Good—I hadn't intended him to.

"My office." I turned and walked away. This time, the pitter-patter of little footsteps behind me was immediate. By the time we made it down four decks to my office, he was in step.

"You know why I want to talk to you?" I asked.

"Yes, sir. Flash—Gerrity—told me he talked to you."

"So you'd know what you could say without giving away secrets. I expect this conversation to go a damned sight farther than whatever he told you was OK to say. I require your full and complete cooperation, no matter how shitty it makes you or any other aviator look. You got that, mister?"

Franklin would have been lousy at poker. More and more interesting by the minute.

Usually, I would have started the same warm-up routine with him that I'd used with Gerrity. Some flying talk, establish a bond, get the basic background, then work up to talking about Gerrity and Worthington and anyone else that came to mind. But the man had already decided to lie to me about something, and I was getting damned tired of scaling that wall of squadron silence every time. I leaned back in my chair and steepled my fingers under my chin.

"You know why I came looking for you. And it's not because you're Gerrity's roommate. I already know most of the story. Tell me the rest or I let the right people know what I already have." I had no idea what I was talking about. But he did.

"I'm going to advise you of your constitutional rights now," I said, following a hunch. I stood up and took two steps over to the filing cabinet, took my time unlocking it and fiddling with a file folder to give him time to think. By the time I turned back around to look at him, fear was starting to set in.

"I didn't know. Not at first. Jesus Christ, this will—look, this can't happen. I'm not taking the fall for something that wasn't even my fault."

"It'll go easier if you're up front about it. That stuff about duty, honor, courage—it still means something to a board." I let him decide whether I was talking about an FNAEB, court-martial, Board of Inquiry, or Administrative Discharge board.

He stared at me for a moment, then became the third person in recent days to take an extreme interest in the state of my deck.

I was going to have to have it field dayed more often if this kept up.

Finally, he reached a decision. The fear had faded somewhat, overlaid by a healthy dose of sullenness and the beginnings of relief. Doing the right thing often looks like that.

"Gina Worthington was a bitch," he started. "And a vindictive one. I know what everyone's told you about her, but that's the truth. Sure, it could have been ugly. But she didn't have to use it like she did."

"What really happened with that Tomcat?"

As I said before, pilots aren't dumb. He caught something in my tone of voice and turned paler than I'd thought possible. "Oh, shit," he said softly. "You don't know, do you?"

"Now I do. Enough, anyway. If you don't tell me, I'll find out soon enough. Your choice."

"Fuck you. I don't give a shit what the skipper says, I'm not going to be lead on this one." He stood up, swayed a second, then the color returned to his face. "You find someone else, asshole." He slammed out of the office. I could hear his feet clattering up the ladder, undoubtedly beating feet back to the ready room. I shoved myself away from the desk and followed him up the ladder.

By THE TIME I caught up with him, it was too late. The wardroom had circled its wagons, and the few aviators left there were on their way out. Faces were closed and hard like they used to be before one of those missions that never happened in Vietnam.

I let the three officers leave without stopping them. Whatever Franklin had told them had been enough. They might not know anything, but they did know one thing.

Not to talk to me.

Jazzman. That would be the quick answer. Catch him now, right after they got to him. If he was in the loop on this at all. Get him to get their young asses back into the ready room now, now, now, before they had a chance to plug any holes in whatever story they were putting out as God's honest truth. Jazzman could get to the bottom of this faster than I could alone.

Unless he were involved. I stopped in the middle of the ready room, considering the possibility. The door opened. A lieutenant—junior grade—walked back in, flipped the popcorn machine off, and left without looking at me.

10

I THOUGHT about going straight to Jazzman's stateroom. He had a right to know his officers were stonewalling and a duty to tell me what he knew. It was just my opinion, but I thought some old-fashioned concepts might count with him.

Then again.

A naval command is a peculiar creature. It's more than a convenient way to organize people and airplanes into neat little boxes in some manual. Every one of them—good, bad, or somewhere in between—was a living, breathing entity with a personality. It's not a constant. And while most of the wardroom contributed to how a command acted, the Commanding Officer was the backbone. His thoughts, his words, his actions colored everything that happened from the moment he stepped up to take command. The bigger the unit, the longer it took to metamorphose, but it happened every time. A good CO could look at his wardroom and read his own faults in each face.

How long had Jazzman been in command? About a year, I decided. Plenty of time for him to put his stamp on the wardroom.

But what were my other options? I considered the possibilities on the way back down to my office.

First, I could call each officer in individually for questioning. Tough call, since by then Franklin's story would have made the rounds.

86

Second, I could go to the Admiral. Oh, lovely thought. He'd understand exactly what I was saying by skipping Jazzman. Good way to torpedo the CO permanently, maybe without any reason to. If Jazzman was who I thought he was, he deserved better.

Finally, I could tap into one reservoir of information that had as much effect on a command as the CO did: the Chief's Mess—the "Goat Locker."

The three senior grades in the enlisted community of the Navy were special. The chiefs, senior chiefs, and master chiefs ran the Navy, often without the wardroom really understanding how they did it. If there was something hinky about the Tomcat problem or Lieutenant Worthington, they'd know.

Only thing was, they were even more close-knit than the wardroom. Most of them had been in this canoe club a hell of a lot longer than the officers they worked for. What'd almost worked with Franklin wouldn't even phase them.

I sat at my desk for a while, thinking. Finally, when I couldn't come up with some clever ploy to use, I settled for one that'd worked before with the Goat Locker. Personally, I wasn't so sure I cared for the tactic—too many ways it could backfire, particularly since I was ruling Admiral Fairchild out as the next step, but it was worth a try.

Always interesting to see how men react to the truth.

CHIEF RAAKUS, WORTHINGTON'S Division Chief, was up on the flight deck, so I tracked down Master Chief Handover, the senior enlisted person in the squadron. He was in the Chief's Mess having a midmorning coffee break and fulfilling his most important role, keeping his fingers on the delicate pulse of the command. And on the ship as a whole. Not much could happen anywhere on *Lincoln* without the Master Chief knowing about it.

The Master Chief intercepted me halfway into the Mess and let me sketch out my introduction before smoothly herding me out of the common area and into his stateroom. On the way out, he refilled his coffee cup and snagged a visitor's mug for me. I got black— he didn't even ask.

It was an encouraging sign, if it meant he had something to discuss that he didn't want circulated around the ship by his fellow khakis. Not so good if he was just trying to keep squadron business private.

He settled into the standard Navy-issue chair in front of his pull-down desk and pointed at his rack. I sat on the edge of it, my weight barely making an indentation on the taut blanket.

"Heard you had an interesting time up in the ready room last night," he started.

I nodded. Of course he knew about it—probably knew more about the whys and wherefores than I did. "Never did find out what caused it, though." I let the statement serve as a question, curious about how much he'd reveal.

Imagine you're a frog, belly-up and splayed out on a wooden cutting board in some biology class. It was like that. I tried to copy his look and fell two lifetimes short of experience.

"Good thinking, coming down here," he answered obliquely. "Some officers wouldn't have thought of it. Maybe Master Chief Reddick was right."

"You know him?" I don't know why it should have surprised me that he knew the man who'd been command master chief when I had a squadron. Aviation is a relatively small community at the top.

He nodded. "We go way back. He mentioned your name a few times—said you were headed out to *Lincoln* as a sand crab and asked me to keep an eye on you."

"Kind of him. What's Vern up to these days?"

"Just what he always said he'd do—fishing, doing some hunting. Wilma's probably going crazy with him around the house."

"If memory serves, his wife was Carol," I said.

Handover nodded. First test passed. "Carol, of course. Mind is the first thing to go after the knees."

"Vern Reddick was a good man," I said reflectively. "Kept me out of trouble more than once." And he had.

"It works that way. Sounds like you could use some help now, too."

"I could, at that. What should I be asking you about?"

He looked at me again, assessing. "Imagine you know how to conduct an investigation, Mr. Wilson."

"I know how to ask the right people a lot of questions."

"Why don't you start off, then?"

"That fight up in the ready room. For some reason, the wardroom didn't seem real eager to share the cause with me."

"You wouldn't expect them to, now, would you?"

"Because?"

"Damned embarrassing, man getting his young ass kicked by a woman."

"Happens. Any idea why?"

"I've got a good guess. Mr. Gerrity, he's OK most of the time. Takes care of his troops, doesn't whine about down-gripes on his aircraft. But he's got a couple of blind spots he needs to get over. My bet would be that Lieutenant Berkshire tripped over one of them."

"Any idea which one?"

"Yep. Her roommate." He shot me a sidelong look, trying to figure out how much I already knew while I tried to figure out if what he knew and what I knew were the same thing. The longer it went on, the more we both figured each other knew. Finally, I fell back on my original game plan.

"Berkshire had to know about Worthington and Gerrity," I said finally. "Gina would have been better at hiding it than he is."

"She was. I don't think Berkshire knew at first. Damn, I'm sure she didn't. The way she is, she would have been screaming bloody murder about it."

"Just the kind of person you like to go on cruise with," I observed.

"Ain't that the truth. She has a lot to learn, that one does."

"Anybody going to teach her?"

"Gerrity might try. But she's a tough one—mentally and physically. Black belt in karate."

"I noticed that."

He nodded. "You would. Mr. Gerrity ought to take note of that fact. I heard they stopped it before she made the point."

"Just barely, from what I saw. Which takes us back to the original question—why were they fighting?"

He sighed. "Berkshire took two bad passes at the boat last night. Somebody said something about maybe Worthington's death breaking her concentration. She snapped back that if it'd been Gerrity who boltered nobody would say that. From what I hear, it got real quiet. Bad enough that she brought it up in the open like that, but then she said maybe it didn't bother him all that much. Gerrity didn't take that well. Said something about if Berkshire were half the man she pretended to be, he'd kick her ass. She took him up on it."

"Gerrity took a swing at her?"

"Not at first. He crowded her a little, maybe. I heard she dumped him on the deck and had him pinned down by the short hairs before anyone knew what was happening. A couple of the guys pulled her off, and he came up swinging."

"She started it, then. Maybe they should have let him have at her."

"The two guys that pulled her off of him weren't real interested in trying to hold her back. One took an elbow in the gut, the other a fist to the balls. The rest of them grabbed Gerrity."

"Not the best way to build team spirit and morale."

"No kidding."

"Jazzman know?"

He nodded. "By now he does, I bet. He hasn't asked me anything—if I find out he's in the dark, I'll turn the light on. The story'll make the rounds soon enough."

"How does this tie into Tomcat 301?"

"Ah." A small look of relief, no more than a tiny crack in the old face. "I was wondering if you'd get around to that."

"Almost didn't. One of the officers let something slip."

"Berkshire was flying 301 the day it had problems."

"And Jazzman let her roommate do the JAG investigation?"

"Yep."

"But why—?"

He cut me off. "Strange, isn't it? Especially when one of the causes of the problem might have been the pilot not preflighting her aircraft. Or postflighting. One thing you can say about Lieutenant Berkshire, though: She's tough in the air. Doesn't take no shit from anyone." He looked at me, gauging whether or not I was paying attention.

"An example?" I suggested.

A quick shake of the head. "Just an observation, Mr. Wilson. You know pilots and how they are. Don't make the mistake of thinking of them as women first. Berkshire is the toughest of them, but Worthington wasn't far behind."

"You'd think they'd have been tight, though. Same problems breaking into the community, roommates and all. I take it they weren't."

"Women. Go figure," he answered, effectively undercutting his early caution about preconceptions. "They got along when they had to, I guess." His eyes hooded over. "The wardroom could tell you more about it than I'd know."

I learn quick. I kept my mouth shut and thought about what the Master Chief had said—and what he hadn't.

A squadron is a close-knit family, far more so than most commands. Fighter pilots have to trust each other implicitly, like cops. When a safety-of-flight issue is involved, a close friend of the pilot involved might be tempted to skim over some relevant facts, maybe laying off the blame on someone else. Jazzman would know that. That's why it made little sense to assign the pilot in question's roommate to do the investigation.

The opposite was true as well. If Jazzman had known that Berkshire and Worthington weren't getting along very well, assigning Worthington to do the investigation also sent a certain message. It boiled down to what Jazzman knew—and when. And how important it might be to Worthington to torpedo Berkshire.

Looking at the Master Chief, I knew I wasn't going to get much further down this road with him. Whatever his personal opinion was about Jazzman, he was still the command master chief, Jazzman's personal assistant on all matters concerning the squadron. Even if the Master Chief hated Jazzman's guts, I wouldn't hear it from him, any more than Jazzman would have heard anything from Master Chief Reddick.

His remarks about Berkshire intrigued me, though. There was something behind them.

"I should talk to Chief Raakus," I suggested.

"You should. I'll send him up to see you."

"But he won't know anything else about Tomcat 301. Not after you talk to him."

The Master Chief regarded me blandly. "He can tell you everything you could ask about the division. Especially about the mechanics of what went wrong with 301. But as to wardroom business—no, I don't think he'll know much more about it than I do."

Which was everything.

I thanked the Master Chief for his time. He issued a standing invitation to drop by for a cup of coffee anytime.

11

YOU CAN avoid anyone for a couple of hours on a ship, even a small one. The converse is true as well. Doc Benning proved it that afternoon.

I was back down in Engineering, looking over the spot where they'd found Worthington, trying to get a feel for the sheer mechanics of getting a 5-foot 8-inch, 132-pound female down in the bilges unnoticed. It looked tough, even allowing for the fact the space would have been mostly deserted while we were in port.

To begin with, most places having anything to do with nuclear propulsion are classified at least confidential. Locked doors, in other words. Not every kiddo with the yen to look at huge steam turbines gets a free look-see.

Second, Engineering spaces are always patrolled. It may be a rover who visits several spaces every hour, or it may be one snipe who hangs around and reads dirty books all night, but someone keeps an eye on things, even in port. There would have been less traffic during the wee hours of the night, when Worthington was transported to the bilges, but it's never totally quiet on a carrier.

Finally, if she'd been killed down here, what possible excuse could anyone have used to get her down into Engineering in the middle of the night? A tryst with Gerrity? Under the right circumstances, that might have done it, but there was no need to. I already knew that Gerrity's roommate had been ashore, and Gerrity himself had confessed to doing the dirty with Worthington in his stateroom earlier that night. Maybe Gerrity'd lied about that, but I didn't think so. Damned complicated to lie about a felony offense as an alibi for murder.

So suppose she was killed somewhere else and brought down to the bilges. That still left a sizable transportation problem. Hard enough to get one perp into the bilges and get Worthington to meet him down here, worse trying to haul a dead body—one with obvious bleeding down the front of it—down ten decks below the waterline and down steep narrow ladders.

So what the hell? How the hell did she get enticed—or moved—down here after she'd been killed?

I looked around the space for clues. I looked again. Nothing in the maze of steel plates and gridded catwalks jumped out at me.

"Looking for clues?"

I stopped myself before I startled. Tempting to blame it on years of training and experience in keeping a cool head, but the real reason was my knees didn't work as fast as my brain. By the time they'd summoned up the momentum to flex, I'd pigeonholed the voice. I turned around.

"Hey," I said.

Doc Benning regarded me gravely. "You haven't told me anything yet."

"Nothing to tell. How did you know I was down here?"

She thought about it for a moment. "I don't know, exactly. It's something I can do sometimes. Find people. I shut my eyes, concentrate, and I get a picture of where they are on the ship."

I had a mental picture of Doc weaving a web from Medical, sending tiny silk suture tripwires throughout the ship. "Everyone?" I asked.

"No. Just some people."

"How long have you been able to do that with me?"

"I don't know. This was the first time I tried. I called your office and your stateroom and didn't get an answer, so I thought you might be down here."

"That simple, huh?"

She nodded. "So what have you found?"

I gestured at the massive, hulking machinery, inviting her to take it in. "No confessions stapled to a feed waterline, no footprints." I pointed at the two catwalks that jagged across overhead, twisting through wicked angles to ladders down to our level. "Two points of access. Hard to see how anyone could get in or out without being noticed, particularly if they were toting a body."

She shook her head. "There's more than that."

My turn to look appraisingly at her. "Didn't know you were such an expert on naval engineering."

"I'm not. But when they hold the mass conflagration drills—you know, the huge engineering-space fires—we have to know how and where the casualties might be coming out. So we can get to them quickly, and so we can stay out of the way in the passageways."

"Aha. So how do the snipes get out of here?"

She thought for a moment, then turned slowly through 360 degrees, peering off into the dingy corners of the space. "Ellison doors and escape shafts. There's at least one on each deck. A straight climb up to the main deck, maybe a couple of decks high. Stryker frames right outside the exit. Look over there—that's one." She pointed at a corner, then walked off toward it. I followed.

"See?" She shoved on the cantilevered door. "It's hinged in the middle so it rotates in the middle of the door frame. That way, if there's an explosion, it doesn't blow open or freeze shut. It just takes a little extra pressure on one side to open it."

"Are they locked?"

"Wouldn't be much point in it, would there? Not for an emergency egress. Are you about done down here?"

I nodded. "I suppose you think I ought to inspect the topside area for signs of recent use."

"We. I thought of it. It's only fair. And you should tell me what you've found out so far."

"Just for the Ellison doors? I'd have gotten around to those eventually."

She regarded me gravely. "Think of me as a paid informant. One who accepts information instead of cash or credit cards."

"Or immunity from prosecution. If I find out you know something and you're not telling me. There're laws about interfering with a criminal investigation."

"And no laws that require me to provide you the services of a first-rate mind as a sounding board. Come on, Bud. You know it'll help you to talk it out."

She was right about that. One of the dangers of being the only NCIS agent onboard a ship was not having a partner to kick things around with. Sure, there was the Master-at-Arms force, and the Chief heading it up was a damned fine professional. But friends—ones like a good partner—were rare.

Sometimes you don't have any choice about who you talk to. When your social contacts are limited to the guys on the other side of a concrete-block wall, you learn to get along with what life hands you just to stay sane. There were times in Vietnam when I probably would have cut off a hand to have someone like Doc Benning on the other side of that wall.

"OK," I said finally. "First, let's go hunt down the other end of this shaft."

She smiled, a rare enough event. I wondered whether it was from winning the argument or sheer pleasure at being involved. "Thanks—partner."

"No badge yet, honey." I leered just enough to let her know it was a joke.

THE TOPSIDE ENTRANCE to the shaft was located on the port side of the passageway. Unlocked, as Doc had suggested. I shoved it open and peered down it. The light at the top penetrated to the bottom.

Doc moved in close and stuck her head in the opening, ducking under my arm after getting a firm grasp on the side of the doorframe.

"Long way down," I said. "How would you do it? Could just toss her down the shaft, I suppose."

Doc shook her head. "I would bet on broken bones, maybe even her neck. If not that, at least some severe bruising."

"No bruises if she were already dead, but you're right about the broken bones. If you were strong enough, you could carry her down slung over your shoulder. Firemen could do it."

"Or use the Stryker frame," Doc suggested. "Strap her in it and lower her down with a rope."

"Maybe just the rope. Tie it under her arms and pay it out slowly. You wouldn't need the frame if you weren't worried about aggravating injuries."

I could see Doc weighing the scenario carefully in her mind. "That would explain the abrasions on her torso."

"One problem with all of the rope scenarios, though," I continued. "Somebody would notice. Even at zero-dark-thirty, you've got the bakers and watchstanders roaming the passageways. Too much chance someone's going to stop and take a gander at what you're doing."

"Yes. No doubt. So we're left with the toss-her-down-the-shaft or the fireman-carry options." Doc's voice hitched on the last phrase.

I patted her twice on the back. Gently. "This is part of it, Carol. You have to do this without thinking about it being Gina. Otherwise, you never get past the grief and into seeing the possibilities."

She straightened up from looking down the shaft and looked down the passageway. I followed her gaze. It was like one of those illusions you get when you have one mirror reflecting into another. Images within images, each smaller than the one containing it. The passageway stretched the entire length of the ship, seeming to diminish to a single point in the distance and broken only by the watertight hatch frames jutting out every six paces, kneeknocker high.

If the perp had been standing in this passageway, he or she could have seen anyone approaching from a long way away. The nearest cross-corridor was four kneeknockers away. Unless—

"He could have secured the hatches at either end of this segment," I said thoughtfully. "Maybe put up a sign that said it was secured for field day or waxing."

"It could have been opened, though."

"Sure, but he would hear the noise of the hatch undogging.

Maybe enough time to tie off the rope to one of the rungs on the vertical ladder and shut the emergency egress hatch."

"That would work. Then he could either duck into one of the offices or pretend to be just another person ignoring the signs." Doc looked down, then suddenly crouched down. "Look." She pointed at the deck.

I stared for a second, then followed her down for a closer look.

Two faint scrape marks scored the old wax on the deck, barely black-streaked in spots. Each was about three-quarters of an inch wide. "Someone's getting sloppy about field day," I said, wondering why so much of this week required me to pay attention to decks.

Doc looked up at me. "Maybe," she said, lightly tracing out the outlines of the marks with one short-nailed finger. "But you know what that looks like. Heel marks."

I nodded. "Either from someone scuffing along the deck and not picking up his feet—or from someone getting dragged."

12

DOC HAD to get back to Medical for two afternoon appointments before we could really finish exploring the intricate causation possibilities of scuff marks. Before she left, she extracted a promise from me to keep her informed on significant developments, the adjective a concession I wrung out of her to preclude the expectation of hourly updates. I followed her down two ladders before breaking off to go to my office while she continued down another deck to her spaces.

I paused before entering my office, inhaling clean. Virtue must smell like fresh wax and Navy industrial spray-and-wipe.

Fernandez appeared at the cross-corridor. He watched me, letting me decide whether to ignore him or not. It's a skill many junior people acquire early on.

"Looks good," I said, pitching my voice just loud enough to reach him.

He nodded at the permission that granted and came around the corner. "Lot better, huh? Bet you didn't know it was that color."

"Nope. Hey, you got a minute?" I asked. "Come on in."

His face stilled, looked a little betrayed. "This about that woman?"

"Maybe. Probably not, though. Just want to ask your advice on who I should talk to, since you know everybody around here."

"I don't snitch, man." He drawled the last word out.

"And I don't ask. Come on." I gestured at the office. "You don't like it, you can leave, OK?"

He followed me into the office, each step steeped in reluctance. He paused in the middle of the room, deciding whether to leave the door open or closed. Finally, he shoved it shut, a little harder than necessary.

"What're you striking for, Fernandez?" I asked. Translation: What do you want to be when you grow up and are paroled from cleaning duties.

"AD—Aviation Jet Mechanic. Soon's I finish ninety days of this shit, I go to Line Division. Working on the flight deck, man."

"Tough job."

"Better than cleaning up shit."

I'd have been willing to bet Fernandez was already spending about as much time up there as the Handler would put up with. Just checking it out, picking up what he could so he'd stay ahead of the pack. There was a reason that his Chief had made him boss compartment cleaner, something you could see in Fernandez. "So you probably already know some shit about the Tomcat, right?"

He nodded, still suspicious.

"You heard about 301 last week? The one that got pulled off the cat for a control surface problem?"

" 'Member that."

"That's what I'm interested in. That lady's roommate was flying it that day, and maybe that had something to do with it."

He shook his head. "Don't think so. Like what?"

"Well, somebody said Lieutenant Berkshire might have forgotten to do a little preflight work on that aircraft before she signed for it. You hear anything like that from the Plane Captains?"

He was mildly pleased at the implication that the Plane Captains conferred with him. Most of the PCs weren't anymore senior than Fernandez, but they'd have at least six months of experience on the flight deck ahead of him.

The PCs were responsible for the care and feeding of the aircraft when it was on the deck, keeping it clean, making sure it was tied down if need be, and riding the brakes in the cockpit when the flight deck crew used the yellow gear to move the Tomcat around on the deck. They checked hydraulic fluid, watched refueling, and washed the sleek beast down to keep the salt from eating into the paint. They usually took possession of their birds by neatly stenciling their names on the underside.

"They talk about it, sure," he answered.

"What about Berkshire? She a decent pilot?"

He frowned. "Maybe off the deck she is. Bitch on the ground. Always whining about something."

"She giving the Plane Captains a hard time?"

"Usually. You heard right about the preflighting. She do it, but not real well." He snorted. "Pretty stupid not to be more careful."

"I think so, too. Any idea why she's careless?"

He shook his head. "No. Just know that she is. Plane Captain complained about her once, and she's been after that girl since then."

"She's not going to know that we talked," I assured him.

"Hell, I not scared of her, man. No way."

"Any chance one of the PCs might have accidentally on purpose left that roll of duct tape in the aircraft? Knowing she was going to fly it, thinking something might take her down a notch or two?"

He got very still. "I don't know nothing about that."

"And if you did, you might not tell me, right?" I added softly. "That about it?"

Fernandez stood up. "Need to get back to work."

"I know. Thanks for talking. It stays here."

He stared at me, open challenge in his face. "I didn't tell you somebody tried to get her."

"If somebody did, you don't know about it." That much was true—I was fairly certain the *chollo* wasn't lying.

I was also fairly certain that he'd now make it a point to find out. If only to show himself that he could.

IGNORANCE IS BLISS, unless you're a Fernandez type who prides himself on having the whole damned boat wired for sound. Or unless you're Commanding Officer of a squadron. I wondered who would know more by the end of the day about Berkshire and her habits as a pilot—the compartment cleaner or her Captain.

I needed to talk to Jazzman again. Needed to, even if he were part of the problem. Especially if he were.

He wasn't hard to find. He was in his stateroom, buried up to his knees in paperwork, and not looking much like he wanted to be disturbed. The sign on the door gave me the clue: "Get lost unless it's important."

I knocked and pushed the door open when I heard him snarl.

"Got a minute?" I asked.

He groaned, put down his pen, and opened his hands in supplication. "If I say no, you'll come in anyway. Not that I would. Anything having to do with Worthington has top priority with me."

"I thought it might. I need to ask you a couple of questions."

He leaned back in the chair and rolled his neck as though trying to work out a kink. "About the fight last night? I heard you were there."

"Not when it started. I walked in just as your officers were breaking it up."

"Yeah. They're both in hack. No liberty until we're on our way back home, and I'm not so certain I'm going to let them out then. Stupid shits—there were a million places on this boat they could go to work out their problems without making half the squadron witnesses."

"So you're more pissed at the lack of discretion than at the fact that one of your guys took a swing at one of your women?"

"You might as well sit." He gestured at the plastic couch against the far side of the room. One corner of a sheet peeked out on the right side. At night it folded out into a slightly-larger-than-single bed. "I told you before, they might as well hire lesbians for all the difference their gender makes to me. Two pilots got in a fight—end of story, the new Navy way. Besides, Berkshire can take care of herself."

"Maybe one on one, but how about in the air? Picking fights with other pilots and beating the shit out of a guy isn't the best way to make sure someone will cover your ass when you need it."

"I know, I know—you think I don't? But exactly what do you suggest I do about it, other than throw them in hack? If I make a big deal about her beating Gerrity up, he loses face bigtime. I pick on Gerrity, and that's sure as hell not fair. The way I heard it, she started it."

"And almost finished it."

He stared at the picture stuck back in one corner of his desk. Wife, three kids—two boys, one little girl—all with that same golden halo he had. "You wouldn't think—hell, who the hell are these women, anyway? Does any damned bit of this make any sense? The three RIOs are fairly normal sort of people, but the pilots—" He shook his head ruefully. "Berkshire's OK most of the time. Hell of a natural stick. But picking fights in the ready room doesn't cut it. And Worthington's dead." He looked up at me. "Tell me this all works out for the best for the Navy somehow. Make me believe it, Wilson, or at least tell me how the hell I'm supposed to pretend that it does!"

I let his words hang in the air. Coming from the skipper, this venting was damned near a compliment. Up to him what happened now, and I'd follow his cue. We could pretend that it never happened or talk frankly about the burdens of command.

"Shit," he said finally. He looked over at me. "You know how it is. Sorry—not your fault. If I'd known it would be like this when I was XO—"

"You would have stuck it out anyway," I finished for him. "Because no matter how much of a pain in the ass a command tour can be, there's nothing that beats it. Nothing."

"Yeah. Be nice if I got to fly a little more, though."

"Then put yourself on the schedule more often. It's your squadron."

"It is, isn't it?" A thoughtful look. "But you didn't come up here to listen to my snivels."

"No. I wanted to ask you about the fight. And about Berkshire and Gerrity. And your Maintenance Officer."

"There're twenty other officers in the squadron. What about them?"

"When I get around to them. Can we start with those three?"

"Sure. What do you want to know?"

"Anything. Everything. Berkshire, for instance. Rumor has it she's hell on the Plane Captains."

He sighed. "She is that. The XO's had her in his stateroom more than once over it. Fucking lazy about too much—her branch work, fitness reports, and enlisted evaluations, just about anything that doesn't have to do with being in the air."

"Preflighting, too."

"So I hear." He rubbed the back of his neck, shot me an irritated look. "And the point is?"

"I'm not sure yet. But she was supposed to fly Tomcat 301 the day it got downed for control surface gripes, and you assigned Worthington as the investigating officer on that case. Not only her roommate, but someone she didn't get along with very well. If you were me, would you wonder why?"

"I guess I'd wonder about everything, if I were you. But the 301 problem—I had a reason for that. Worthington knew a hell of a lot about the guts of an airplane, more than most of them."

"Her degree, right?"

"Exactly. You don't use that theoretical stuff much out here, but it did give her a better feel for how things that move in flight work. She was damned near psychic about mechanics and aerodynamics. Berkshire was the better pilot, mostly because of her reflexes, but Worthington could outthink her in the air. Anyway, Worthington was a good choice, and I knew she'd do a damned thorough job. She was as hard a worker as Berkshire is a slacker. Besides—off the record—it did make a statement. One woman screwed the pooch on preflighting, another one did a good job on the investigation. It balances out, like."

"Were you worried at all that Worthington might slam Berkshire on the preflighting?"

"I thought she probably would. And it needed to be said. I'd feel the same if it were a guy or one of the gals. And no, if you're working up to asking the question—I don't think that Berkshire killed

Worthington over something in the JAG investigation." He rooted through a pile of papers, then fished out the copy I'd given him. "You read it. She was almost done with it, and there were no career killers in it."

"But she wasn't done with it, was she? Or she'd have turned it in already."

He shrugged. "Typing, spellchecking—maybe her printer was on the blink. It wasn't due for another two weeks, anyway."

"And from your understanding of her, she wasn't the type to turn in a rough draft?"

"No way. It would have been letter-perfect with even margins. I told her she could use the yeoman with the typing part, but she was working on it on her laptop."

"Think she would have talked to the Maintenance Officer about it?"

"I'm sure she did. Another AE grad, her boss. They probably had a lot to talk about."

That surprised me. "How did they get along?"

"OK, as far as I could tell. The usual gripes from the MO, but what's new? You're talking about a man with a serious FMC fixation. I imagine he pushed on her to keep it up, she maybe resisted cutting corners. If he'd gotten too out of line with it, she would have told someone."

"The Master Chief would have known?"

"Along with Maintenance Control, the Chief's Mess, just about anyone else. You don't keep secrets in a squadron for long, not about something like that."

"Just about something like two pilots screwing each other."

A glare. "I told you I didn't know about that."

"But you suspected. Just like you suspect there's something else going on with that Tomcat."

"Why do you say that?"

"Because there is. I can smell it, taste it, almost touch it. There's something no one's talking about, and it shows up in officers fighting in the ready room, in sloppy maintenance practices, and in one dead pilot."

"You have a problem with me, I suggest you talk to CAG. Or the Admiral."

I stood up. "I ought to hear it from you first, sir."

He shook his head. "You're on the wrong track."

"I'm not. You're about to be." I left him staring at a stack of fitness reports.

13

LATER THAT day, fresh out of smart ideas, I took advantage of a break in the flight schedule to get out on deck. The sky was partly cloudy, the seas relatively calm. Twenty knots of wind gusted across the flight deck, half of it generated by the ship's own course and speed. All in all, a beautiful day to be at sea.

Hornets and Tomcats crowded the area around the island, the protrusion that stuck up twelve decks above the flight deck and housed Pri-Fly and the Destroyer Squadron Commodore, the DesRon. Three E-2Cs occupied their normal spots just aft of the island, close enough so that the massive fifteen-foot-diameter radar dishes mounted atop their fuselages almost touched. Yellow gear, the ubiquitous towing and servicing vehicles, trundled around the deck, rearranging the aircraft into a pattern more pleasing to the handler, who watched the moves from his windowed space at the base of the island.

I walked toward the aft end of the carrier, feeling as always dwarfed by the ship. As small as it looks when you're trying to hit just the right combination of airspeed and descent angles to snag the three-wire, on foot it is truly massive. Two football fields in length, the edge of the flight deck towered ninety feet above the ocean. If they ever add a ninth wonder of the world, it ought to be an aircraft carrier.

A small city, a captive population contained in a pressure cooker.

Turning on the heat brings out the best—and the worst—in the inhabitants. More bests than ashore, perhaps, but that just makes the worst stand out.

Like with Gina Worthington. The human faults and normal peculiarities of the people around her were being magnified by the circumstances. The MO's preoccupation with FMC raised to an obsession, Gerrity's affair with her now a felony. And maybe some irritating little habit of Gina's—her meticulousness, perhaps, or her chip-on-the-shoulder assertiveness, hell, maybe even the way she wore her hair, turned out to be a reason to kill her.

I paced the flight deck for awhile, thinking. Wonderful philosophy, but it wasn't doing much to move this case off my desk. I decided that walking the flight deck was just complying with Doc's orders that I start getting more exercise and paced up and down the hot tarmac until the Air Boss cleared the deck for the next cycle. When I went back into the rabbit warren inside the skin of the carrier, I felt mildly virtuous and a good deal more at peace.

IT DIDN'T LAST. Four telephone messages were taped to the outside of my office door, left there by the Master-at-Arms force. Unlike Fernandez, they didn't rate a key.

I peeled the messages off slowly, trying to avoid taking off more paint. All were from the chief of staff, requesting in increasingly large adjectives that I see him in his office at my earliest convenience. At my very earliest convenience. ASAP—the military equivalent of the medical order STAT. "As soon as possible." And the final message: "Buster," pilot slang for "Bust your ass getting here!"

In my case, any busting would involve knees, although the Admiral might be tempted to break off something sharp and pointy in me if he was really that pissed. I balanced courtesy with independence and selected the appropriately brisk pace up the ladders to flag country.

"Where the hell have you been?" The Chief of Staff—COS—threw his pencil down on the desk and glared at me. "Hell, you damn near caused a man-overboard drill!"

"On the flight deck. And I would have heard the 1MC if you'd put the word out for me," I pointed out.

He snorted. "Right. I'm going to broadcast the fact that the Admiral wants to see you."

"There a problem with that?"

"Why don't you ask the Admiral yourself, seeing as how he's been waiting for damn near an hour for you?" The COS pointed at the Admiral's door.

I studied COS's flushed face for a moment. "You need to get more exercise, Captain. Liable to stroke out if your blood pressure keeps spiking like this."

"Fuck you, Wilson. Just get in there."

I waggled one finger at him. Taunting COS is sort of an old hobby. "Now, now—remember our policy in the new Navy. Don't ask, don't tell."

I stepped out of his office and headed for the Admiral's cabin as he started to stand. There are times when a surgical strike is preferable to an out-and-out war.

THE ADMIRAL WAS only slightly more pleased to see me. He did the usual number, letting me stand in front of his desk while he finished signing one important document after another, finally deigning to notice my presence.

"Thanks for keeping me updated, Wilson," he said.

"You're welcome." My tone was nothing if not meticulously neutral. If he were counting on the deer-in-the-headlights reflex response to flag disapproval to turn his statement into a reprimand, he was going to be disappointed. Maybe in a prior life.

He glared. I waited politely for the Admiral to continue.

"I was being sarcastic."

"I wasn't." A non sequitur, certainly, and one that he barely paused to consider.

"I told you to keep me informed."

"At this point, I suspect the Admiral knows everything about the case that I do," I answered.

"Which isn't much."

"Exactly."

"Would it be too much trouble," he began, laying on the sarcasm heavily now since I wasn't playing his game, "for you to occasionally stop by my office and tell me what progress you've made in this case? I'm referring, of course, to the murder of Lieutenant Gina Worthington, in case you might not be certain exactly which of your oh-so-pressing matters is causing me some concern. That is, if it doesn't interfere with your exercise periods."

Interesting. So at least part of COS's annoyance was self-induced. If he'd wanted me down in Flag Country that quickly, he could have sent one of the mess cooks up to get me. I spared a few seconds to consider that.

"Doctor's orders, Admiral. At my age, one starts to seize up without regular mild exercise." A cheap shot, one that added an edge to his glare. I knew Admiral Fairchild was only two months older than I was.

"Perhaps you'd like to apply for a medical transfer off of *Abraham Lincoln?* It could be arranged," he said.

I waved one hand nonchalantly, dismissing the problem. "Won't be necessary, Admiral. But I do appreciate your concern."

He leaned back in his chair and considered me carefully. Finally, after a silence he obviously intended to be disconcerting, he said, "Do you have any suspects?"

I nodded. "Several. But no evidence and no real clear motives. Just a number of oddities that bother me."

"Like what?"

"It really is too early to make them public."

"I'm not the public, you idiot!" He shoved himself out of his chair, hands flat on his desk, and leaned across the desk, shouting. "This is my goddamned ship and you'll goddamned well keep me informed. Do you understand that?"

"And risk your being accused of exerting command influence over the course of this investigation, Admiral?" The magic words, the silver bullet, the one factor that'd given rise to the transformation of NIS into NCIS. You didn't want to use it often. It killed more than it should.

He sat down abruptly, his eyes still fixed on mine. "Are you accusing me—"

I cut him off. "No, sir, I'm not. I don't want anyone else to be able to, and the only way I can make sure that happens is to keep you out of the loop."

His high color abated slightly. "One of my staff is involved?"

"I don't think so, but I'm asking some hard questions about one of your squadrons. Sometimes shit rolls downhill, sometimes it gets pushed uphill. This time, you want to stand clear."

He broke the eye lock and stared off at the plaques on his wall. Over twenty-five years of military service, some of it in combat, and now I was raising one of the oldest tenets of naval command. When something goes wrong, the senior man is responsible. Period.

"Why?" he asked finally. "Wilson, I'm damned if I can figure out what the hell you're up to. You could have ended my career in Hong Kong, but you didn't. Yet every time we talk, I'll be damned if I can figure out why. You don't like me, you don't cooperate, and you're generally an obstreperous pain in the ass. So why? Can you answer that, at least?"

"May I speak frankly, sir?" I asked.

He nodded permission.

"Admiral, with all due respect"—the old exculpatory litany came easily to my lips—"I think you're an asshole about a lot of things. You expect me to ask how high when you say jump, you don't listen to liberty briefings, and you're generally on my ass about a lot of things that are damned well none of your immediate business. You've pressured me, threatened me, and you have the gall to object when I don't heel immediately."

"That's an explanation?"

"Not all of it. In spite of all that, Admiral, I happen to think I'd want you on this ship if we went to war. Or"—a vision of the Hanoi Hilton flashed into my mind—"worse," I concluded. "You said something to me right after we got underway about not liking me but that you thought you needed me. Consider the sentiment reciprocated. What's good for the United States Navy is good for NCIS, and that includes having you in command."

"You're protecting me." There was quiet astonishment in his voice.

I nodded. I'd almost told the Admiral he'd have made a damned fine POW but stopped the words before they'd come out, certain that they'd never sound the way I intended them to.

"From what?" he asked again, this time with a note of real concern in his voice.

"I don't know. Not yet, at least. And until I do, I'd like a free rein. Sir."

He looked off in the distance again. "So we don't like each other, but you want me to trust you with my career."

"You already did once. Whether you admit it or not, you know you can."

"Hong Kong." It wasn't a question.

"Yes, sir. You may dislike me—hate me, even—but you trust me."

He thought about that for a moment, then sighed. "Strange world."

"There're stranger."

"I guess you'd know."

"I think you do, too."

An odd sort of silence fell between us, one that felt as familiar as it felt disconcerting. I could almost hear him mulling it over, finally coming to a decision. "OK." He looked up and met my eyes again. "You're right—about what, I'm not exactly sure, but you are. Keep me—" He caught himself in time, almost smiled. "I was about to ask you to keep me informed, but I guess we just agreed you can't really do that, didn't we?"

"I'll tell you everything I can, Admiral, as soon as I can."

"That will have to do, Capt.—Mr. Wilson."

"Is there anything else, Admiral?"

He shook his head. "I'll get the Chief of Staff off your ass, for now. All bets are off after this is over with, though."

"That's good enough."

"Very well." He cleared his throat, then added, "Thank you for coming by. This has been—interesting." He stood up from the desk again, more slowly this time, and held out his hand. I took it, shook it firmly, and said, "I appreciate your time, Admiral." I left before either of us could start wondering what the hell had just happened.

14

FERNANDEZ WAS pointedly not waiting for me when I got back to my office. Instead, the three inches of the deck nearest to the bulkhead three kneeknockers aft of my office were getting his close personal attention. I admired his style. He was close enough to see if I went into my office yet far enough away to avoid any apparent association with me, positioned at the intersection of the closest athwartships passageway so he could see anyone approaching.

I left the door ajar. He gave me five minutes, long enough to make sure no one was watching and that I hadn't just stopped by to pick up something and leave, then slipped in as unobtrusively as a cat burglar.

"Hey," I greeted him.

"Hey." He hesitated for a moment.

I pointed at the chair before he had to decide if he had to wait to be asked to sit down. "Take a load off."

He dropped down quickly, as though it'd been his right all along. "I found out something interesting," he said.

"Yeah?"

He nodded. "Real interesting," making sure I understood this was a no-shitter.

"About 301?"

He almost smiled. "They make the flight schedule up the night before, you know," he said casually, watching my face carefully. "Put those pilots' names on it in pencil, then type it in later at night."

"And?"

"Then they make a bunch of copies and put them under the pilots' doors at night—you know, like mail service."

"Still doing it that way, huh?" Except in my earliest days, it'd been a blue mimeograph machine. "Damn."

"Night before 301, somebody else was on the schedule to fly. Not that one that took the flight—somebody else." Every second, he got closer to actually smirking. I let him enjoy it.

"You know who?"

He nodded, savoring the moment. "Senior officer. Most senior around here."

"The Admiral?"

He looked faintly disappointed. "No, man. Not him. Skipper."

"Jazzman? You're sure?"

"Heard it from the Plane Captain herself. Skipper told her to be sure the bird looked real special good the next day—joking with her, like. She washed it, shined it all up—pissed her off when that bitch came out and started ragging on her, all that work."

"Plane Captain say why they switched flights?" I asked.

"I asked her that," he said smugly. "She didn't know, but Air Ops yeoman told her it got changed before they copied the schedule out. Didn't know why."

"Wow." I stared at Fernandez, grateful that some instinct had tumbled me to his importance in the scheme of shipboard life. Lots to be said for getting a clean office and a new reliable source of information in the same fell swoop.

He stood up, moved toward the door. He stopped with one hand on the door knob, assessing me to be sure I understood the importance of what he'd just told me. "Could have been real bad, the skipper flew that bird," he pointed out.

"No shit," I agreed. "Anybody else know this?"

He shrugged. "I didn't make no big point about it."

"So the Plane Captain, the yeoman in Air Ops, and probably a couple of officers in Air Ops," I said.

"That about it, man. Maybe that bitch pilot—maybe not."

"I owe you one," I said.

He nodded, slipped out of the office, and shut the door silently behind him while I considered the possibility that I'd been smarter than I'd planned in not telling the Admiral anything.

So what was it now? Maintenance carelessness or planned sabotage? Did Worthington uncover something in her investigation that put her at risk? If so, from whom?

And why wasn't whatever it was in her JAG investigation? Despite what Jazzman said about her being a perfectionist, the report looked to me like it was finished. I pulled it out of the folder and read through it, looking for misspelled words or awkward phrasings that might indicate she'd wanted to do some more work on it.

Nothing. Even the margins and spacing between headers were neat and correct. As far as I could tell, it was ready to submit. But appearances aren't always reality.

Back in Vietnam, I'd learned a little about what lies underneath the faces we show to the world. Things you can't see in normal circumstances—deep rills and lofty crags in a man's personality—get accentuated. You cut him off from all contact with his fellow prisoners, beat him until he's blind from pain and bleeding from every orifice, starve him, torture him, and tell him his country's abandoned him, and he gets unpredictable. Sometimes the ones you think won't make it turn out to be heroes, tap-coding strength through solid rock to you, making you hold on that one more minute. Other times, the ones you think will come through it don't. Facades crack and crumple, everything glommed onto our public face through nature and nurture comes sliding off and lies in fragments on the ground around you. You're left with the bedrock, what makes a man really who he is. When you can't take anything more from him without killing him, you do.

Life's more complicated when you get past the survival instincts.

People are like pearls, layers of material accreted around a grain of sand.

It was the sand I was interested in, not the pearl. That's what would tell me why there was trouble in Jazzman's wardroom, whether or not the Admiral would have survived the Hanoi Hilton, and who killed Gina Worthington. Unfortunately, getting to the middle of the pearl requires grinding off the bright-shiny layers on top of it. And there wasn't much chance I was going to be able to put the entire ship in a concentration camp any time in the near future.

Thinking about it, I decided there might be another way.

"You want to *what?*" Admiral Fairchild didn't look particularly impressed with my brilliant idea.

"Put some pressure on some people, sir. Stir things up, see what happens."

"On who in particular?"

"I don't know," I repeated. "Wouldn't have to do it this way if I did. But I think Lieutenant Commander Worthington's death is tied in some way with that JAG investigation she was working on. And the guys who attacked me." I left out the parts about whether or not Jazzman had been an intended victim in the whole potential mishap. "At least, that's the only thing I can find in her recent past that seems to offer some possibilities. And, since they seem to have a predilection for sabotaging aircraft, I figure I'll play to their strengths. Give them a chance to go after an aircraft I'm going to be in." Other than Gerrity, I added silently. And I wasn't quite ready to throw all that in the Admiral's lap—if I did, he'd have to do something about it.

"What is it exactly that you want me to do?" Fairchild asked.

"A little misinformation, that's all. Put the word out quietly that you've got a soft spot in your heart for retired aviators and that you're going to let me get a couple of flights in the backseat of a Tomcat. Then get on the CCTV and tell the ship we're making great progress on the case and expect an arrest shortly."

"Cold day in hell, Wilson. Your swim quals and ejection seat quals are seven years out of date."

"How do you know?"

He had the good grace to look embarrassed along with annoyed. "Because I checked, OK? That make you happy?"

"And why—if I might ask—did you care?"

He was silent for a moment, and a flush colored his neck, creeping up toward his face. By sheer force of will, he stopped it below the jawline. "I see you up there, you know. Hanging around Pri-Fly, walking the flight deck. I know what I'd feel like if—damn it, Wilson, when I saw how far out of spec you were, I let it drop. Seven years—if it were just two or three, maybe so."

So maybe my instincts about the Admiral hadn't been that far off. Still . . . "That last senator that was onboard—anyone check his seat quals?"

"You know that's different."

"I know, you know—maybe the rest of the ship doesn't. It makes the story more plausible anyway."

"I suppose so. OK, you win. I'll tell the staff that I'm probably going to let you backseat on a couple of flights. It'll get around fast enough. And you write down what you want me to cover on the CCTV. And when." A small smile then. "One of the advantages of being an admiral, I get free airtime whenever I want it. And there're damned few people on this ship who can question anything I do."

I nodded. We both knew that I was one of them.

15

Y OU'LL BE going with me," Jazzman said. He stood in the
doorway to my office, body lines hard and taut. "I don't
know how the hell you convinced the Admiral to let you do this,
but I'll be damned if I'll be the one standing tall if something happens, trying to figure out what happened in midflight."

"Good. Be nice to get backup," I answered noncommittally,
pointedly not noticing his annoyance. "Appreciate your taking the
event yourself."

"Like you said—I ought to write myself into the flight schedule
more often." He stayed. Glaring at me.

"Something else?" I asked.

"Now that you mentioned it—just why the hell do you have
enough free time to do this? Aren't there more important things on
your daily schedule than trying to recapture your youth?"

I leaned back in my chair and tossed the pencil on my desk. It
worked for COS, maybe it would work for me. "I wasn't aware that
you had input into my activities. Don't recall inviting it, at any rate."

He crossed the room in two steps, leaned across the desk at me.
"Worthington. That name mean anything to you? Because it sure
as hell does to me."

"So you think carving out a couple hours for a flight means I'm
neglecting to tend to my own business, right?"

"Do you know who killed her?" he snapped. "Until you do, I'd say that there's more than enough onboard the ship to keep you occupied."

"It was probably the same person that almost killed you."

That stopped him for a moment, but not for long. "You want to explain that?"

"You want to sit down and lose the command attitude?" I pointed at the visitor's chair. "Thought we'd agreed to trust each other. Just a little."

The anger seemed to drain out of him. Instead of a CO on the warpath, I saw a man maybe fifteen years younger than I was, carrying the load of commanding a squadron of high-octane birds and personalities.

"Sit down," I said more quietly, remembering. "There're some things you ought to know."

TEN MINUTES LATER, Jazzman was getting wound up again. It was that instinctive male reaction to fear or agitation that made everything come out looking like anger. I'd gone through my suspicions with him about Tomcat 301, including the fact that it had been the one he'd been slated to fly that day until he sniveled out. I glossed over Fernandez's identity, hoping to leave him with the impression that I'd talked to someone in Line Division, the Plane Captains' workcenter.

He jumped out of the chair, started for the door, and converted the vector into pacing around my office. "God damn it, I'm going to—"

"Do what? What can you do, other than what you're doing right now, which is talking to the suspicious, nasty mind that started asking all these questions in the first place?" I pointed out. "We still don't know who left the duct tape in 301. Remember, Gina's report said the technician claimed to have checked the bird before signing off the MAF, and that there was no duct tape left in there."

"Yeah, but QA didn't check it."

"Which doesn't mean he wasn't right. Look, Jazzman, I hope I'm real wrong about this. But the way I see it, someone was trying to make sure you had some problems with that flight. Serious problems, maybe. If that duct tape was left in there intentionally, we're coming damned close to attempted murder."

"You are wrong, you know. That tech left that tape there by mistake. Which leaves you with absolutely no leads on her death."

"Maybe so, but this is the one incongruity that I can find in the last month or so before her death. We push on this a little, something may turn up."

"Or we may end up in the drink when I miss something on preflight," he pointed out. "You're taking a chance, you know. If I were this person, I wouldn't use the same method twice in a row."

"There's that. But the plan is that we do find out. Better yet, that we see someone screwing around with the aircraft the night before."

He opened his mouth to argue, then shut it abruptly. His face paled. Finally, he said, "You know what you're saying, don't you? It was one of my people. Someone in the squadron."

"Not necessarily. Yours isn't the only Tomcat squadron onboard. Even the techs in the other squadrons would probably know enough to be able to pull it off. It could even be coincidence that it was the bird that you were supposed to fly."

"My name's stenciled on the side."

"But you're not the only one who flies 301. Look, Jazzman, I'm not saying this is some Perry Mason stunt that will have the perp falling on his knees and confessing, scared into it by our stunning brilliance. But it's somewhere to start. And, as it stands now, you're not going to actually have to ferry me around the sky. We're just going to put our names on the flight schedule and watch, OK?"

"Long shot."

"Maybe. Not if it works. Just keep quiet about it and play along. Hell, you can even bitch and moan about it in public—that'll just make it more convincing, as far as I'm concerned."

He shook his head, unconvinced.

"Tell me," I said, "why did you snivel out of that flight? After all the complaining you do about not getting enough stick time, I'd have thought that'd be the last thing you'd do."

He looked uncomfortable. "Not feeling well, I think. And I'd already been on the flight schedule once that week. It didn't seem that urgent, getting another hop."

"So you flew that week? Hell, one mission's just barely enough to get you hot. What day?"

He frowned. "The day before, I think. Why? What difference does it make?"

I ignored his question. "Anything wrong with your bird that day? On the deck or in the air?"

"I don't remember anything—oh, wait, yeah. I had a problem with a hard point on the wing—one of the weapons stations. Ended up jettisoning a Sparrow." He shook his head and grimaced. "I'm trying to repress it. You got any idea how much paperwork is involved when you dump live ordnance in the ocean?"

"Can't say that I do. Back in my day, we were supposed to come home with clean wings. Just as much hassle back then if you didn't dump."

He dropped into my visitor's chair, the initial hostility gone. "At least you got to shoot. Not like me." He reached out and picked up a pencil from my desk, tapped the eraser on my desk, then started rolling it back and forth between his fingers like a cheerleader handles a baton. "Fifteen years in the Navy, and I've never fired a shot in anger."

"Anger doesn't have much to do with the real thing. Sometimes, a little. But not most of the time."

He looked at me doubtfully. "Come off it. Vietnam would have beat the hell out of flying exercises and running blue-loaded CAP missions."

The blue-painted missiles and bombs were dummies. Same weight, same avionics connections as a live round, but they were designed to simulate the real thing. A pilot could conduct the entire attack or engagement, but he would be shooting blanks.

"You're carrying a full combat load out here," I pointed out.

"Like it makes any difference. Amnesty International could have written our rules of engagement."

"Which are?"

"Short version: Don't shoot."

"And just what is it that you're not shooting at?" I asked, exasperated. I was getting singularly tired of being out of the loop, having cryptic operational conversations with pilots in which only one of the parties knew what the hell was going on. It would have been OK if that one party had been me.

He leaned back in the chair, a slightly surprised look on his face. "That's right, I'd forgotten—you're not briefed in, are you?"

"There's a thing called 'need to know.' They think I don't."

"The only pilot with any combat experience onboard, and they don't bother to tell you what the hell's going on? That sucks."

"I'm with NCIS now, not on staff." The bite in my voice was because Jazzman might have been reading my mind, parroting back to me some of the same things one part of my mind kept bringing up. Hell, I'd paid my dues—more than any man or woman on that ship. I had a right of some sort to know, a moral one if not a legal one. Admiral Fairchild ought to have understood that.

He leaned forward and stopped rolling the pencil around. "There's a submarine out here. An Oscar. Been hanging out in this part of the ocean for better than six weeks. We wouldn't have even known it if the electronic snoops hadn't started picking up some weird ELF—Extremely Low Frequency—communications."

"An Oscar? What the hell's a cruise missile ship doing out here in our playpen?"

A self-satisfied expression crossed his face. "I thought you might wonder about that. The Oscar's got only one purpose in life—to kill surface ships. One torpedo shot'd break *Lincoln*'s keel."

"When did the Russians start deploying out of area again?"

"Earlier this year. Nobody's saying it, but this might be the start of another Cold War."

"You better hope not." Jazzman's attitude was bothering me a lot. Combat wasn't nearly as fulfilling as he seemed to think. People shot at you, you shot back, and sometimes—I cut the thought short.

"We wouldn't be having these funding problems if we had an enemy," he muttered, looking vaguely disappointed in me.

"Jesus, Jazzman. Things haven't changed that much. War's a bad thing—that's what we try to prevent."

He stood up suddenly, now distant and cold. "Of course it is. I'll let you know what time we're briefing." He left.

What the hell was that all about? Was Jazzman a frustrated Cold Warrior, an officer who figured he'd missed out on all the fun during Vietnam? God, did he think flying combat mission after combat mission when you're dead tired, dodging flak and praying you didn't shit your pants, writing letters home to the wives and parents of dead friends, was a good thing? It sounded like it—and that bothered me almost as much as Worthington being dead.

Almost.

MDI WAS WORKING overtime. By that evening, I was getting colder looks than I thought possible from Jazzman's squadron. Seemed like every technician, every pilot, and every last damned pencil geek in the squadron knew Jazzman'd been ordered to let me get my jollies.

Not that I minded that. Made the odds better that the word would get back to the one person I wanted to know about it.

If there was such a person. I considered that possibility for a moment. It was entirely possible that the duct-tape-in-the-Tomcat theory was worthless. Could have been just what everyone thought it was—a mistake, an accident, a careless maintenance tech. In which case I'd lost nothing and just gained the mere possibility that I might actually get airborne without a stewardess and without sitting backward in the dark in a COD or sideways in a helo.

Correction: two small downsides, not worth worrying about. I'd piss the Admiral off some more and have to get close to flying without actually going.

Was it worth it? Annoying the Admiral didn't bother me. I'd been doing that since I was a boot Lieutenant Commander eons ago. The flying part, though—maybe. Getting fitted out in the loaner gears, going through my own rituals—every aviator has them, running the gamut from the order in which he adjusts his ejection harness straps to tucking one particular lucky rabbit's foot in its own special pocket—tightening down the straps and feeling them bite just short of pain into my crotch, knowing they'd ease up some when I strapped into the aircraft—all details associated with carrier aviation. For a moment, I wondered which would be worse: to not fly at all or to get that close and not go.

I'd never really accepted the fact that my flying days were over, I realized. That refusal had pulled me through months of grueling physical therapy after Vietnam, let me fly when most of the docs said I was lucky just to be able to walk without lurching. Even during my retirement ceremony, the flags snapping in the wind across the carrier deck, listening to the nice words and flattering summaries of my career, I hadn't believed it.

Being assigned to a carrier with NCIS—hell, it was easy to pretend that I'd just been left off the flight schedule that day and to ignore the funny clothes I wore. I even tended to wear turtleneck shirts, the kind that I wore under my flight suit during—

Stop it, I told myself sternly. OK, maybe it's time to let that sink in now, but not right this second. You'll suit up, walk through the wind on the flight deck, tarmac hot under your boots, maybe even strap your middle-aged Walter Mitty ass into the back seat of that Tomcat, and go with whatever happens. There's not a chance in hell that they'll let you take another cat shot.

But they might, some tiny part of my mind insisted. They might.

16

THAT AFTERNOON, I was still puzzling over Jazzman's outlook on life. I'd thought I was getting to know the man—hell, I was figuring him for a sure shot at the stars, but now I was wondering whether that was such a good idea.

Gil Shaughnessy. I hadn't followed up on our conversation up in the tower, and it looked like my stock with Jazzman was falling. Maybe whatever'd been on his mind could help me understand what was going on in Golden Boy's brain.

I caught Gil down on the flight deck, screwing around with the Handler and looking more relaxed than I'd seen him in days. He looked up when I walked into the room, gave a friendly wave, and finished telling the Handler a rude joke.

I laughed at the punchline, which'd been ancient when I was a pup and hadn't gotten a hell of a lot funnier in the subsequent decades. Finally, when he looked over my way, I cut my eyes toward the hatch leading out to the flight deck.

He stood up slowly, uncurling from the hard plastic chair he'd been filling up. "Guess I'll go out and make sure all the noses are warm," he said casually to the Handler. He looked over at me. "You wanna go? I'll show you how a real flight deck works—knock some of that rust out of your brain."

"Hell, that's all that's holding it together." I followed him outside.

We walked aft, ostensibly to examine the arresting wires. The thick cables that snag the tailhooks on carrier-based aircraft get inspected often. Jolting tons of aircraft to a dead halt fatigues the metal something awful, and you don't want one of those puppies snapping. Not if there's a person within a mile or so. The line will snap across the deck, cutting anything in its way in half. Aircraft, yellow gear—and people. People especially. Anyone that gets in the path of a breaking arresting wire under tension usually bleeds out on the deck before Medical can get to them.

"What you said the other day," I said finally, after we'd finished a good fifteen minutes of generational sparring and male bonding. "About Jazzman."

"Yeah." Gil crouched down on the deck and picked up a small bolt. He muttered something obscene and held it out for my inspection. "You have as many FOD problems when you were flying?"

FOD—foreign object damage—is slang for anything laying around on the flight deck that's not supposed to be there. Let that bolt get sucked into an engine and you're looking at a seriously hurt bird, not to mention the casualties if the jet starts throwing turbine blades at people. A real danger—and a lousy try at changing the subject.

"Yeah, sure did. One thing we didn't have though."

Gil looked at me with a quizzically resigned expression, hearing the other shoe drop somewhere off in the distance.

"Tap dancing. I've seen more of it in the last forty-eight hours than I saw in ten cruises."

The Air Boss sighed and slipped the bolt into his pocket absentmindedly. "It's not always that easy, you know."

"What, interfering with a murder investigation? Hell, you couldn't prove it by me. Seems like the whole ship and every swinging dick on it—correction, every swinging genitalia, 'cause this damned sure cuts across the sex line—is doing a fine job of it. Tell you what. When we get back, let's put together a Rockettes line. And you're going to be the lead attraction."

Not many people on the boat could talk to Gil that way and get away with it. I couldn't have either except that I was right. I watched him decide whether to get pissed or honest.

"I'm not going to be the one that sends him down. I know what you're asking, and I've probably got the answer you're looking for. But you got no witnesses to that statement, and you won't ever have them." Gil looked stubborn—bothered, but stubborn.

"Tell me where to start," I said finally. "That much is all I'm asking."

Gil walked over to a huffer, a massive, mobile air compressor used to turn over jet engines, and examined the stencil on it. The last inspection date was current. He examined the tires carefully, then looked up at me from next to one wheel. "You want to know about weapons. Not the dummy loads, the real thing. I figure you'll get around to checking those out eventually, so I'm not giving you the whole thing."

"How far back do I want to go?"

He shook his head. "Not far. This cruise."

"Jazzman's been shooting when he wasn't supposed to?" Given my last conversation with him, it wasn't hard to believe.

Gil straightened up and looked out at the sea. It was calmer today, almost glassy between the gentle swells. "You'll figure it out. I've said all I can say and still live with myself. And with the rest of the Navy."

"Aviation, you mean." I was suddenly fed up with the pervasive code of silence. Not so long ago, I'd have been on the inside, and I wasn't sure which pissed me off—being an outsider or having people make cryptic, meaningful statements at me.

"That's all I can tell you, Mr. Wilson. And I'm afraid I'm going to have to get back up to the tower—first cycle starts in thirty minutes." Something that looked a little like pity backlit his eyes. Whether for me or Jazzman or for life in general, I couldn't tell. I decided not to take it personally. He'd done what he could.

THE ADMIRAL AND I agreed that he'd call Flight Ops at 2000 and tell them to put me on the schedule the next day for a Fam flight— a familiarization, normally not conducted at sea but safely ashore from one of the Replacement Air Groups. We set the hour that late to allow me time to catch some sleep and to get in position. Jazzman would be contacting Air Ops himself to make sure that he was assigned to Tomcat 301.

I racked out for three solid hours, more than enough rest to carry me through the night. If I'd actually been planning on flying the next day, I might have been worried, but we all knew that the Fam flight was just a ruse.

We did, didn't we? I considered the large thermos of coffee I'd set down on the Air Boss's chair and tried to believe it myself.

By 2000, I was on the 0-10 level, standing up next to the glass, staring down at the flight deck from the darkened spaces. Tomcat 301 was parked forward, within view. I had a clear view of her right side from my vantage point since her nose was pointed at the starboard side. Most of the approaches to her were also in plain view, although there was one little arc obscured by the yellow gear cluttering the deck. That was a problem, but not a major one. Anyone trying to get to 301 would still have to walk across a clear area, even if he or she was hidden behind the yellow gear at first.

Although most of the flight deck was deserted, a few technicians still buzzed around, checking chocks and chains, refueling aircraft, and generally performing the myriad care-and-feeding duties of any squadron. There weren't so many people out there that I couldn't keep them all in view, although the rising moon and the clear, hard stars kept distracting me as the night deepened.

I had just given up trying to decide whether one particularly bright star was Betelgeuse or Cassiopeia when a flicker of movement caught my attention. Something, someone, near Tomcat 301. I moved from between the two Air Boss chairs to the forward window.

A brown-shirted figure approached Tomcat 301 and crouched down by her nosewheel. There was nothing furtive about the movements—the person walked straight toward the aircraft, glancing around in the normal pattern that kept experienced flight deck personnel alive during ops. It was an impossible habit to break, even when flight operations were secured during the evening. Aviation mechanics would occasionally start engines to check repairs, perform periodic maintenance, and investigate pilot gripes, posing a danger to anyone who relaxed up on the roof. Just because there were no aircraft landing and taking off was no excuse for relaxing one's scan. It was a very natural explanation for Mr. Brown-Shirt continually glancing around the flight deck.

Of course, there were other ones as well. I found myself hoping that wasn't the case this time.

Brown-Shirt knelt down at the nose wheel. From what I could see, he appeared to be running his hands up and down the strut, occasionally yanking on a structural component. Apparently satisfied by what he found, he moved to the port wheelwell and stood up to reach inside it. I watched, swearing quietly, replaying in my mind what I'd seen.

Brown-Shirt had walked empty-handed up to the aircraft. I hadn't seem him take anything out of his pockets or try to remove anything from the aircraft, although I couldn't see every motion where he was standing now. I pulled out my green wheelbook and jotted down a few notes about the time.

Finally, Brown-Shirt moved back around to the starboard wheelwell. I saw him go through the same routine.

Stranger and stranger. My scenario called for someone to be leaving things in the aircraft or tinkering with the hydraulics lines or any one of the many moving parts that keep it airborne. But from what I could see, Brown-Shirt was simply checking the aircraft over. It didn't make sense.

Or did it?

What if you needed somewhere to stow something overnight? Something you didn't necessarily want to keep in your locker or under your mattress, or anywhere else in squadron spaces? If you had custody of a Navy fighter jet, wouldn't you think about taping the package to the inside of one of the avionics or wheelwell compartments, sticking it well back into the dark recesses where it wouldn't be easily seen by a hurried preflighting pilot?

And what if you were interrupted just as you were finished by someone you didn't like particularly well anyway? Might you forget to take your duct tape with you, partly by mistake and partly because you wouldn't mind seeing her dumped in the ocean? And maybe you might want to look later, when no one was around, just to see if your package was still there or if you'd left something else in there.

It made sense.

The figure finally moved away from the aircraft, moving with that same combination of confidence and caution that I'd recognized before. This time, though, Brown-Shirt turned toward me and walked toward the hatch that led into the island. His ball cap blocked my view of his face.

He couldn't have seen me, not with the lights out inside the tower. The chair behind me would have masked the outline of anyone moving in the glass-encased edifice, and the windows were reflective.

With the full moon already two-thirds of the way up to its zenith, the deck below was awash in faint light. I stared down at Brown-Shirt, trying to decide why the rolling swagger looked so familiar. I picked up the telephone and dialed Jazzman's stateroom. He picked it up on the second ring.

I groaned out loud and swore quietly, calling myself a number of biologically impossible names, then hung up the phone without answering his greeting. Things had just become a lot more complicated as I stared down into the face of my favorite *chollo*.

17

AN HOUR later, I called Jazzman again and denied that I'd tried to call him earlier. I just needed a relief for a while, I claimed. If he could cover for two hours, I'd grab some rack time and relieve him again at midnight, giving him plenty of time to satisfy the safe-for-flight guidelines for pilots on the next-day's flight schedule.

He showed up fifteen minutes later, vaguely grumpy and short with me. I couldn't blame him—standing late-night watches from the tower wasn't what he'd worked fifteen years to achieve, not even when it involved his own aircraft. Command tours might involve late hours and long nights, but the hours and timing were of his own choosing. After all, there were only six Captains and an Admiral onboard that were senior to him.

I left him up there without telling him about seeing Fernandez and trudged back down the miles and miles of ladders to my office, depressed. Until that moment, I hadn't realized that I'd dreaded this moment, the point at which I knew who'd killed Worthington. To have to bust Fernandez—well, this sort of thing was why cops were, by definition, cynics.

Surprise, surprise. Fernandez was waiting for me, leaning against the bulkhead around the corner at a maintenance shop, his eyes half-closed over some remnant of excitement. It had been about fifty minutes since I'd seen him on the flight deck. I wondered if he'd been down here the entire time.

As soon as he saw me, he started down the passageway toward me, apparently ignoring me unless you noticed the way his eyes flicked over me. As we passed abreast of each other, he said sotto voce "Gotta talk. Now. Unlock the door—I'll be back."

A reasonable precaution. He'd already established that hanging out in the passageway outside my office was totally unacceptable. It struck me that the covert nature of our relationship might entail the same kind of excitement he might have found running with a gang in Los Angeles.

TEN MINUTES LATER, the door opened noiselessly. Sometime during his field-day operations, my young friend had decided to oil the hinges on the door.

He shut the door behind him and paused, so excited that he was damned near vibrating. He took time to enjoy the moment, then strode decisively over to my desk. He reached inside his chambray shirt and pulled out some smudged copies of a Tomcat maintenance manual. I could see that this little episode was clearly taking on blockbuster proportions in his mind.

"What is it?" I asked.

"Read it," he said smugly. He'd found something, something important, and taken action independently to get it to me. Looking at it from his point of view, he was a hero.

Fernandez dropped into the chair, resigning himself to showing less capable minds what had transpired. "I got to thinkin' 'bout that bird—301, the one was down hard. And how that roll of tape end up there. Convenient, like. So I went an' looked."

"For more duct tape?"

"Naw, maaannn." I was certain of it now—I'd dropped ten points in his esteem, easily. "At the book—the maintenance book. Seeing what maintenance they was doing that they need duct tape for, like whether it's cycle maintenance or something else. Not a lot of stuff need duct tape."

I leaned back in my chair, silently swearing at myself for not thinking of the same thing. "Go on."

"That bird was on cycle maintenance the day before. Nothing on that needs duct tape." He pointed at the pages I held and began reciting the cycle maintenance items from memory, counting the checks off on his fingers, the words coming quickly. An impressive performance for a nondesignated airman who hadn't yet escaped his compartment cleaning tour. Finally, after he ticked the last one off, including a summary recitation of the tools required, he said, "So I knew something was off about it—just not right, you know?"

I nodded. I'd had that same feeling a number of times when I was trodding down the wrong path. "And?"

"I went back out to look at that bird." He fished a flashlight out of his back pocket. "Go at night, so nobody be asking why I'm climbing up inside of her. White light, though, not red. Wanted to see if I could see that gummy shit on the inside panels somewhere." He looked at me pointedly as though demanding a response.

"Good idea," I tried.

Condescending disappointment. Clearly I'd missed whatever had seemed obvious to him.

"Like if someone wanted to be hiding some shit on the boat, man. 'Nuff places around, but sometimes you don't want to be leaving no shit out where somebody can—like—find it."

"Steal it, you mean."

He nodded. "That."

"Drugs."

He nodded again encouragingly, pleased that I'd managed to follow his thinking. "So I go on up in there looking. Don't see shit at first. I'm putting my hands all over it, looking for this tape shit."

"And you found it?"

He looked, if anything, more pleased with himself. "Nope. But somebody's been doing some painting on that bird. Along the right wing, a touch-up on the undercarriage."

I wasn't following. "So what the hell does that mean?"

He sighed. "It means that's why the tape was there. For masking off the part you don't want to paint. That's how you do it. I came down earlier, you're not here." The last sentence was delivered in an accusing tone, like he'd caught me asleep on watch.

"I'm not here every hour of the day," I pointed out reasonably.

"You're here now." He pointed at the papers. "Now that's some shit," Fernandez said admiringly. He beamed at me.

For once, I had to agree. It was indeed some shit.

More importantly, Fernandez had pointed out something I hadn't truly followed up on—the duct tape and the aircraft. And with Gil's hints about Jazzman, maybe somebody was painting out evidence around the weapons station.

When you're stuck, you have to go back to the few things you do know, starting with your physical evidence. In this case, that's about all I had. Besides too many suspects.

18

"STILL REMEMBER how to get into your gear?" the young pararigger asked me.

"Think I can manage." And I found I could, even though a few of the straps and buckles had changed position.

An ejection seat harness is the ultimate lifesaver for a Navy aviator. Basically, it consists of a set of broad, nylon straps that truss you up from shoulder to crotch, the straps running over your shoulders and then down along the insides of your crotch. For men, getting the lower straps carefully positioned can spell the difference between a happy sex life and singing soprano.

As part of the dream that never dies, I'd brought my old A-4 helmet with me on cruise. It was still festooned with the rubberized tape and reflective strips we'd used back then. The parariggers had stripped out the old hardened foam lining and refitted it for me. Compared to the modern, sleek ones the Tomcat drivers used, my brain bucket looked like a Model T. My old call sign was still stenciled across the brow, faded now but still legible: Bam-Bam.

One pararigger rapped affectionately on the helmet that was still on the parachute-folding table. "This baby's been around, huh, sir?"

"It's seen better times."

"Still structurally sound, though. I'd bet on it lasting another ten years or so before you want to think real seriously before you use it.

We tinkered with it a bit." He pointed out the modifications they'd made to allow the new communications gear to attach, the new chin strap they'd riveted in.

I let the pararigger check my straps and harness, then picked up the helmet and slipped it onto my head. I noticed the difference immediately, even though it'd been six years since I'd worn it. There're some things you never forget, and one of those is the way your helmet fits on your head. A small protruding patch of foam on the back on the right was gone, the surface now smooth and cushiony hard like it was supposed to me. I didn't miss the slight feeling of pressure being gone, but I noticed its absence much more than I would have noticed its presence. The inside had a clean, chemical smell of newly hardened foam.

I looked around the rigger loft. How many times had I been in a compartment just like this, studying the long rows of ejection harnesses hung from pegs? Each aviator has his own personalized set, carefully fitted and tinkered with to provide the maximum comfort.

"New flight suit, huh?" the rigger asked.

I nodded, disliking the stiffness, the way the fabric rustled when I moved, remembering that it usually took a number of washes before a flight suit got as soft as the one Admiral Fairchild wore. You had to maintain a careful balance between safety and comfort— each washing reduced the fire-retardant chemical impregnated in the fabric, but only slobs never washed them.

I'd completed my go-fly outfit with a blue, Nomex turtleneck. The elastic at the neck was still taut and snugged up against my skin a little too tightly. I ran one finger around the inside of it, trying to stretch it out.

"You're a go, sir," the rigger said finally. He looked me over one last time, checking for anything he'd missed. "Looks real right on you."

"It should." I'd been strapping myself into airplanes and flying missions over Vietnam before this young man was anything more than a speculative gleam in his father's eye.

"Be something for you, won't it? Getting back up there after all these years." The rigger's expression changed for a moment, dissolving into something more human. "You might have known my dad, sir. Brinker McCauley?"

He couldn't have stunned me more if he'd hit me over the head. Brinker, the man who'd lived next door to me at the Hanoi Hilton, my lifeline to the rest of the human race. If this was Brinker's son, he had to be—

"You're Teddy? Teddy McCauley?"

He nodded, slightly less surprised than I had been. "You know my name?"

"Hell, how could I not? My God, if I'd known you were on this ship, I'd—"

I'd have what? I wondered. Somewhere inside I knew.

How many nights had I lain on the cold cement, my ear pressed close to the concrete walls, listening to the tiny taps and scratches we used for a language. Brinker had two kids, and he'd spent hours talking about them, telling me how much he loved them, describing every tiny detail about them he could remember, from this child's first bowel movement to the Flintstone napkins he'd bought for the boy's fifth birthday party. I'd have adopted the boy—young man, now—taken care of him, made sure he had someone he could turn to, done for him whatever Brinker would have if he'd made it out.

Looking at him now, I could see the echoes of the thirteen-year-old I'd met when I'd come back from Vietnam. I'd gone to Minneapolis to visit Gracie in person, to tell her what her husband had meant to me and how he'd proved himself to be one of the very finest human beings to have ever lived.

And to offer my personal condolences.

"How long have you been in the Navy, son?" I asked.

"Almost four years now." He shrugged, looked faintly embarrassed. "I was kinda wild as a teenager. I figured the Navy might straighten me out some."

"Has it?"

He nodded. "I got accepted to ROTC at Notre Dame. I start this fall."

"You're going to fly, then." I could see it in his face, feel it in the way he touched the gear, loving the feel of it and jealous of the men who wore it.

"I think so." He smiled. "It's in the blood, isn't it?"

"In yours, it would be." Behind me, I heard Jazzman make a sound. "Listen, I guess I've got to go fly. When I come back, I want to talk to you. Your father—he was a fine man, Teddy. And he loved you and your mom more than I can possibly tell you."

He pretended to fiddle with a strap that didn't need adjusting. "I'd like that, sir. If you've got the time." I saw his eyes mist slightly.

"I've got all the time in the world for you, Teddy. Anytime. When I get back—" For a moment, I forgot that I probably wasn't going flying anyway, that this was all an elaborate charade.

And that answered my earlier question. It was harder to get so close and not fly than to pretend I'd just been inadvertently left off the flight schedule.

I held out my hand. He took it, his grip strong and tight. Jesus, Brinker would have been proud. I pulled him close to me, gave him a brief, hard hug like the one Brinker'd given me the day we walked out of our cells and turned our faces up to the sun.

JAZZMAN DIDN'T ASK any questions or volunteer any comments as we went up the ladders toward the flight deck. He paused just inside the island before opening the blast door that would let us out onto the tarmac. I could already hear the metal skin of the ship vibrating in response to the engines turning just yards away.

"I didn't know either," Jazzman said, his hand resting on the dogging lever. "If I had—"

"You would have what? Made life easier for him? Taken his father's place?"

Jazzman nodded. "Something like that. We still take care of our own."

"Somebody doesn't." I shut my eyes for a moment, willing myself into control. The unexpected encounter with Brinker's kid—Jesus.

You don't have a long life expectancy as an aviator unless you have that peculiar knack of compartmentalizing your life. Once you step out onto the flight deck, you've got to lock everything else in your life behind a leakproof wall. Your girlfriend or wife, the paperwork waiting for you, the lousy bean burrito you had for lunch—anything that can distract you from the task of staying alive in the most dangerous flight environment in the world has to cease to exist. You let it distract you and you miss the first vibrations that spell a stall or the shudder of an engine unbalancing. You don't notice that your wingman is getting too damned close or that a particular patch of sky is starting to look shimmery like something's moving in it. Bang, you're dead, and it's nobody's fault but your own.

I concentrated, almost surprised at how easily it came back to me. Seconds later, there was nothing else in the world except an aircraft waiting for me. I nodded at Jazzman, knowing he understood.

A speculative look crossed his face. "You're thinking we're going to find something wrong with that bird, aren't you?" he asked.

"Maybe, but we kept a pretty careful eye on it last night. Odds are that it's fine."

"Some problems don't show up until you're airborne, you know," he said carefully. "For what it's worth, I think there's a lot of validity to your theory. Be a shame not to test it out completely."

I hadn't realized until that second that I really believed that I was going flying. "You're right. Be a shame."

"Well, then. Let's go preflight."

We stepped into the Handler's office and checked on the aircraft we'd been assigned. Tomcat 301's Plane Captain was waiting for us there, shepherded us out to the aircraft like neither one of us had ever been on a flight deck before. I watched Jazzman stifle his amusement at the PC's officious attitude.

Tomcat 301 was parked just forward of the island. Its smooth skin shone, the paint glossy. It radiated good health and airworthiness like an Olympic athlete, almost begging to be let off the deck to get back into its natural element.

I followed Jazzman around as he went through the preflight checkoff list. Same basics as on the A-4—avionics dogged down, fuel, check for hydraulic leaks, examine the struts and wheel well.

Jazzman took it a step further, undogging panels and checking for FOD, going through every step twice, banging on parts of the airframe at random and listening to the sound his fist made. He even examined the pitot tubes, the small structures that measure speed through air, as well as the base of each antenna.

Finally, he turned to me and said, "If there's something wrong with this aircraft, I can't find it."

"Looks like you checked everything," I agreed.

"Everything I can see on the ground." He looked off in the distance for a moment, as though weighing his options. "Of course, it could be dangerous to fly it. If someone's been messing with it, I mean."

"Could be."

"You willing to take that chance?"

I nodded.

"Me, too. Let's go." He reached for the step that folded out from the airframe.

"You going to get in trouble over this?" I asked, not really wanting to know.

He shrugged. "Probably not. The Admiral's the only one who knows this was all for show, right?"

"Right. He didn't feel the need to share it with the Air Boss or CAG."

"Well, if he's real unhappy, he'll let me know. In the meanwhile, I suggest you get your ass up here so I can give you a quick cockpit fam and we can get the hell out of here before someone figures it out."

I climbed up beside him and paid attention while he pointed out the RIO controls, the ejection-seat handles, and the myriad other bits and pieces of gear that are tucked away in the cockpit of a modern fighter jet. From his tone, I guessed he'd done this a million times before.

Just like with the flight suit, some of it was familiar with minor modernizations. It didn't take long until I felt completely comfortable with the layout.

I climbed into the back seat and let the Plane Captain fuss over the attachments and flight suit harness. It clips to the seat at a variety of points. The back of the seat contains the parachute, the seat pan holds a life raft. If we had to eject, my seat would fire a split second before Jazzman's and an equally long period of time after explosive charges blew the canopy out of my way.

We hoped. At least, that's the way it was intended to work. Otherwise, your neck and head try to occupy the same airspace as a large, solid piece of tempered glass. Just like in *Top Gun*.

Ten minutes later, Jazzman fired up the engines and we began a slow, stately taxi toward the catapult.

19

THE TOMCAT quivered on the catapult, eager to get airborne, both throttles shoved forward to full military power. I turned my head sideways to watch the yellow shirt snap off a salute, then drop to the deck on one knee, his arm outstretched and pointing toward the bow. I turned my head forward and braced it and my back against the seat as the aircraft started to move, remembering enough to know that taking a cat shot could put a hell of a cramp in my neck if I didn't.

The F-14 is a hell of a lot heavier than my old Skyhawk, but she accelerates damned fast. To reach the airspeed she needs to stay airborne, she's got to be traveling forward fast enough by the time the catapult flings her off the pointy end of the ship.

Tomcat 301 dropped ten feet as we left the ship and hung in the air for a moment, deciding whether or not she was going to stay airborne. I don't care how many times you do it, that two seconds while the wings grab for lift and the engines fight for airspeed are invariably gut-wrenching. You find your hand reaching for the ejection handle, knowing that if you've just taken a soft cat you've only got a couple of seconds to get out.

Lift and airspeed finally overcame gravity and drag. Jazzman nursed the aircraft up, careful not to demand too steep a climb rate and stall. By the time I started breathing regularly again, we were at five thousand feet and climbing.

"Like you remember it?" he asked over the internal communications system, the ICS.

"Oh, yeah," I managed. "Still the biggest E-ticket around."

A slight chuckle. "That old cliché. Some of the youngsters don't even remember E-tickets. Disney's gone to a different system. Plays havoc with your slang. Hold on—"

The Tomcat curled into a sharp right-hand turn as Jazzman cleared the pattern. I listened to him chat with CDC, acknowledging that Tomcat 301 had two souls onboard and giving our fuel state to the Operations Specialist. Jazzman requested and was given a vector to the area designated that day for ACM—Air Combat Maneuvering.

"So, now that we're up, whaddya want to do?" Jazzman asked.

"How about letting me drive?"

"Yeah, right. You going to climb over that seat and come up here?"

"Would figure out a way to do it if you said yes," I admitted. Even though it's a two-seater, the flight controls in a Tomcat are only in the forward seat, a small fact that countless wanna-be military aviation shows have overlooked. All I could fly from the back seat was radar and a chaff dispenser.

"Well, since this is a Fam flight, how about I show you what she can do?"

"OK. Aerobatics, you mean?"

"Something like that. By the way, what did you have for lunch?"

"Don't remember. I guess I will when I see it again," I answered, smiling. Yeah, right—like I was going to get airsick.

"Don't say I didn't warn you." Jazzman yanked the nose of the Tomcat up and kicked in the afterburners. I damn near grayed out from the G-forces. It's one thing to read the specs on the rate of climb of an airframe, another to actually experience a horrendous rate of climb with about zero speed over ground.

Jazzman took us to the top of a loop, gradually shedding airspeed and rolling over until we hung inverted, staring down at the ocean, motionless for a split second. He kicked her over gently, just nipping the edge of the stall envelope, and let her pile on the airspeed as we headed for the deck.

My reflexes were way wrong. Nurtured and ingrained in the Skyhawk, I didn't have a feel for what the massive surface area of the Tomcat's wings could accomplish. As we passed the point at which the dive would have been unrecoverable for a Skyhawk, Jazzman toggled the swept wings forward, increasing our lift and slowing us down, and pulled the nose up. The Tomcat shuddered, then performed, pulling out and regaining level flight.

"Jesus," I managed. "You got some spare wings back on the boat?"

"They just feel like they're going to come off, but we haven't lost one like that yet." I heard the satisfaction in his voice, the pride in the wondrous power of this airframe.

We spent the next thirty minutes jinking and twisting in the air while Jazzman demonstrated to me irrevocably just how far out of date I was. It was a heady, exhilarating experience, one that left me with a ground-pounder's awe of the pilots that flew these birds and a quiet pride that I'd been one of the people who'd gone before.

And a sense of closure, the way retiring from the Navy had never done. While I was fairly sure that I could learn everything I needed to know to fly the F-14 safely, I finally faced the fact that I no longer had the reflexes or eyesight to fly combat air patrols. The fifteen years that separated me from Jazzman made all the difference in the world.

Maybe it was like that with other things, too, I thought, as I tensed my stomach muscles and grunted. Not from a digestive disorder, but a maneuver called the "M-1," designed to keep blood flowing to the brain when the pilot in front of you is pushing the envelope on G-forces. It prevents the creeping gray at the edges of your vision and the loss of consciousness that can kill you faster than the aircraft can.

Jazzman whipped the Tomcat around in a tight turn, slinging her tail assembly through the air like he was playing crack-the-whip. I finally lost consciousness for a few moments, only dimly aware of the headsup he was transmitting over the ICS. Not for long, but long enough. For a moment, when I came to, I though I'd busted some small vein in my eyes or around my face. My vision was blurred and wetness streaked my cheeks.

Time changes too many things. I resisted where my train of thought was leading me, then gave up.

That was one of the problems with the Worthington case. I was seeing it through my own filter of experiences, reflexively exonerating the officers because of what I'd been through in Vietnam and in my own tours of duty, looking with suspicion at the young *chollo* who'd done nothing more than engineer his own escape from a life he didn't want and take some pride in doing a damned good job of cleaning decks. The interweaving relationships between Gerrity, Worthington, Berkshire, and Jazzman—this was a different Navy, built on the foundation my generation had left them but substantially different in many ways.

I tinkered with the radar, watching the lozenge-shaped radar paints fuzz in and out of focus as I played with the knobs. When I got back down on deck, I was going to have to start from the beginning, reassessing the entire case with an open mind. I'd gotten too much backward—airmen hiding packages in wheel wells and avionics bays instead of leaving rolls of tape there by accident, Fernandez acting as my independent partner-conspirator in ferreting out information. Hell, I'd even misjudged Admiral Fairchild. He'd hated my guts, I'd thought, but he'd taken the time to look up how current my seat quals were.

I said a silent prayer to the gods of the air and wiped the area under my eyes. Jazzman carefully didn't watch.

Admiral Fairchild. Now just why—I got my head back in the cockpit where it belonged and finally heard the squawking voices coming over Tactical.

Jazzman cleared his throat. "I—um—I think the Admiral finally noticed we launched."

"No shit." The voice coming over Tactical was quite recognizable. "I take it he's not too pleased."

Jazzman caught my eyes in his rearview mirror. I saw the amusement in his. "I'm not too damned sure exactly how he feels about it," he said thoughtfully. "He sounds a little upset, but he's not ordering us right back to the boat. And it sure as hell took him long enough to notice we'd launched. You know Pri-Fly is usually dialed up in his cabin, and usually he's got the Plat camera going on his CCTV. Mighty convenient that he didn't notice."

"Hey, how the hell do you get this sea-clutter off of here?"

"You tweak and peak, friend. What, do I look like an NFO?"

"There's a couple of contacts off to the north," I said. "I thought they were just garbage, but now I'm not so sure."

He sighed. "We're transmitting our radar info back to the ship automatically, you know, Link 11, all that fancy stuff? If there's anything of interest, they'll let us know."

Two seconds later, they did. The TAO in CDC interrupted Admiral Fairchild. Politely, respectfully, but firmly, to ask what the hell we were holding up to the north and why we'd drifted out of our designated area. I listened to Jazzman trot out the usual excuses for being out of area, knowing they didn't work any better now than they had twenty years ago. The TAO pretended to listen, then cut him off with an order to vector toward the two contacts.

I heard Jazzman's voice change. It went cold and flat, the noncommittal, casual drawl of a fighter pilot at work. He rogered up on the vector and executed an immediate turn along it while responding.

"You want to fill your backseater in on what's going on?" I asked. I was starting to feel definitely edgy.

"Pay attention," he said crisply. "You've been fucking around with that thing long enough. You figured out how to give me range and bearing information off it?"

"Sure, but—"

"Then verify the distance to that piece of shit you've been staring at. Now."

I did it, calling off the figures and stifling the questions. There's only one person in command in an aircraft on a mission, and it sure as hell wasn't me.

"How much do you remember about ESM?" Jazzman said. It

wasn't really a question—more like a demand for an immediate, no-notice briefing.

"Enough. I see the gear back here."

"Take a look at it, see what you don't understand."

I did as he asked and reported that most of the buttonology seemed at least slightly familiar.

"Good. Now don't touch it, but watch for any hint—and I mean any—of the following signal." He rattled off pulse repetition rates and sweep rates, a string of numbers that identified the character-istics of a particular transmitter. "You recognize what it is?"

"No, not specifically. But from what you're telling me, I can make some guesses. It's a fire-control radar of some sort, right?"

"Could be," he said noncommittally. "Just keep your eyes open for it."

"This have anything to do with the brief I got thrown out of last week?"

No answer.

"You going to tell me anything?"

"No, actually, I'm not," Jazzman said finally. "You know I've got weapons control from up here. I don't think we'll need it—the only thing I need right now is a damned smart RIO who knows what he's looking for. You've got about ten minutes until you have to be that person."

20

IVE MINUTES later, I was almost as good as I'd been when I'd left the Navy. Flying the single-seater Skyhawk, I hadn't had a lot of this fancy electronic shit that Jazzman's RIO relied on, but I'd spent some time in an Intruder, which did. Smaller aircraft, simpler ESM and radar gear, but I was willing to bet that I probably knew more about tweaking than Jazzman did.

I started feeding him routine information at six minutes, letting him get used to hearing my voice and trying to generate some teamwork damned fast. I heard his voice start to loosen up as he realized I probably had been able to puzzle the gear out. I kept a continuous watch on the ESM gear, finally figuring out how the automatic alert functions worked. I'd scribbled the parameters of interest in grease pencil on the canopy.

By the ten-minute mark, we were starting to act like a team. Not first-string, maybe, but age and experience count for more than youth and reflexes in some situations. I just hoped this was one of them.

When the signal finally blipped across my screen, it was almost anticlimactic. By then, judging from the speed and altitude readers on my radar ghosts, I'd managed to puzzle out that the contacts were aircraft. A real tactical coup. Like surface ships or submarines would be cruising at 10,000 feet.

What worried me was not knowing what they were. Jazzman

probably didn't either—not exactly, at least—but at least he had a better idea than I did. I considered pressing him on the point, figuring the more I knew the more effective I'd be, but in the short time we'd been tactical together I'd decided that he knew that I knew I should know. He'd tell me if he could.

"Variant Bears," he said finally. He paused as though considering what else I might need to know. Not everything—that was clear from his tone. "There might be some long-range air-to-surface missiles we're interested in, too. And these Bears—you see how they keep fading in and out on the scope?"

"Stealth technology?" I asked.

"Maybe. Might be avionics instead. We don't know."

"OK." And it was. Now I knew to pay very careful attention to the radar paints and to scream bloody hell if it looked like anything was separating from the original trace. Like a missile.

This was how a pilot should die. In the air, fighting back, doing what he'd—damn it, or she'd—been born and bred to do. Not with a knife in the gut and laying in some dirty pool of water so far from the sun. At least if my death involved water, it'd be the bright clean salt of the Pacific where I'd return to the food chain and the great cycle of life.

At that moment, getting a taste of life that should have been gone from me forever, I hated the person that'd killed Gina Worthington more than I'd ever thought possible. I had what she should have had.

"Nothing?" Jazzman asked.

"No." If he'd been used to flying a single-seater aircraft, he wouldn't be expecting a continual chatter of data from the back seat.

"Keep me posted."

Like I'd forget. I clicked the mike twice in acknowledgment.

THE ONLY THING we killed during the next two hours was time. Fifteen minutes after we'd started vectoring out, *Lincoln* had launched two more F-14s and had four F/A-18s chaffing and whining on the deck. While the Hornet's a nifty little fighter, it sure can't match the Tomcat in sheer endurance. Even so, I was a little relieved when we made our approach on the tanker before taking a close and personal look at the deck. Twenty minutes after we'd refueled from the KA-6 tanker, Jazzman did a nifty job of nailing the three-wire on his first pass.

After we were back inside the ship and had returned our gear to the Paraloft, Jazzman asked me to come down to his stateroom. The spooks in Intel were chafing to get a word with us, but he waved them off. After all, we'd seen damned little except some ghosts.

"So a good time was had by all," he said, waving me toward a standard gray Navy chair.

"As good as it's been in a long time," I acknowledged. "Thank you." I started to say more, then stopped. It would only embarrass one or the other of us.

"When you grayed out up there," he began. He paused for a moment, assessing me. "It happens, you know. To all of us from time to time, if we're not expecting it."

"It happens."

"Well, I just wanted you to know it's not unusual. Not in a Tomcat in the back seat."

"And not when it's been a couple of years since you've been balls to the wall, either." I shrugged, appreciating his attempt to placate the male fighter-pilot ego, but not really seeing the point.

"Right before you came to, you muttered something about Gina," he continued. "I was wondering—sometimes, you get up there, more things make sense. You know."

"Ah. So you want to know if I had any profound insights into the case while we were chasing sea-clutter?"

He nodded.

I thought about it for a minute. I had, in one sense, since I'd realized I had to shed some of my preconceptions about the case and the people involved in it. But did that qualify as an investigative piece of the puzzle or a realization of my own shortcomings? The latter, I decided.

"Sometimes you just have to look at things from a whole new perspective," I said finally. "You get up there, it reminds you of that."

"Doesn't sound like much."

"What, you expect me to find some clues in the cockpit? A written confession, maybe some fiber evidence that ties it all together?" The minute the words were out, I regretted them. Jazzman had done me a favor, and he didn't deserve any of my smart-ass crap for it.

He stood up. "We'd better get down to Intel."

I pushed myself up out of the chair, feeling the muscles in my back complain at having to stretch again. The lumbar support system in the Tomcat left as much to be desired as the one in the Skyhawk had.

"I'm sorry," I said.

"Nothing to be sorry about," he said coolly. "You did me a favor today, too. That McCauley kid—I'll keep an eye on him."

But there was. And I didn't think he knew how much.

21

FLYING ALWAYS makes me ravenous. I notice the same thing after being on a smaller ship. It must be the body's continual attempt to compensate for the movement of the aircraft or the ship that burns up fuel. Regardless of the reason, after an essentially unproductive session with the Intel spooks, I headed for the dirty shirt, the forwardmost officer's wardroom on the ship, and the only one in which flight crews were allowed to wear flight suits.

Not that I would have worn mine down there. Something had finally clicked into place during that last flight. I'd kept the flight suit on during the debrief, then gone back to my stateroom and carefully folded it up and put it away in a drawer. Part of my past went with it.

The Dirty Shirt was crowded, and I knew that it would be as soon as I smelled the pungent tang of carrier pizza wafting down the 0-3 level. Every Thursday, the mess cooks—assisted by the squadron for that week—shoveled steaming pizzas out as fast as they could to the hordes of officers jamming up to the hot carts and in the serving lines. Pepperoni, onions, green peppers—heck, even some godawful combination of pineapple and Canadian bacon, a particular favorite of the California crowd—pies sliced large disappeared down young gullets as fast as they came off the line. At its peak, pizza night looked like a feeding frenzy.

I snagged a chair at the end of one table. The men and women seated there noted my presence and just as quickly screened it out. I eavesdropped, noting that the usual trace of envy I felt at hearing them talk about the life of a young pilot was gone. I hadn't realized how it ate at me until I no longer felt it.

One of the young male pilots was bitching about his Maintenance Officer. I heard just enough to convince me that his MO was probably in the right. For all that they're always the bridesmaid and never the bride, most MOs have a damned good sense of what's required to keep their birds flying safely. And most of their division and branch officers go to great lengths to point out that their primary duty is to fly jets—not fix them.

This young man's MO evidently had a hard-on for getting aircraft down into the hangar bay to work gripes. I mulled that over for a minute, wondering why some part of my mind kept insisting that I pay more attention to the pilot's whining. Sure, it was easier and safer to work on aircraft down in the hangar bay, away from most of the dangers and distractions of the flight deck, but it could be a pain in the ass clearing a path for the aircraft to an elevator, making sure there was space in the hangar for it without getting it buried behind a few hangar queens, and then getting it back up for full power tests, but—

Something finally clicked. Moving aircraft, moving bodies. Suppose that my theory that Gina had been lowered into the engineering spaces after she'd been killed was right. The scuff marks near the Ellison door seemed to support the theory, and I'd already proved that it was feasible by doing a test run with Doc Benning and Fernandez. But I hadn't put enough attention on what happened immediately before that—where was she killed, and how did the perpetrator manage to transport her through the passageways of the ship without being noticed? Instead, I'd let myself get caught up in the personalities and dynamics surrounding them and misled myself with my own preconceptions. Fine sleuthing was one thing, but hard evidence was a hell of a lot harder to screw up.

I picked up my plate and walked over to the nearest garbage can and pitched it in. Swinging the lid of the trash container open, watching the paper plate spiral down to smack gently down on the other plates gave me a chill. Garbage, tossed away. That's what she'd been to someone on this ship.

22

COMING DOWN off the adrenaline high of the flight, stripped of my naval officer prejudices by the last flight, everything about the Worthington case took on a new clarity. I hadn't seen what I didn't want to. Now I starting looking at the people who had a motive to kill Gina Worthington again, trying to puzzle out what I might have missed before and wondering about the skinhead connection.

Gerrity. Suppose he'd been a little less than fully forthcoming about his last argument with her. Maybe she'd been bothered by what they'd done, decided to call it quits for the sake of her career. How would he have taken that? Not well, I suspected.

And the Maintenance Officer—more than enough bad blood there. A good-looking woman, one that had a peculiar sort of genius in the one thing that set him apart from other fallen angels, and a hot stick at that. Knowing how virulent the short-man's syndrome could be, and how floridly it was manifested in this particular man, what might have started as acute dislike might have blossomed into something more deadly.

Even the women had their share of candidates. Berkshire, for starters. If anyone disliked Gina Worthington as much as the MO, it would have been her dear roomie. Enough to kill her? I felt myself shy away from the idea, invoking some reflexive male protective instinct that decided women didn't kill women that way, and resolutely followed my train of thought down the obvious paths. On cruise, in close quarters, flying a lot of missions and trying to balance out life on the boat, minor sins can escalate to deadly insults. Come in drunk once too often, puking in the washbasin and stealing clean clothes from your roomie later and sometimes something snaps. I remembered more than one violent confrontation with a roommate on cruise during Vietnam where we'd come to blows over something as trivial as who farted. I'd grown a good deal more tolerant since those days.

Who else? Jazzman? His comment about the Navy recruiting lesbians. Maybe having women in his squadron made completing his tour without incident a good deal chancier that it might have been otherwise. And this thing about the weapons—what the hell had Gil been talking about? I jotted down a note to follow up on that.

Everything that applied to Jazzman went for the Admiral, I supposed. Still, even with that, neither of the two were leading my list. Several reasons for that.

First, both of them had more to lose than gain from a female dying on the cruise. And a man doesn't usually get to command or to the flag ranks unless he's proved that he's got some degree of self-control. Sure, maybe they'd both engaged in roommate fisticuffs in their earlier days, but I was willing to bet that they'd both outgrown it.

Second, as far as I could tell, neither of them had any particular interest in Worthington as a female, while all of my other candidates did. The MO, for instance. Just because she was female she was an affront to everything that mattered to him. From what I'd seen of him, at least some small part of his bitterness would be due to the fact that he'd be someone Worthington would never even consider as a male partner. On some level of testosterone, that had to eat at him. Berkshire—maybe in competition with Worthington for the role of hotshot best-of-breed. Gerrity—obvious.

And there were other possibilities as well. It could have been someone almost entirely unconnected with her, that most elusive of suspects without a motive. Maybe somebody that hated having women invade this formerly exclusive male club had decided to do something about it. Maybe a psycho, one that enjoyed murder and had been curious as to how offing this one-of-a-kind victim would feel. Or maybe another type of crazy that was convinced she was reading his thoughts and sending mental commands to him via the CCTV. If that were the case, this was going to be a hell of a lot tougher than the classical scorned-lover scenario.

I decided to focus on the physical evidence. Duct tape, how Gina got down into the bilges, and the source of the semen were a good deal easier to figure out than human motivation. I brainstormed ways to follow up those lines. Ten minutes later, I was still staring at a piece of blank paper.

Then again, there are a lot of good things to be said about the classics. Especially the older detective series. You know, the ones where the hero calls all the suspects into one room and lays out his results, finishing by pointing out the guilty party. Or, in a twist, tricking one of the suspects into inadvertently revealing himself to the assembled party.

I tried to imagine Hercule Poirot or Miss Marple tricking any of my suspects into confessing and couldn't see it. Still, it might be worth a shot. It wasn't like I had a whole lot of other avenues to explore.

It took me two hours to arrange a time when all parties could be present and the Admiral's conference room was available, but finally I was set. At 1300, immediately after the midday meal, Jazzman, the MO, Lieutenant Berkshire, Lieutenant Commander Gerrity, and the Admiral would assemble for a briefing. I didn't let any of them know that the others would be present, hoping that omission might increase the sweat factor. God knows, sometimes it's better to be lucky than good.

I passed the hours before the meeting reexamining what I knew so far. It wasn't much. Try as I could, I couldn't find any single reason for any of my suspects to kill her. Sure, they all had gripes about her—something I was beginning to suspect was far more common among Lieutenant Worthington's acquaintances than I'd originally thought. But none of it seemed like a real good reason to kill her.

Confronting the fact that Gina Worthington had been a less-than-perfect human being was one of the more difficult parts of the case. I'd made the same mistake that a lot of people undoubtedly had, wanting to see her just a little bit larger than life. Before my flight with Jazzman, I hadn't realized it, but I'd seen what I wanted to see in her. A tough, competent pilot, a strong naval officer, someone with the balls to be among the first to join our elite fraternity of fighter jocks.

Reality was different, just as I'd learned it was for the men I flew with. To nonaviators, what we did daily for our living was virtually incomprehensible. Even on the ship, they attribute to us qualities we could never have, not as long as we are human. And, while I would have thought it heresy to say it, even think it, ten years before, that's what we were. Human, no more, no less, with all the foibles and frailties that went along with that condition.

And so was Gina Worthington. Instead of a paragon of human virtue, she was a woman who could be a complete and utter bitch. Leaving aside the fact that her oh-so-charming roommate might have deserved it on occasion, I was still left with the fact that Worthington had committed some serious breaches of our standards of conduct. Like sleeping with Lieutenant Commander Gerrity on the ship, compounding the offense by doing it on her duty day. Like the mishap with Tomcat 301 and missing the fact that the duct tape had no business in the airframe, something even AN Fernandez had thought to check out.

And, finally, her attitude toward the MO. Gerrity had made it clear that she had a temper and rumor had it that her discussions with the MO verged on insubordination. While privately I might agree that the man was a complete and utter ass, I would never have tolerated or condoned her blatant disrespect. Had I been his CO, the MO and I would have shared harsh words behind closed doors about his treatment of the women onboard, as well as his somewhat questionable fudging of FMC, but in public I would have backed him absolutely. Not a single other member of the crew would have suspected that I was anything other than extremely pleased with his performance.

I kept coming back to Jazzman. While I was coming to like the man more and more personally, the deficiencies in his style of command bothered me. The brawl in the ready room, the laissez-faire that the junior pilots felt about taking shots at the MO—yes, even Berkshire's preflight sloppiness. These things all had a common source, and beyond a doubt it was Jazzman.

But did that make him a killer? Not directly, no. Not until Berkshire missed something on preflight and racked up her Tomcat, along with her RIO.

It also made it more difficult to plan out my grand investigatory scheme. After two hours of hard thinking, I came to the conclusion that the goal of the session was to turn up the pressure, maybe convince somebody to do something stupid in the next twenty-four hours.

The way the investigation had gone so far, odds were it'd be me.

THEY WERE BARELY civil to each other. Respectful, even accustomed to being around each other, but the temperature in the briefing room was nearer to absolute zero than a Supply Officer's heart. I was encouraged by it.

I resisted the urge to start off by saying "I suppose you all know why I've called this meeting." I settled for simply thanking them for making time for me. I followed that with "Since you were the people closest to Lieutenant Worthington, I want to bring you up to date on what I've learned so far."

The MO leaned forward aggressively. "I wouldn't say that we were exactly close, but as her immediate superior, I appreciate the courtesy." He made it clear from his tone that courtesy might be the last thing he'd expect from me. I saw him glance at the Admiral, seeking approval like a lap dog.

The Admiral frosted him without saying a word. He could do that. I knew from experience.

Jazzman stirred a bit in his chair, uneasy at the look the Admiral was giving him but looking oddly relieved. Again, the fact that the MO would have taken that tack with me spoke volumes.

"At least, that's part of the reason," I said "The other thing is I wanted to read you all your rights at the same time. Save me hunting you down individually."

The Admiral was the only one who remained impassive, partially because I'd briefed him earlier but mainly because he was just that sort of guy. The other reaction could be classified in two general types: hostility from Berkshire and the MO, shock and pain from Jazzman and Gerrity.

"Most murders are committed by someone who knows the victim," I continued. "There is, of course, an outside chance that someone else did it. This is not an arraignment or even a notification that I intend to file formal charges against you. But since you are, at this point at least, my leading suspects, I'm required to advise you of your legal rights." I stood up and passed around an Advisal of Rights form. "Please read along with me as I explain your rights. Afterward I'll ask you to print your name, social security number, and rank at the bottom, and sign in the spot indicating that you've been so advised."

The MO took a deep breath in preparation for what I was sure would be a prolonged and vigorous protest. Jazzman caught the movement and forestalled it with a sharp shake of his head. Berkshire seemed to have shrunken into herself, whether distancing herself from the entire situation or preparing to strike, I had no idea. Only Gerrity seemed to give a true reading. He was pale, shaken, and almost crying. Still, Jazzman managed to control him telepathically as well.

And wasn't that interesting? Despite the signs of disorder I noted in his command, he was still able to achieve a mind lock with at least two of the three officers from his command who were present.

Admiral Fairchild did his trained flag act during the entire briefing session, present but silent. I collected the forms, noting that not a single one of them had elected to waive their constitutional rights, another indication of unit cohesiveness. Whatever other problems there might be in Jazzman's squadron, at least they could still fight as a team.

"Thank you," I said finally. "You'll each have a chance to speak with a JAG officer later today."

"You said you were going to brief us," Gerrity said. "You said."

I gave him a long, hard look to make sure he was paying attention. "I just did."

23

I TOOK the forms back to my office and locked them in my safe. I was uncomfortable holding the first step toward accusing one officer of murdering another. As right as this step felt, operating under my newfound clarity, it opened up something sore and aching in my gut.

The physical evidence—I stood at my desk and looked at my blank sheet of paper again. No guardian criminal investigator angel had stopped by and outlined a plan of attack.

Guilt. Major procrastination guilt tempered with anger. Next to my thinking pad was the white supremacist case file. I picked it up, wrote "put away files" on my blank paper, and sat down to thumb through it. Maybe working on a different case for a while would unleash a flow of deductive insight on the Worthington evidence. At the very least, I owed it to my snitch to make sure he wasn't endangered by my preoccupation with someone who was already dead.

The case file was satisfying thick. Sworn and unsworn statements from my informant, criminal background results on the Nazi wannabes, and a list of physical evidence I'd found. Mostly stuff floating around the ship. I'd taken flyers and hate literature over to the Regional Office for fingerprinting while we'd been in port, and the results matched up with two of the skinheads. Not enough for the JAG to prefer charges, but a good start.

Time to talk to my little snitchlet again. So far, he'd proved relatively reliable, if not particularly productive. That lid of marijuana mellowing in my evidence locker—the one I'd found in his pocket—was sufficiently motivating to ensure some cooperation at least.

I shoved the file back in the cabinet, then leaned over and put a neat, professional checkmark next to the reminder on my blank pad. A satisfying moment, but a bust would have been better. Or an idea.

PETTY OFFICER COLBURNE was a dirtbag. Most snitches are, and there was a strong possibility that one of his little playmates had been my assailant.

Nevertheless, he was *my* dirtbag, and I had to make sure he stayed relatively sane and healthy while he was working for me. Most days that just meant being careful about being seen with him and generally reassuring him that I'd get him transferred the second it looked like his role in the investigation was compromised. And being firm that now was not that second.

Whenever I wanted to meet with him, I'd leave a phone message at his workcenter, asking him to call Petty Officer Lindball. Every week, I checked the alpha roster, the alphabetical list of people on the ship, to see if a real Lindball had checked onboard. Hadn't so far. We'd meet in one of a variety of spaces, and the telephone number on the message gave him the location—deck, frame, and compartment—and it was always at the same time, 1700. Colburne seemed relatively happy with the system. I think it added a touch of mystique to the process of setting up shipmates for a hard fall.

I don't have to like snitches. Just use them.

I glanced at my watch. Since I hadn't talked to him since the aborted surveillance attempt, he was bound to be getting edgy, wondering if I was pissed and if a report chit was on its way to his skipper at that very moment based on the aforesaid lid. Time to do a face to face, assess his continuing value as a snitch, and find out what my favorite racists were up to.

I didn't like them any better than my snitch.

Two hours later, I wandered down to the fifth deck and quietly slipped into a pump room. Barring a catastrophic failure, the odds of anyone checking out the small, intermittently noisy compartment were nil.

Pumps. Brinker had covered them in some detail, but the exact classification of this one escaped me. Whatever it was, it was of the intermittent sort, gurgling and snorting quietly for several minutes before bellowing for a few seconds. It seemed to be doing that quite efficiently—or at least regularly—but the idea that some piece of critical machinery onboard *Lincoln* needed a pump that sounded like that bothered me.

Just as the hatch started to swing open, the pump gave a particularly obnoxious belch. The hatch slammed shut, then started to open again slowly.

"Hurry up." I tried not to sound annoyed, since the damned thing startled me every time it went off. Scratch one covert meeting place off the list.

He sidled into the room, hugging the bulkhead to stay as far away from the pump as possible. And he was an engineering rating. This particular pump clearly wasn't in his area of responsibility.

"You weren't there." The tone was accusing but faintly groveling. It was one of the things I disliked most about him, along with the dirty brown hair that somehow managed to hang lanky in his eyes even burred down for his skinhead buddies. Eyes the color of a shallow stream after a bad storm. Good teeth, though—I'd give him that much. Probably why he tried to smile at me ingratiatingly so often.

"I got held up. What happened?"

He shifted uneasily against the bulkhead, moved farther back into a dim corner of the compartment. "Just what I said. The next mission planning."

"And just what is their next caper?"

He shook his head. "We haven't decided. More tagging, I think."

Wonderful. A real vicious militant group. Their idea of fomenting unrest was to spray paint racist slogans on bulkheads. They were especially fond of the back of toilet stall doors.

"Anything else?"

"I think they're starting to get suspicious," he whined. "Jim gave me this look when I walked in—sort of meanlike. If they come after me, it'll be him."

"Did they say anything about that female pilot that got stabbed?" I wasn't entirely sure why I asked, just that it seemed to matter.

"Jim did. He said it was a clean, professional job. Like we'd want to do."

"Anybody bragging about doing it?" Too fast, too fast. This guy already had the screaming willies. I tried a bored, patient tone. "Probably not. That's out of their league, right?" It usually worked with him, implying that his great criminal connections weren't all that impressive. He'd start bragging a little, trying to sound like more than he was. Which was nothing.

He looked down at the deck. My attention, which had started to wander away from this futile little encounter, started to track again.

"They said something about you. That before the shit hits the fan, something would have to be done." His voice was soft, barely audible above Sneezy the Pump.

"Like what?"

"You know. The MAAs too."

I crossed the pump room in three steps and stood up close to him. "Remember when we had that last little chat about cooperation and what it's going to take to keep your ass out of the brig?"

He nodded, fear now overriding his perpetual hangdog expression. "Am I going to get in trouble for being there?"

"Not if you play straight with me. I think you're holding out, that's a different matter." I shrugged. "Once this is finished up, you're off the boat. The same day. But you fuck around, and you're not my responsibility anymore."

"You're on the list, that's all. Of the ones who'll have to be neutralized."

"How?"

"They didn't say. Just that you were." His words were coming faster, starting to tumble over each other. "Look, I gotta go. I got watch in half an hour."

"What about Lieutenant Worthington?" I asked, sure now that he wasn't telling me everything. We'd been through this ploy before. Sometimes I just saved up the inconsistencies and hit him with them all at once.

"I gotta—"

"Talk!"

"She was a spy," he blurted out, the pressure behind his words increasing. "For the Russians. Jim, he said someone else found out about it, put a stop to it."

"Who?"

"I don't know, honest to God, I don't know, I don't know—"

"You'll find out. Today. Because if you don't, I'm going to have Jim brought down to my office in handcuffs and I'm going to find out myself. He'll know where I got the information, won't he? The way he was looking at you? I find out from you, you get safe passage off the boat. Otherwise—" I let him imagine what that might include.

"They won't tell me! You can't do this, I—"

I opened the door, checked the passageway, and stepped out of the compartment. Like I said, I don't like snitches.

24

NOTHING LIKE a little enlightened self-interest to motivate a recalcitrant sailor. Two hours later, I received a frantic, whispered telephone call from "Petty Officer Lindball," urgently requesting that I meet him up on the flight deck.

By that time, I'd arrived at the conclusion that I needed to do a little more to motivate my erstwhile suspects as well. I couldn't seem to entice anyone into monkeying around with my aircraft, so maybe something simpler might do the trick. God knows there're a hundred ways to die on a ship at sea. The problem was staging an enticingly vulnerable situation that I could survive. The flight deck was a good source of possibilities. Until I had my escape route planned out, though, I wasn't taking any chances.

I went up thirty minutes before I was to meet my snitch and took two senior Masters-at-Arms with me. They were briefed to disappear when I told them to. Hopefully, Colburne would be late—he usually was—and wouldn't see them.

How to safely arrange to die? I wandered around the flight deck, looking at the opportunities. Too many of them were too certain. Finally, an idea—the first decent one of the day—occurred to me.

"What're you doing up here?" The voice was familiar, a rasping Southern drawl that destroyed any trace of charm.

I turned and looked at the MO. "Any law against getting some air?"

He glared at me. "You don't have more important things to worry about?"

I sighed. Why was it that everyone on this ship from Admiral Fairchild to Airman Fernandez seemed to have an idea about how I was supposed to run this investigation? And why did they all feel compelled to seek me out, monitor my activities, and share their thoughts with me?

I turned my back on him and crouched down at the edge of the elevator, examining the black nonskid around it under the glare of yellow-gear headlights. The two Chief Petty Officers accompanying me watched, murmuring quietly as they tried to figure out just what it was that interested me so much. The MO, bless his tiny little heart, had decided that the entire evolution required his personal supervision. I let him edge in a little closer than the chiefs.

"Hmmm." I made it sound like something had just occurred to me and got down on my knees to examine the deck more closely.

"You see something?" The MO started to take a step closer, then paused, evidently having watched enough cop shows to be aware of the possibility of destroying evidence.

"Maybe." I looked up at him.

From this angle, the MO looked almost normal, if you ignored the spate of tiny shaving pimples under his chin and the markedly black hair growing out of his nose. A sight not many people had ever seen, I suspected. I looked him up and down. It felt odd to have him look tall.

My eyes noticed something, insisted on coming back down to his midsection. I resisted for a moment, then gave in, hoping whatever it was I saw would become obvious to my conscious mind before Napoleon got antsy and started accusing me of being some sort of pervert. I squinted, turned back to the deck, then looked out across the flight deck as though I were thinking, keeping his midsection in my peripheral vision. What the hell—suddenly, it leaped out at me, just the way a SAM suddenly materializes out of a gray sky.

The bottom of his left-side belt loop was frayed and ragged, the material separating from the overstitching that bound it. Not something you'd normally see in the mirror, not unless you had one mounted on the floor. And not something I would have expected to see on the uniform of Napoleon.

What could cause that? I looked away, now satisfied that I'd at least pinpointed whatever trivia my eyes found interesting.

"You didn't bring an evidence kit out with you," the MO said pointedly.

I gave him a hard look. "Since when are you an expert?"

He sniffed. "Common sense, if you ask me."

"I didn't."

"What?"

"Ask you."

One Chief made a snorting noise, the kind you get when you stifle a sneeze or a chortle.

I patted my pocket. "Got a knife?"

His hand went to his belt automatically, fumbled and groped, feeling for the knife sheath that had frayed the loop. "Hold on. I'll have someone bring you one up."

The brisk breeze suddenly turned icy. I got to my feet slowly, moved toward him. "Never mind. It's not important." He'd gone from being a pain-in-the-ass short shit to something a good deal nastier.

"When did you lose your knife?" I asked quietly.

"Sometime last week." He looked puzzled but not guilty.

"Where?"

"If I knew that, it wouldn't be lost. Would it?"

Silly theory. There're hundreds of knives on a ship this size, one clipped to every plane captain's belt and tucked into aviators' flight suits. That's not even counting the ones in the galleys. Still, I couldn't help wondering what Doc Benning would come up with if she had to do a forensic analysis of the MO's lost knife and Lieutenant Worthington's wounds.

One of the Chiefs cleared his throat pointedly. I glanced at my watch, then nodded at him. The Chiefs started strolling back toward the island, leaving me alone with the MO, who showed no signs of disappearing.

"Go away," I said finally.

"Why?"

"I have things to do that don't involve you. You hang around me now, you'll be interfering with a criminal investigation. That enough reason?"

He glared. "You don't own the entire flight deck, do you?"

"No. But this part I do. Do I have to get the Admiral to tell you to stay the hell out of my way? I have to tell you, this is suspicious behavior on your part. Especially since you're suspect."

"Hell with you." He pivoted and stomped off. The nonskid on the flight deck soaked up the noise his boots made.

I walked forward, toward the forwardmost helo landing spot on the port side of the ship. Why Colburne was suddenly willing to meet openly was a puzzle. Willing, hell—he'd been downright insistent. All I could chalk it up to was a growing fear of being caught below decks by the men he was betraying.

An F/A-18 Hornet was sitting parked on the spot, chocked but not chained. I was fifteen feet from its nose when I heard the first familiar sound. A whir-clunk, then the low growl of a General Electric F-404 turbofan engine turning over.

The first rush of air fluttered my shirtsleeves, almost indistinguishable from the wind blowing across the flight deck. Almost. There's something peculiarly insistent—something no aviator ever forgets—about the air being sucked down the throat of a jet.

Within seconds, the noise built to a scream, the gentle tug of air to a gale pulling me toward the aircraft's starboard engine. Instinct kicked in, and I dropped to the deck, lessening the surface area I presented to the wind.

Despite what they taught me in flight deck safety courses, going low wasn't enough. It never has been. As the turbine noise climbed up the acoustic spectrum, I started skidding and rolling across the flight deck. The nonskid ground skin off my face and hands, quickly sanding off large patches of clothing and skin. I flailed, disoriented except for one reference point—the direction of the aircraft pulling me toward it.

Something hard slammed into one hand, and I grabbed hard at

it, locking my fingers and palm around it like a lifeline. A tie-down chain for the Hornet, still secured to a padeye in the deck.

The thick steel links slipped through my hands slowly but inexorably. I got my other hand on it, and my rate of movement slowed even more.

Slowed, but didn't stop. Sooner or later, the last precious link would touch my palm and slide across the sweaty skin. I was halfway down the chain now, blood on my palms making my grip even more tenuous. The chain started moving through my hands a little faster.

The suction force pulled harder, jerking me up off the deck. I was airborne, suspended between hundreds of sharp rotor blades and the tarmac, tethered to the flight deck by the tie-down chain like a balloon.

Knowing what was happening sent my mind skittering into sheer, raw panic. I'd seen two sailors eaten by jet engines during my active-duty years. They went into the gullet of the jet as men, came out the other end a stream of bloody hamburger strewn out sixty feet behind the aircraft, no single chunk larger than two inches across. If you didn't know who they were going in, you had to hold a muster to find out who'd been chewed up.

Suddenly, the flight deck rose up and smacked me in the face, scraping the side of my face that was already raw. The chain stopped moving under my fingers. I finally noticed that the engine was spooling down.

Someone grabbed me roughly by the shoulder and turned me over on my back. I looked up into Master Chief Handover's face and saw his lips moving. He was standing up, his pants legs blown tight over his legs—but he was standing. It might be enough. Still deaf, I tried to convince myself I could let go of the tie-down chain.

I couldn't. Some part of my mind was still convinced that would kill me.

The Master Chief put his fingers over mine and gently peeled my hands off the chain, not forcing my fingers open but gently reassuring me by his own movements that it was safe to let go. I uncurled my fingers, feeling the tendons pop and creak, the blood seeping back into the crushed tissue.

"Ready to stand up?" he asked.

I nodded, reached for his hand. He deflected the gesture and grabbed me by the elbow. "Think you might want to get those hands looked at first." He assessed me candidly. "And the face. You're going to be an ugly bastard for the next couple of weeks. A live one, though."

"Who—?" I couldn't get the rest of the question past my throat—it'd seized up something bad. The Master Chief appeared to understand what I meant.

"They got him," he said, turning me slowly around, his hand still on my elbow, to face the aircraft.

I saw a rat-faced green-shirted technician caught solidly between my two Masters-at-Arms. Blood was running from his nose and from the corner of his mouth. I walked over to my posse.

"He tried to escape," one of the MAA said calmly. "Attempted murder—I guess he would."

I was more interested in what I saw thirty feet behind their captive. Goggles and a cranial helmet obscured the face of the other man, but they were pulled uncomfortably low over his face. And he was walking away, the opposite of the natural reaction of any witness to an almost fatal accident. He glanced back once over his shoulder and I saw the gleam of perfect teeth. Colburne—it had to be.

"Get him." I pointed at him.

The two MAAs looked confused. Steadier on my feet now, I started lurching after my snitch, intent only on getting my hands around his slimy little throat. If he hadn't set me up, then he'd have two seconds to explain before I choked the living shit out of him.

Colburne broke into a run, heading aft. It made no sense. He was on a ship in the middle of the ocean, about as unable to escape as anyone had ever been. Even if he could have made it back inside the skin of the ship, I still would have been able eventually to hunt him down. If nothing else, he'd have to eat sooner or later.

Still, he ran anyway, sprinting off toward the stern of the ship like a bat. The two MAAs exchanged a startled look, then looked at me. Or tried to. I was already moving past them as quickly as I could on a banged-up knee. I heard them follow and quickly gain on me.

I chased him down the flight deck, adrenaline masking the feeling of cartilage crumbling in my knees. He gradually increased the gap between us as we headed aft. The MAAs drew even with me. I managed to point at Colburne, gasp out a "get him," and they pulled past me. By the time our little procession had reached the arresting wires, he still had a thirty foot lead on them.

Colburne danced over the wires as nimbly as a hurdler running a familiar course. He reached the stern and hopped over the side of the flight deck, disappearing below its edge. The LSO platform. The MAAs skidded to a halt, as I did immediately behind them. I could feel the dull black hole around my patella where adrenaline masked pain. I knew I'd pay for it later.

"You want us to pull him back up here?" one of them asked me. Colburne was at the far end of the platform, his back to a metal plate, eyes as fixed as a rat trapped in a corner.

"No. Just stand by." I eased myself over the edge of the flight deck and down the short ladder that led to the platform.

"Don't come any closer." His hand darted to his belt again, then to his pocket. He pulled out a small pocket knife. "You still don't get it. Even after I told you."

I read him his Article 31 rights, including his right to remain silent, to consult an attorney, and such. He cut me off halfway through the recital. "I know my rights. You want to know anymore, you ask the skipper. He's the traitor to this country, protecting that spy. You ask him." He shut up.

"Jazzman?"

He refused to say another word. I let the MAAs cuff him and take him down below.

25

I HAVE no idea why he'd say that," Jazzman said stiffly. "And yes, for the record, I do understand the warnings you read to me."

"I can understand the skinheads wanting to kill me," I said. "But this business about a spy—he was talking about Worthington."

Jazzman was oddly still. "She wasn't a spy."

"If she were a good one, you wouldn't know it."

He exploded then, moving from utter immobility to angry pacing. "This is absurd. She wasn't a spy."

"No. But we're getting away from the point of this discussion. Why did Colburne say you knew about it?"

Jazzman sighed and some of the bones under his facial skin seemed to soften. "It's always the Commanding Officer's fault, isn't it, though? When something like this happens. Officers brawling in the ready room, drugs on fighters—regardless of who was actually behind it, it's my command and my fault. So much for my career."

I waggled one finger at him. "You know, that disappoints me. I thought you'd probably say something like that, then follow it up with deciding to resign."

"Wouldn't you?" he flared. "I might as well—there's no future for me in the Navy now, not with all this happening on my tour of duty as skipper."

I looked at him steadily and thought back to the flight. Jazzman, taking the chance to take me up one last time, understanding what

175

it felt like to be grounded, showing me the edge of the Tomcat's envelope. The flash of clarity I'd had after we'd landed, how I'd started seeing all the players in an entirely different light, and how much that was like what I'd learned about people after spending two years in a cold rock prison on the ground. People were both better and worse than I'd ever believed possible, and it surfaced under pressure.

Like in a POW camp.

Like during a command tour.

"No," I said finally, feeling sadness wash over me. "No, I'd never resign if I knew I had done nothing wrong. I'd make them throw me out kicking and screaming, fighting every step of the way. Like we did in Vietnam. Like Gina did in your squadron."

"I didn't kill her."

"Not directly. I do believe that. It's called command climate."

"I'm not putting up with this nonsense," he snapped. He started for the door, yanked it open, and stepped out into the passageway.

I let him go. He might be able to run away from me, but I suspected that he'd find it a hell of a lot harder to escape from himself.

BY 2100, THE ship was starting to feel confining and cramped. Since I'd cleared off-hours forays with the Admiral, I hobbled up the ladder to the flight deck, hoping that the massive presence of the sea would soothe me. Between Colburne, the Hornet, Jazzman, and being banged up, I was feeling filthy. Besides, I have a thing about getting right back on that horse that threw me. And almost getting killed wasn't a reason to put off my plans.

With no flying that night, the flight deck was as quiet as it ever got. I could hear the sea pounding against the carrier's hull, feel the slight shudders as waves reached thirty feet up from the ocean. *Lincoln* barely deigned to acknowledge the force of the sea, limiting herself to a few gentle shudders befitting the queen of the ocean.

The flight deck was secured, as it normally is during heavy weather. The clouds spit out an occasional raindrop, but the worst of the storm had passed. I breathed in the heavy, sweet air, clean and wet, holding the promise of better weather in another twelve hours.

I turned and stared up at the bridge and could make out a blur of faces staring back from five decks up. The Captain hadn't been happy about having me out on the weatherdeck, not with the seas running so strongly that finding me if I went over the side would be a virtual impossibility, but he'd given in to the Admiral's insistence that I be allowed out. He was probably on the bridge now, one of the faces staring down at me, watching to see if I disappeared into the foaming march of waves that stretched from the ship to the horizon.

I took my time, walking forward almost all the way to the bow, stopping only when I could feel the sea spray being blown up onto the deck, then turning around and heading back aft, walking between the number-one and number-two bow catapults. I paused for a moment, studying them, and could almost feel the tension ratchet up another notch on the bridge as they tried to read my mind and figure out what had caught my attention. Nostalgia wouldn't occur to the professionally safety-paranoid mind of a ship's Captain.

I finally continued walking back aft, veering toward the starboard side and eventually coming close enough to the island to pass out of view from the bridge. I wondered whether the Captain himself would venture out onto Vulture's Row to monitor my progress. If I'd been him, I would have, although I was fairly certain he'd see nothing more than a retired old aviator creaking around the flight deck trying to pretend he knew what the hell he was doing out there.

Aft of the island, tie-down chains snaked across the deck, eight of them per aircraft. The Plane Captains had been lugging them out all day, four chains at a time draped around their necks and over their shoulders, struggling up ladders onto deck from wherever their line shacks were located in the ship. The chains formed a maze of neat 45-degree angles between tie-down points on the aircraft and the padeyes on the deck, pulled taut enough to prevent even the heavy Tomcats from rolling around if the carrier started pitching.

Thank God they'd been there earlier. Was *my* tie-down chain still over on the port side? As cool as I was playing it, I couldn't entirely repress a shudder.

Aft of the orderly array of E-2C Hawkeyes was the aft elevator, still lowered three decks down to the hangar bay. A Tomcat was tied down to it. The storm must have come up too quickly for its Plane Captain to find yellow gear and get it towed into the hangar, getting it out of reach of the salt spray. He—or she—would have a nasty freshwater washdown to perform the next day, removing the salt residue before it could start the insidious process of corrosion.

I walked toward the elevator, with no particular purpose but acutely aware of the three-deck drop down to the hangar bay, purposely not glancing behind me or up at the island.

I heard the sound of feet pounding on the deck behind me too late. A split second later something hit me hard in the back, catapulting me forward to the edge of the yawing abyss. I tried to stop my forward motion and turn to look behind me in the same movement, flailing my arms to regain my balance.

It almost worked. I teetered on the edge of the flight deck for a moment, just starting to get my center of balance back over the wet nonskid, when my right knee crumpled. I scraped the inside of my left leg on the edge of the flight deck, made one last desperate grab at the edge of it. At the last moment, I managed to twist around and get a glimpse behind me. All I could see was a dark figure running back toward the island.

My stomach knew before I did that it was hopeless. I fell.

26

I T SEEMED like much longer, but I hit the net maybe a second later. Face down, with two strands of barricade rope stretched across my forehead and my chin, I looked at Airman Fernandez.

"Good work," I managed to say with what I thought was an admirable degree of equanimity.

"You right 'bout the time. Good thing you wasn't early—had a problem getting it rigged." He shook his head. "Give some extra time next time."

Levering myself up into any semblance of dignified posture was not possible. I rolled across the net like a log, caught the edge of it in my hands, and was just contemplating executing a skin-the-cat maneuver when Fernandez rolled a metal maintenance platform up.

"Don't do nothing else stupid," he muttered.

"Wasn't stupid." I managed to exit the net feet first. "You have any problem getting the other Plane Captains to cooperate?"

He shook his head, not in answer to the question but in rebuke. "You the next victim, almost."

"I noticed that. But you guys prevented—" I looked around for the rest of the line division people. "I thought you said you needed help to set this up? Where're the other PCs?"

"Didn't need *your* help," he said. "Not so hard, getting the spare net out. Not many people around. Just told them I was checking for holes."

"You ever rigged a barricade net before?"

"I seen it done. Once."

"You did this by yourself?" Suddenly, an idea occurred to me. "Fernandez," I said slowly, quietly, "maybe it's not a healthy thing you're doing. Helping me out."

He looked away and I knew the truth. It shamed me that I hadn't thought of it earlier.

In the junior enlisted circles in which he moved, getting too friendly with the onboard NCIS agent wasn't safe. Half the people he shared a forty-man berthing compartment with probably would have decided that he was a narc. The other half would just dislike him for it on general principles. The minor sins and peccadilloes they commit on the ship—and off—often bring them to my office under less than optimum circumstances.

No, I hadn't done Fernandez any favors by depending on him. And I'd just assumed—from his confident assurances that he could rig the net—that he'd coordinate his efforts with some of his friends in line division. Now, looking at it again, I saw why it couldn't possibly have worked out that way. And the degree of risk he'd taken by rigging a net—which he'd just incidentally never done before— to keep me from playing Humpty-Dumpty on the hangar bay deck.

"We're going to have to do something about this." I stepped back into the shadows as Fernandez carefully and methodically unrigged the net. "It's not safe."

He looked over at me, his face half shadowed by the bulk of the steps. I saw what he'd tried to keep from me—the worried tension over his own safety. I swore quietly at myself.

Like I said, you trust a *chollo* once, he's yours. The converse was true as well. By getting him involved, I was now committed to his safety as well. The flight today had taught me something of what that meant.

The flight. Suddenly, an idea.

"Fernandez, what's the gossip about my hop today?"

He shrugged. "Long preflight, they saying. That 301 PC—she's all nervous, wondering she gonna get in trouble, you climbing over her bird."

"She clean?"

"Her?" He snorted. "Man, you talking serious born-again. Bitch done been praying for my soul last two weeks."

"You're certain."

He gave me a look I deserved.

"Then come back by the office as soon as you get that net stowed. I've got something in mind that might save both of us some problems down the road."

He looked at the net, then at me.

"Not again. This time, it's something you might already know how to do."

DOC BENNING WAS waiting for me outside my office. From the look on her face, I was about to get beaten up again. I wasn't up to it.

"What?" I snapped.

She looked at me clinically, reaching out to grab my jaw and turn my head from side to side. "A little first aid will prevent infection and scarring. Hold out your hands."

"They're OK."

"Let me see them. You wouldn't know OK right now if it bit you on your ass."

"I—"

She grabbed my wrist and turned my hands over, then scowled.

"I washed it out. It doesn't hurt." I tried to flex my fingers smoothly and couldn't.

"You ran off the flight deck before the corpsman could get to you. Then you disappear. In the last ten hours, you couldn't find a few minutes to stop by Medical and see if you were really hurt? What is this, some sort of macho thing?"

"I had some things to take care of." The defensive tone was because she was right.

She sighed. "Unlock your office and invite me in. I'll take a look at your wounds, give you something for them to prevent infection."

"A house call?"

She looked at me levelly. "Consider it the sort of thing that partners do for each other. Like letting each other know what's going on, calling for backup, maybe even asking someone they trust to cover their back."

That hurt more than the damp sterile gauze she was dabbing at my face.

"Look," she said, wadding the pad and tossing it in my very empty garbage can, "if you want to go solo, just say so. You get eaten by a Hornet, it's not my fault. But you die of septicemia from not getting the damage looked at, that's my business. You got that?"

I tried to nod, but one of her hands was clamped around my chin, keeping me from flinching away from whatever she was dabbing on my face. Maybe she felt the motion—she didn't press me for an answer.

Finally, she turned loose my face. "Roll up your sleeve."

"What for?"

"Or drop your trousers, if you prefer. You need a tetanus booster."

I groaned. "I hate shots."

Carol sighed.

27

MOST LAW-ENFORCEMENT officers know the advantage of working with a partner. While I hadn't been at it as long as my crusty TV heroes, it made sense. Somebody to talk to on those long stakeouts, share theories and facts with, and cover for you when things went real wrong.

Like Fernandez just had. Like Doc Benning.

If I didn't come up with a reasonable explanation for being on the flight deck—and for who tried to kill me—it would just alert the one person I didn't want to tumble to the scheme. Given the fact that I hadn't managed to winnow out the pool of suspects, the priority had to be protecting my ace number-one assistant, my Chicano Dr. Watson.

I finally tracked Fernandez down on the flight deck, hanging out around a Tomcat, and motioned at him. Fifteen minutes later he showed up in my office. It started with a vein jumping at the corner of his jaw and progressed to toe tapping and rustling around in his seat. By the time I finished laying out the scheme, I was seeing a first. I'd have been willing to bet that Fernandez hadn't looked that nervous since early puberty.

I didn't blame him. My guts had been strung tight all day, and the knee I'd banged was complaining. The only thing that the plan had going for it was that it was the only one I could come up with.

"Can you do this?" I asked.

He nodded, froze down the nervous tension I saw in his face. Chilled out, but nerved up, like he must have been before when the gangs started rumbling. "No big deal. Just a little face, man."

"OK. It gets bad, you just tell them you're ready to confess. I'll come down and get you out. I swear."

He tried hard to look bored. "But something happen to you, I be in a world of shit."

He had a right to know, I decided. Two weeks ago, I'd decided to trust him with the key to my office. This was more important. "I'm not the only one that knows what's going on. You'll be taken care of, as much as we possibly can."

"Who backing you up?"

"The only guy who's not on my list—couldn't be, not the way things went down. The guy with the stars on his collar."

"Texaco man." If anything, the fact that Admiral Fairchild now knew of the existence of Airman Fernandez only wound him up tighter. "Shit. Some kinda shit, man."

"You don't have to do this. There're other ways to do it."

He shook his head. "Not as good. Won't work like this will."

He was right, and he knew I knew it. He looked up at me, and I felt the duty to safeguard his trust settle on me as firmly as the oath I'd once taken to defend my country. I reached out both hands, took his one hand, and bore down hard. His hand tightened in mine. "POW oath, Fernandez. We all get out of this together."

I didn't tell him the rest of the promise we'd made. We all got out together—or none of us did.

"Let's get this shit moving," he said, withdrawing his hand and settling himself down to work. "Five minutes, then you come up. I be by the bird."

FIFTEEN MINUTES LATER, it was all over. I'd strode out onto the flight deck, making my normal brisk progress from bow to stern, stopped at Tomcat 301, and busted Fernandez for trying to shove me off the edge of the flight deck, calling him names and swearing about a drug deal. My partner got hustled down to the brig faster than I'd seen MAAs move in years. I made it real clear that nothing accidental was to happen to him, that this would be a high-profile case and there damned well better not be a mark on him or anything for his defense attorney to be screaming about later. I thought I'd impressed the MAAs—but I couldn't be certain.

WITH FERNANDEZ SAFELY—I hoped—out of the way, I went back to looking for hard evidence. With that would come some hint as to the right direction to look for motive.

I started with what I knew—that Worthington had been found in the bilges. Based on my observations with Doc Benning and my little experiment, I was willing to bet that she'd gotten down there via the Ellison doors. For that to have happened, she had to be dead—or at least unconscious—at the time she was moved. Time for a little independent verification before I ventured too much further down this path.

I rummaged through my evidence locker until I found the right bottle. It was the latest addition to crime fighting, a reagent that fluoresced on contact with blood. Unlike the stuff we usually used, using it didn't require a blacklight source. I didn't have to understand all that to know what it did.

I walked down to Engineering and made my way through the vaguely remembered path of twisting metal catwalks. After two wrong turns, I was back on the lower level, staring down at the metal grating I'd first seen her body on. It seemed like so long ago, but it had been only three days.

As an experiment, I squeezed the spray bottle. A thin mist shot out, hung for a moment in mid-air, then slowly settled onto the grate. Three bright spots of green appeared on the old metal, startling splashes of color out of place in the black-and-white world of Engineering.

I heard movement above me and looked up to see snipes gathering on the walkways above, staring down at the intruder in their realm. I waved. Most of them turned away and pretended to study the gauges and manifolds that protruded at odd angles from sinister-looking masses of metal. Two sailors, younger than the rest, waved back. Not fully inculcated into the snipely tradition, a state of affairs that would be remedied as soon as I got my ass out of their spaces, I suspected.

Moving back along the walkway, I tried a few other spots, just as a control. Only one other spot fluoresced, near the first ladder leading up to fresh air. Probably from when they'd transported her out of Engineering on the Stryker frame, I suspected. In my new show-me mode, I tested several other spots along the route I'd seen the corpsmen take, with no positive results.

Moving back down to the first three spots, I started back along the walkway toward the lower end of the escape hatch, spraying periodically as I went. I found two more spots in the next ten feet, the one farthest away from the body the larger of the two. Then, just outside the Ellison doors, I struck gold. Or, more properly, green. Streaks of puce ran down the edges as though the snipes had turned to some form of agro-engineering and planted grass on the lower levels in an effort to do something about the stale air.

I shoved open the Ellison door and looked at the deck. It looked clean—too clean, maybe, for a space that was used only in emergencies and drills, although I couldn't be certain. If my deck consultant hadn't been incarcerated, I would have asked him for an expert opinion. Barring that, I tried to put what he'd taught me in the last several days to good use.

I knelt down and ran my hand over the tile. It had a smooth feel to it and left only a small trace of grit on my palm. No shit in the corners, I imagined Fernandez pointing out, and the streak marks of less-than-professional mopping were still evident. I stood up and tried to visualize a prosecutor putting my erstwhile partner on the stand as an expert witness.

I held the spray bottle out and gently depressed the trigger. Mist again, then the small compartment seemed to be flooded with light. The deck, the grating, the rungs on the long ladder bolted to the bulkhead, even the walls lit up. Doc Benning had been right.

I looked up the shaft that stretched up three decks to safety. The ladder was bolted close to the wall, leaving minimal space for anything other than the ball of the foot to rest on each rung. Countless operational tests conducted by expensive contractors had probably proved conclusively that a snipe fleeing a fire would damned near hardly even need the rungs, being propelled upward as much by sheer terror as muscles.

At eighteen or twenty years of age, it was a quick two-minute climb to safety, even hauling a buddy along and wearing a fifteen-minute oxygen mask. For someone my age, it represented a comprehensive cardiovascular workout.

I hooked the bottle around my belt and started up the ladder. Straight up.

Ten feet above the deck, I looped one arm over a rung and pulled out the bottle with my free hand. One spot on the wall lit up. Still on the right track.

I proceeded up the next fifty miles of ladder in a similar fashion, wheezing and swearing at the pain in my knee. Approximately four days later, I reached the top. If I'd have been a snipe trying to get out, the ship would have been decommissioned before I'd reached safety.

Exiting the escape shaft proved even more problematic, since the ladder simply terminated four feet above and to the side of the Ellison door at the top. I followed my now-proven procedure, anchoring myself with one arm and using the other to shove the door open. I slid one foot off the ladder, transferred my weight, and finally found the handhold that was intended to support the rest of my body. I eased out of the shaft, still swearing at engineers that built safety features for teenagers.

The corridor was still and silent, as quiet as it ever got on ship. At the far end of the passageway, someone was walking forward toward the enlisted galley, one of three onboard. I did my spray routine in the corridor again and paused to marvel at modern science. Even with the heavy traffic in this passageway, my miracle spot tester still found traces of blood. I wondered how long the effect would take to fade, and whether some compartment cleaner was in for an interesting surprise the next day.

Would it—suddenly, my keenly honed analytical senses reminded me of a relevant paradigm that could provide enlightenment on my current investigatory methodology. All those years of training and study finally paid off. My kindergarten teacher would have been proud.

Hansel and Gretel. A trail of bread crumbs. Since the evidence of blood had persisted for so long next to the entrance to the escape hatch, there was at least a chance that a trail of now-invisible blood stains could lead me to the place Gina'd been murdered.

I took two steps aft and squirted. Bingo. Experimentally, I took two steps forward past the Ellison door and squirted again. Nothing. So, unless the nuclear engineers who owned this part of the ship made it a habit to drag sides of freshly butchered beef up and down the corridors during their off-hours—something I might actually have not put too far out of the possibility if we'd been on a submarine—I thought there was some merit to the theory that Gina had been killed somewhere aft of the Ellison door.

But on this deck or another one? After verifying that no blood traces fluoresced on the deck forward of the doors, I started laying down a careful path aft, playing Hansel with a spray bottle of green mist. I tracked her faint bloody path back aft four frames and then lost it.

I checked the deck and saw no appreciable difference in the cleanliness of the linoleum on one side of the kneeknocker when compared with the other side. Even if it had been recently thoroughly field dayed, I was beginning to think that my magic mist would have had little difficulty. Based on that assumption, I studied the doors and hatches in the immediate area.

One frame forward, a ladder well led up to the next deck. I misted the area and got no reaction. Back to the doors.

Two were labeled with cryptic Navy jargon, the sequence of numbers, dashes, and letters that spell out to the trained eye the exact location of the hatch and what the compartment behind it was generally used for. Another set of letters spelled out the damage-control characteristics of the hatch, whether it was watertight or not. And the kind souls who inhabited the spaces would sometimes even put signs on the doors, stenciled or painted with varying degrees of proficiency.

At the spot where the green traces ended there were two doors, one on either side of the passageway. The one on the port side—4–135–7–Q, if you want to be exact—was a watertight door labeled "Teletype Repair." Why, exactly, a repair shop for something that no longer even existed in a modern communications shop needed a watertight door, I wasn't exactly certain.

Across from that, another watertight door sported the rating insignia of a Photographer's Mate. An unlit red light was placed immediately above the hatch and a sign next to the door warned everyone to keep out if the light was lit. A darkroom.

Since the red light was out, I tried the dogging lever that held the hatch shut. It moved under pressure, and I swung the hatch open and fumbled for the light switch that should be next to the hatch. Dim red light flooded the compartment. I shoved the hatch open all the way to let the white light from the hallway in.

The compartment was longer than it was wide, with the hatch located at the forward end of the compartment and the length extending forward parallel with the corridor I'd just walked down. Two processing tables jutted out from the wall opposite me. A double metal sink filled the entire end of the compartment. The shelves above it were empty.

I stepped in, already afraid I knew what I would find. The darkroom appeared to be unused, one of those stray compartments that no one can find out who owns and that no one wants to take responsibility for cleaning and inspecting. The label on the compartment checkoff list said that S-3 division was responsible for maintaining it, but I doubted that any cook had set foot in here in months.

I put off the moment as long as I could, then lifted the trusty spray bottle.

Even under the bastard mixture of fluorescent light from the passageway and red darkroom bulbs, I could see the deck turn brilliant green. With a sick feeling, I walked toward the sinks, certain the entire compartment would soon resemble an obscene abattoir's greenhouse.

28

IT DID. From overhead to deck, the compartment was awash in different shades of puce, verdigris, and alfalfa. Higher up on the bulkheads, blood had spattered in a gentle, arclike pattern. The lower starboard side was completely green, with a large, brighter smear in the middle of a four-by-five-foot area.

I groaned and leaned against the bulkhead. For some reason, this graphic evidence of how Gina had been killed, even more so than the sight of her pale face in the bilges, shook me. It had seemed almost antiseptic before, once you got past the presence of the body. The knife wounds and slashes had been washed clean by the bilge water, and, as with most dead bodies, I had had a clear sense that— whoever and whatever Gina Worthington had been—she was gone.

Where, I'll leave to the chaplain. But the sense of loss I'd felt then was nothing compared to the rage that the physical evidence of her murder invoked.

Evidence. I directed a few foul words to myself, realizing I'd forgotten the camera. While it might be enough for me to know that I'd tracked down the location of her death, the rest of the judicial process would sooner or later demand a record of the physical evidence. Short of impaneling a jury and airlifting them out to the carrier within the next thirty minutes, photographs would have to do.

I stepped back out into the corridor and grabbed the nearest sailor. "Guard this room," I said harshly. "You know who I am?"

The startled sailor nodded. Most of them did, I thought bitterly. Probably more than knew who Lieutenant Gina Worthington had been.

Even fewer would have known who she really was. A week earlier, I would have put myself in that category as well. It bothered me that it had taken her death for me to really understand who she'd been.

Once I was certain the sailor knew how serious I was about guarding the room, I tromped back up the two levels to my office. I would grab both the Polaroid and the thirty-five millimeter, since it looked like the darkroom might be off-limits for awhile. That way, at least I'd have an immediate evidentiary record of the bloodstains.

As soon as I reached the 0-1 deck, I looked down the passageway to my office, half expecting to see Fernandez backing out of my compartment pulling a bucket. Instead, Commander Burroughs, probably number one on the list of people least likely to be standing outside my office, was pacing back and forth impatiently in front of my door. I watched him for a moment, almost relieved that he was there. The MO would undoubtedly piss me off, giving me an opportunity to vent. He probably hadn't counted on being a therapeutic relief valve, but he was about to experience that pleasure.

I walked down the passageway, almost eager to tear into him. He saw me immediately and kept his eyes locked on me as I advanced down the passageway. No pretending he didn't see me, giving me the opportunity to politely ignore him, as Fernandez would. Such is the arrogance that comes with making commander.

"What do you want?" I made the question harsher than it should have been, giving him fair warning. Under the circumstances, it was the least I could do. I waited for him to piss me off.

His mouth opened and his lips started to move, and I finally deciphered what I was seeing on his face. An anger that matched my own, an uncomfortable mixture of embarrassment and desperation. Not what I would have expected from him, nor did any immediate explanation occur to me. I sighed. Maybe catharsis would have to wait.

Finally, after a few seconds of delay, his words started coming out. "You don't have to make this any harder than it has to be," he said defensively. "I'm here voluntarily."

I slipped my key into the lock, turned the knob, and shoved the door open, applying a little more force than necessary. The hatch banged back against the bulkhead. Not as good as yelling at someone, but it looked like it would have to do for the moment. "You talked to the JAG officer?"

He looked puzzled for a moment. "No, why would I do that?"

"Then I don't have anything to say to you," I said roughly. "You've been advised of your rights, and I suggest you avail yourself of them."

"This isn't about Worthington," he said. "At least, I don't think it is." He settled down in my one visitor chair without asking. I stood over him for a moment, glaring down at him, then moved behind the desk and slumped into my own seat. Physically, it wasn't as comfortable as his office chair was, but I'd a damned sight rather be sitting on my side of the desk than his.

"Then what is it? Be advised, I'm not in the mood for any games right now. And I've got some business to take care of, as well."

He studied me for a moment, as though wondering whether to continue. By then, curiosity was starting to nibble away at the edges of my temples.

"Look, it's been a rough day," I said by way of explanation and excuse. And, just maybe, apology. "I am a little pressed for time." I glanced over at the locker where my cameras were.

How long would the fluorescence last? I didn't remember exactly—about thirty minutes, I thought I recalled. Not that it mattered, particularly. I still had my trusty spray bottle and could always recreate the evidentiary trail if needed. This stuff was a hell of a lot better than good old Luminol, which only fluoresced under blacklights. Although some defense attorney somewhere would undoubtedly make a point to mention how new the stuff was to the jury. It might even confuse them enough—

The Maintenance Officer interrupted my train of thought. "We have some weapons missing." I could tell from his voice that he liked telling me that even less than I liked hearing it.

"Weapons." With an effort, I tore my thoughts away from the eventual trial of Lieutenant Worthington's killer and concentrated on him. "What kind?"

"Sparrows. Two of them." He stopped and rustled papers in a manila folder he was carrying. "Here." He handed me two sheets of paper.

I studied them for a moment. It was surprising how little had changed since the days that I'd been on active duty. An ammunition transaction report still looked basically the same, cryptic lines of numbers and letters that indicated ordnance had been expended, received, or transferred to another command. The codes change occasionally, as new weapons are introduced to the system, but the purpose remains the same—providing continuous, wall-to-wall accounting for every piece of naval ordnance a squadron held.

I found I could still translate most of the entries. I studied it for a moment, trying to figure out what it was that caused him concern. "As far as I can tell, you expended two Sparrows in aerial combat maneuvering. So what?" I laid the two sheets of paper back down on the desk.

The MO looked annoyed. "Of course that's what it says. The only problem is that was a no-fly day for us. Remember the fleetwide safety stand-down that AIRPAC ordered after that last F-14 was lost? Well, that's the same day. Therefore, the ordnance was not expended on that day."

"So it's a typo. Don't tell me you've never had that problem before?" I leaned back in my chair, starting to be convinced that the paranoid little Napoleon in front of me was even more of a pain in the ass than I originally suspected. Hard to believe.

He snorted. "That's what I thought at first, too," he admitted. "But a certain AA in Lieutenant Berkshire's division just happened to screw up badly enough that I thought he needed some extra military instruction. So, since he was an ordnanceman, I put him to work doing a bulkhead-to-bulkhead inventory of all of our weapons. Everything." A satisfied smile crossed his face. "Took him about ten hours."

"And?"

"And the Sparrows are missing, that's what." His face was starting to turn red. "Listen, I've been in this business a few years. I know how to run my department."

"So the gist of it is that you have two weapons missing and a report that says they were expended on a day when you know they weren't. That about it?" Probably a typo, I decided, suddenly weary of the small man in front of me. Seven-day clocks, gallons of paint—I decided that the MO needed to get a life.

"There's more. After I found this discrepancy, I went back and balanced all the flight schedules and after-action reports against the naval ammunition logistics control records. There's no way to account for that expenditure—none at all."

For the first time, the arrogant belligerence on his face started to fade. I could read where his thoughts were going. The maintenance officer that lost control of his weapons inventory would be sure to see it turn up in his fitness reports. Aside from a maintenance-related fatality, there was no surer way to kill his career.

"You're certain?" I shouldn't have asked.

He looked annoyed. "Of course I'm certain. Do you think I would come to you if I weren't?"

"Any ideas?"

He shook his head, the uncertainty and apprehension showing more clearly on his face now. "No. I was going to ask Lieutenant Berkshire about it, but after yesterday—" His voice trailed off, and I followed the path of his thoughts.

After my brilliant performance in the Admiral's conference room, he meant. Since Lieutenant Chelsea Berkshire had been one of the participants, the MO had deemed it prudent to come to me first. I gave him credit for that.

"We'll have to look into this," I said slowly, hoping he caught the use of the plural subject. By coming forward and exposing a potentially serious deficiency in his department, the MO, whether he knew it or not, had just turned himself into one of the good guys.

At least professionally. I still didn't like the little shit worth a damn.

"What are you going to do?" he demanded, back to being the man I loved to hate.

"Investigate," I answered loftily, trying to give the impression that I knew exactly where I would start. Which would be, I admitted at least to myself, probably talking to Lieutenant Berkshire.

The MO stood and put the manila folder on my desk. "I'll leave this with you, then. It's a summary of the records indicating exactly where and how we've expended ordnance since the last bulkhead-to-bulkhead inventory." He turned to leave, and then hesitated at the hatch.

"I see Airman Fernandez up here quite a bit," the MO said, his back still toward me. "I was wondering—does he work for you? I mean, in some official capacity?"

"Yeah, I throw all of my snitches into jail." I tried to make it sound convincing. Forestalling any suspicions that Fernandez might have been a snitch was the whole point of tossing him in the hoosegow. I hoped it worked a hell of a lot better on his peers than on his superiors.

The MO turned back to face me. "I think that's probably bullshit," he said in the softest voice I'd heard from him to date. He looked at me appraisingly. "It might work with the troops, though."

I leaned back in my chair, regarding him gravely. My estimation of him went up another notch. "But not with you?"

He shook his head. "Not a chance. That boy joined the Navy to get away from that sort of stuff. You watch his work around here—he's young, okay, but he's got a lot going for him. At least in my book." He studied me for a moment. "If my opinion counts for anything with you."

That's the problem with people. You figure you've got them pegged, stuck them into neat little compartments, and all at once they break out of them of their own will. I let the MO see the surprise on my face.

He stared down at the deck. "I've got a son about his age. At least, almost his age. Fifteen, going on twenty-five." He shook his head, his mind somewhere far away. "You do the best you can with them. Sometimes it's enough, sometimes it's not."

I reached a decision. "Commander, do you have a few minutes?" I said gravely. "I could use a witness for what I'm about to do."

He looked up at me uncertainly, jarred slightly by the unexpected courtesy. "Of course, I'm available to assist on anything you might need." His tone was stiff, probably the closest he ever got to friendliness.

"Good. Hang tight for a moment." Like there was any other way the MO would hang.

I rummaged through the locker, extracted the two cameras, and made sure that they both had color film in them. "Come on. I want you to watch me take some pictures."

29

A S WE traipsed back down to the darkroom, I gave the MO a brief description of what he would see. There were no words, however, to really encompass the enormity of it all. That would have to wait for the actual experience.

The sailor I'd left guarding the compartment had settled into a stance somewhere between at ease and leaning against the bulkhead. He looked vaguely relieved and annoyed to see me, and I figured he had been good for at least another fifteen minutes before he got fed up with standing watch on an empty darkroom. I thanked him, got his name, and made a mental note to send his department head a nice memo on him.

I undogged the compartment, pulled the door open, and peered in. The green fluorescence had faded partially, with only a few darker streaks remaining along the lower bulkheads. The blood smear pattern higher up on the bulkhead had completely faded. "Hold this," I ordered, handing the MO the thirty-five millimeter. I backed up across the corridor and took a picture of the entrance to the darkroom, then stepped forward and started snapping shots of the interior. "Faded, some, but I need this for the record."

Five minutes later, I'd finished what I thought was an adequate evidentiary record. I motioned for the MO to hand me the spray bottle. He handed it to me, stepped forward, and peered into the compartment. "You saw me take pictures of that, right?"

He nodded. He looked slightly pale, I noted, but I expected the next demonstration would have more impact.

Starting with the bulkheads nearest the hatch, I misted the area with the reagent. The green sprang into sharp relief, a long, smeary trail on the deck, the two large blurs on the bulkhead. I lifted the bottle up, hoping the compound wasn't toxic, and sprayed it at the upper wall. The green blood-spray traces immediately materialized.

"Dear sweet lord Jesus," the MO said softly. "It was here."

I nodded, relieved on some level to find that I was not the only human being in the world to experience such a strong reaction to the evidence of carnage. "Pretty ugly, isn't it?"

"And the sink—do you think—"

"That was one of the worst spots," I answered. It felt like picking at a scab, painfully peeling back the layers of detachment and objectivity I tried to overlay on myself. I felt the tears start in my eyes and tried to surreptitiously rub them away. Of all the people to see me lose control, the MO was the last one I wanted it to be.

"You'll have to find him," the MO said. The observation struck me not as trite, as it might have. Instead, it was merely an affirmation of what we both knew was true—that some bastard was going to have to pay for her death. And heavily.

The gonging demand of general quarters cut short my evidentiary inspection. The first notes sounded, accompanied by the stark, bald announcement that there was an unidentified air contact to the north, inbound. Moments later, the thundering pounding of feet rang down the corridors as five thousand sailors and officers raced for combat stations. We plastered ourselves against the bulkheads and watched at least two hundred sailors tromp through the green shit on the decks. The last traces of my bread-crumb trail disappeared, carried off to all sections of the ship by the running sailors.

The MO grabbed me and pulled me back toward the hatch. We both stepped just inside the kneeknocker, trying to stay clear of the sailors racing for battle stations.

"Don't you have somewhere to be?" I asked the MO, raising my voice to be heard over the stampede.

He nodded. "Maintenance Control. I'll head up there as soon as there's a break in the traffic."

I nodded. My own general quarters station was in my office, not nearly as urgent an assignment as that of most of the men and women running down the corridor.

Five minutes after the GQ went down, the flood of humanity trickled down to a steady drip. During GQ, a traffic pattern imposes some sort of order on the normally random movements of its inhabitants. To go forward and up on the ship, you're supposed to use the starboard passageways. Down and aft, the port ones. Stay to the right and across ship passageways, hugging the bulkheads, and you'll usually avoid serious injury trying to get to your battle station.

As soon as he saw the traffic start to abate, the MO nodded and slipped out of the compartment. I watched him disappear down the passageway, an arrogant bantam rooster strutting.

Or something more.

I finally eased out of the compartment myself and dogged the lever down on it. I slipped the chain and lock I'd brought with me for that purpose through the metal door handles and padlocked the scene of the crime.

As I walked down the passageway toward the up ladder, the sound of hatches clanging shut reverberated. All around me, the ship was sealing up for battle. The watertight doors and knee-knockers I so despised turned the massive ship into a honeycomb, a series of small, watertight compartments that could withstand a hell of a lot of structural damage. Though it might complicate my egress back to my office, it made the ship virtually unsinkable. Like Styrofoam.

At six-foot-two, I can see over most crowds of people. Looking down the passageway, I thought I saw the Ellison door move.

Odd. No one should have been going in or out of it during General Quarters. The required walks to their battle stations took the engineers down the normal ladders and stairwells, and the emergency escape hatch shafts wouldn't normally be used. I paused at the ladder leading up to my deck, wondering. If I took the time to investigate right then, I'd soon be cut off from my office. That would mean I'd have to phone in a muster report from wherever I ended up to the duty officer, since an affirmative report from every battle station was required before the captain would declare General Quarters set.

A pain in the ass, and one that might earn me a few snide comments from the Admiral, but certainly not an unpardonable sin. Besides, I decided, under the circumstances, investigating Lieutenant Worthington's death took priority over most routine evolutions.

I turned away from the ladder and headed back down the passageway. The Ellison door was now shut. I placed one hand gently against the right-hand side and shoved, swiveling it out, then looked down the shaft.

The three-story vertical hole through the ship was lit by one overhead light immediately above me. Near the bottom, it was gloomy. Opening the door had provided some additional illumination, and I saw a reflection off something light.

Something blonde.

Looking down from above, I couldn't see the person's face, nor could I tell how tall the person was, nor even if it was an officer or enlisted person. Nevertheless, I knew who it was. Immediately.

Even from that distance, I could tell that the blonde hair was longer than regulation. At least for men. Out of two hundred women on the ship, I doubted more than twenty percent or so were blonde. Even fewer would be that peculiar shade of melted butter shot with silver.

Without pausing to consider the consequences, I swung myself into the shaft and grabbed the ladder with one hand. Once I had a foot firmly set along the rungs, I shifted my weight, letting the Ellison door slam shut behind me.

Negotiating the escape ladder twice in as many days wasn't my idea of fun. At least this time I was going down. I moved more rapidly than I had last time, grateful for the gentle assistance of gravity. When I was ten feet down the ladder, I heard the door at the other end of the shaft bang shut. I kept going, a thousand reasons why this was a very bad idea suddenly occurring to me.

Still, I could think of no good reason why Chelsea Berkshire would be headed for the Engineering spaces during General Quarters. That she used the same shaft through which Gina Worthington was lowered to her death was peculiar.

More than peculiar. Damned incriminating, if I did say so myself.

By the time I reached the bottom of the ladder, I'd formulated a tentative plan. Find a telephone, call in the muster report. Track down Lieutenant Berkshire somewhere in the maze of catwalks and machinery and demand to know why she was in Engineering. Finally, after I'd gotten her explanation, I'd go see Jazzman.

Engineering had put this plant on line since the last time I'd been down here. It was as noisy as the day we'd found Worthington's body, deafening. Or at least, it would have been if I hadn't already been half incapacitated by too many years spent around jet engines. The noise probably bothered me less than it did normal denizens of this place.

I opened the door and stepped onto the steel-plated deck immediately outside it. The catwalk on which I'd first seen Worthington's body stretched off to my right. Another one led immediately forward, tracking around the edge of the compartment. Three steps away from the emergency hatch, the steel plates were replaced by iron grating. I could see the bilge waters, lower than they'd been that day, gently lapping at the supports.

Which way? Probably around the bulkhead, I decided. The path to the right would have led immediately below the upper-level watches, and whoever had come down this way—Berkshire, I was sure of it—would not risk being seen by the engineers.

I moved to my left, and followed the catwalk that ran between the bulkhead and two massive pieces of equipment. What they were, I wasn't exactly certain, but they appeared to be something like a condenser.

The catwalk divided at that point, one branch running between the two condensers. The air was noticeably hotter there. Impelled as much by instinct as a growing sense of claustrophobia, I walked between the two condensers, hoping to find a path to a more clear area of the Engineering space.

Not that that was likely. There was damned little open space there.

The catwalk took a sharp right turn ten paces forward and dead-ended into a small, metal-railed platform in front of the fire pump. I was certain it was a fire pump—the brass metal plate on it said so.

A dead end. I turned to retrace my steps, dreading squeezing between the condensers and the bulkhead.

I had a split second of warning before something crashed into me, a movement that flickered overhead so briefly that I was barely aware of it. Reflexively, I took a step back. Lieutenant Berkshire leaped down from the nearest condenser, landing lightly on her feet on the metal grating. The impact of her landing was lost in the general din.

She regarded me levelly, a cold, assessing look. I tried to return it in kind, feeling a bit like a dog that's just caught a Volkswagen. OK, years of chasing cars, and you finally catch one. What do you do with it? Same issue. I'd crawled down the escape hatch looking for Berkshire, and here she was. I wondered for a moment what I could say to avoid seeming completely inane.

Finally, I settled on the obvious. "What are you doing down here?"

I saw her hand slip inside a pocket of her flight suit. Without answering, she withdrew a knife. It was a switchblade—she proved she knew how to handle it immediately. It flicked open with a nasty flash of light.

Alone, in a strange compartment on a ship, facing a young woman I knew to be well versed in martial arts, I did the only sensible thing. I ran.

I had a three-step lead initially, but within seconds I felt her hand clawing at my back. I found an additional burst of speed from somewhere and managed to stay out of her reach for a few more seconds.

I twisted back along the way I'd come, passing up the emergency hatch and taking the right-hand path. The catwalk ran straight for almost fifteen feet before it intersected with an up ladder. I pushed myself, shoving harder than I thought was possible and, at the last minute, whirled around and put the ladder between the two of us.

She still hadn't spoken. We played feint to either side of the ladder for a few seconds, then she made a charge around the right side of it. She held the knife in her forward hand, leading the way.

I let her come closer. Finally, her reflexes kicked in and she noticed I wasn't moving. It was too late for her then to come to an immediate stop. As she got within range, I hauled off and kicked her in the groin as hard as I could.

Okay, maybe not the preferred tactic against a female, but judging from her reaction, it was fairly effective. She doubled over, moaned, and then tried to straighten. I took advantage of the opportunity to start up the ladder.

Jesus, she was quick. Within seconds I heard her feet clattering up the ladder behind me. Slower, yes, but moving faster than I was.

The top of the ladder was fifteen feet away. I felt my right knee quiver, threaten to give out, and I swore.

Something gripped my ankle and yanked down hard. I stumbled, almost fell off the ladder, and then lashed out with the same foot, trying for her face. She was too far below me. I managed to connect with the knife, though, and saw it flip out of her hand.

That's the problem with using a professional grip on a blade. When held lightly, it becomes an extension of your hand. You gain maneuverability and quickness, but you lose something—a firm grip.

Or in this case, the whole knife. I kicked at her again, and saw the knife hit the grate below, poise for a second, then slide into the bilge waters.

She pulled back long enough for me to regain possession of my foot. I started up the ladder, wondering where in the hell the watch-standers were. At General Quarters, there should have been eight sailors in this space, maybe more.

There were three levels to the Engineering space, each one a mass of gratings and catwalks. It resembled a tree house more than anything, a tree house in hell.

At the top of the ladder, the catwalk ran right and left. I chose the left, since it looked like it would take me to the center of the Engineering space. Berkshire followed me up, moving more slowly, but still closing the distance.

Damn it. The catwalk dead-ended again, another small platform. Off to the left, a curving ladder led over the top of an auxiliary boiler.

The boiler was two stories high, a massive, square configuration of silver gray. At the top, the steam drum was painted white.

Still no sign of any of the watchstanders. And I didn't know how long I could hold her off.

I reached for the ladder and started climbing at a 45-degree angle onto the top of the boiler. I could feel the heat radiating from the metal, making the ladder rungs almost uncomfortably hot. At the end was another platform, this one located close to the boiler safety valves.

There was a thin metal railing around it, waist high. I backed myself into one corner of the square platform and waited.

Berkshire's blonde head peeked over the edge, and she scampered quickly up the ladder. She stopped, now only four feet away from me.

For the first time, I saw a smile on her face. It was an ugly thing, alive and full of menace. In some ways, more frightening than the death mask I'd seen on Worthington's face.

She advanced slowly, her experience with a size-twelve EE boot in the crotch having taught her something, at least. I remembered what Jazzman said about her reflexes and was surprised that I'd even gotten that shot in.

"Go ahead and scream," she said. The smile never flickered. "They can't hear you. They never can."

"You killed her."

She nodded. "No one else would. All those big, brave fighter pilots—not one of them had the balls to do what had to be done."

"Why?"

She studied me for a moment, moving forward slightly, raising her hand to distract me. I kept my eyes on her, ducked under the railing, and stepped back onto the boiler. Heat radiated up through my shoes, already painful. "You won't get him, you know."

"Why?" I demanded.

She moved faster now and was standing at the spot where I had been. I backed up, struggling to keep my balance on the broad, curved top of the boiler.

"It had to be done," she repeated. She eased herself under the railing and followed me.

We stood facing each other, feet wide apart to maintain our balance. One more step back, and I'd put the steam safety valves between us. Small barriers, barely knee high—less than the knee-knockers she hurdled over daily. Anyone with the strength to lower all one hundred twenty-five pounds of Gina Worthington down the escape hatch would have no problem vaulting over those.

Something Brinker had said to me long ago suddenly flamed into my mind. In those endless hours of deadly boredom, that time between torture and starvation when all we had was each other, we'd talked. Brinker had had his eyes set on command and had already started his qualifications. That included familiarizing himself with the Engineering plant. As a former surface sailor, he'd had an easier time of that than most.

I'd made him memorize the intricate performance envelopes of the Skyhawk. In revenge, he'd quizzed me endlessly on the details of a steam engineering plant. Patiently walking me through the temperatures, pressures, and flow rates necessary to sustain combustion in a boiler.

The steam safety valves—those had been worth two weeks of discussion in our hurried tap code in the Hanoi Hilton. They were there to relieve the pressure if the boiler ever got out of control and would release superheated steam into the air rather than let the steam drum explode.

I concentrated on my peripheral vision, trying to see if the three valves in front of me—looking for all the world like chimneys with spark arresters on them—matched the lessons he'd drummed into my brain. There. There was what I was looking for. A thin chain led up the side of the valves, running down the side of the boiler and terminating within arm's reach of the platform we'd descended. Manual release valves, built into the system in case the automatic boiler controls failed to function.

Berkshire was walking slowly now, moving carefully toward me. I doubted that the loss of her knife would slow her down any. From what I'd seen in the ready room, she knew more than enough ways to kill me with her hands.

Still, the kick in the crotch had made her cautious. That worked to my advantage and bought me a couple of seconds. Just as she started to move toward me, I launched myself over the edge of the boiler and grabbed for the chains running up to the relief valves.

I had a last glimpse of her puzzled face before the mass of the boiler blocked her from my view. I caught the chain with one hand, felt my hand start to slip off it and the links bite through scabs, re-opening the wounds from the tie-down chain. My free hand touched the surface of the boiler, and I finally screamed. I swung for a moment, feeling the chain slip through my grasp, then hit the guard rail below. The impact hit me midshin. I wavered for a moment, perched on the railing, then teetered over to fall on the platform.

As soon as I touched the chain, I'd felt resistance. It yielded a moment later. A shrill scream, louder than a ship's whistle heard at close range or a foghorn, blasted through the space. I turned loose of the chain immediately.

The boiler safeties vent to the stack, shunting the superheated steam safely out of the compartment. At least they were supposed to, since the steam can cut through skin and bone like a hot knife through butter.

I heard Berkshire scream. The sound was cut off abruptly, as though some giant hand had stifled her voice. Moments later, her body pelted over the side of the boiler and landed over my legs. The narrow metal railing caught her at the base of the neck. Her head snapped back at an impossible angle and stayed that way.

There are few wounds more horrifying than burns. A pinhole

leak somewhere in the pipe, not big enough to fill the compartment. But big enough.

I looked away immediately, tried to control my stomach, and lost the battle. I leaned to one side and puked. In the brief seconds I'd seen her, I'd stored up fodder for decades of nightmares.

The steam had sheared off skin and flesh, exposing her facial bones and partially destroying them. The right side of her face was gleaming bone, the eye boiled away, with a few bits of charred flesh clinging to her ear. Her hair was gone on that side, and the acrid smell of it mixed with the peculiar chemical scent of the steam. Most of her flight suit was burned away on that side, although some flesh still remained on the bones. Her breast tissue had separated from her ribcage, folded over, and hung loosely against her stomach, held there by only a thin strip of skin. The rotator cup on her shoulder gleamed white against charred flesh. The one thing about burns— they produced sterile wounds.

The left side of her face was not much better. There the steam had had less time to cook the flesh and split the skin.

Farther back along the left side of her skull, a few strands of blonde hair, miraculously uncharred, curled.

"Hey!"

I looked up. A sailor was looking down from the upper level, his face a horrified mask.

"What the hell are you—" Like most sailors, he chose actions over words. Five seconds later, he was standing next to me. "Oh, Jesus," he said. He reached around one stanchion and extracted a sound-powered telephone from its cubbyhole.

"Trust Jesus." For some reason that seemed important. I wondered why the air was so gray.

30

O F ALL the things I hated about Vietnam, the heat and humidity were at the top of the list. My cell was sweltering, hotter than I'd ever felt it before.

Voices from out in the passageway reached me, barely distinguishable, the words incomprehensible. The guards, forming up into groups of six, waiting until everyone was there.

Pigeye—his Vietnamese name was something that sounded like that—was the worst of them. Something in his eyes said he took particular pleasure in seeing us afraid, and he smiled when we screamed. Of all the guards at the Hanoi Hilton, I hated Pigeye the worst.

I could hear them outside the cell now, all six of them. Waiting.

Oh, God. I prayed, wondering if anything or anyone ever heard me. *Not again. It's too soon. I can't*—a cool breeze blew in through the high, barred window. It made me afraid for a moment. Anything out of routine was dangerous for us, anything at all. A change in the food, a new addition to the endless list of rules and regulations we had to follow to avoid beatings, even a shift change. Change was dangerous, and a cool wind in that hellhole was most definitely change.

Then it started raining. It must have been rain, I decided. I turned my face up to it, felt the wetness slide in drops over my tight skin, the breeze drying it and cooling me off even more. The sensation was so sheerly luxurious I quit wondering about it. I was finally insane, or some other altered state, an answer to too many prayers to take me out of my body for as long as the guards had me.

"Bud," I heard one of them say. I tried to shut my ears. *Dear God, if this is you, don't let them make it stop.*

Slowly, it occurred to me that I had never heard the guards address me by my first name. That, along with most of my humanity, had been ripped away from me the day I showed up here.

"Bud, come on." A hand touched my shoulder gently. I tried to run away from whatever new prelude to terror this was. We'd all experienced the sudden, irrational changes in demeanor from the Vietnamese, but—

"He's coming to," the voice said. I squinted my eyes hard against reality. "You're in Medical," the soft Southern drawl continued. "Bud, you're on the *Lincoln.* There was an accident. Do you remember?"

I groaned as consciousness came flooding back. I wasn't in the Hanoi Hilton at all. The rain, the breeze—a wet cloth on my face and the ship's normal circulation system. For just a moment, I mourned the loss of that unexpectedly poignant moment.

"There." The voice held a note of quiet satisfaction. "I told you."

I opened my eyes slowly, squinting them against the bright lights. Blurred faces above me swam into focus. Beyond them, the pale green expanse of bulkhead, that peculiar color found only on Navy ships.

"Dim the lights." The hard light in my face faded to a bearable level.

I cracked my eyes open the rest of the way and tried to concentrate on the faces in front of me. The voice I knew immediately—Carol Benning. Finally, I could make her features out.

"How do you feel?" she said quietly.

I tried to speak, but all I could manage was a croak.

"Water. Here," she answered. Something poked at my lips. I opened them, closed around it, and sucked. The fluid trickled into my mouth, soaking parched tissues. I held it there for a moment, flashing back briefly to the rain dream, then swallowed. Water slipped down my throat soothingly.

After a few more sips, I thought I'd try again. "Berkshire," I tried tentatively. The word was mostly recognizable.

Doc Benning nodded. "Do you remember that?"

"Sort of." I tried to get one elbow underneath me so I could sit up. Doc Benning put one hand on my chest and held me down. It didn't take much force.

"No moving. Not until I've had a chance to finish examining you."

"I followed her," I said, concentrating. Bits and pieces of the scene in the boiler room popped into view, isolated still shots as though they'd happened to someone else and they were barely related to each other. I filled in the gaps.

"Engineering. She was trying—there was a knife and it's in the bilges." I stopped, realizing I wasn't making a whole lot of sense.

Doc Benning nodded gravely. "You were at the boiler," she continued for me. "She followed you up there, and you found a way to trigger the steam valve safeties."

The vision of Berkshire's face swam in front of my eyes. "She's dead." It wasn't a question.

"The snipes are looking for her knife now," Carol said. "The Masters-at-Arms are with them—don't worry, they'll preserve your precious evidentiary chain."

Even in my *non compos mentis* state, the hostility sank in. "I think she killed Worthington—no, I'm certain of it."

"I think so, too. What I don't know is why."

I tried to shake my head and regretted the movement as soon as I made it. "I'm not entirely sure. But I know who might know."

Thirty minutes later, against every bit of forceful medical advice Doc Benning could muster, I left. I was moving slowly, and the flash burns I'd sustained across my face made me feel like I was wearing a tight mask. Still, the more I moved the more my muscles loosened, and the feeling of being deathly ill resolved itself into a series of specific pains and bruises.

According to Medical, there was nothing crucially wrong with me. Scrapes, bruises, and some first-degree burns. I'd let them hold me captive long enough to cover the burns with gauze. My face felt greasy as though I hadn't taken a shower in weeks. Months, maybe. At one time in my past, I'd been able to judge how long it had been between showers simply by the oil on my skin.

The ladder up to the 0-3 level was a bit more difficult. That damned right knee—normally I could blackmail it into cooperation, but this time even the worst threats of the Stairmaster didn't work. I ended up hitching myself up one foot at a time, letting my left leg do all the bending and hauling my right leg behind me like a stroke victim.

Two ladders later it was easier going in the passageway. I hitched a little over the kneeknockers but still managed to give a reasonably credible imitation of a walk down to the VF-54 ready room.

I didn't bother knocking, but simply shoved the door open and strode in. As close to a forceful stride as I could make it, at least. I figured I owed the entire squadron damned little courtesy, since one of their pilots had tried to kill me.

Silence is a palpable thing. You can feel it, touch it, almost mold it in your hands. Particularly when you're the cause.

I looked around the ready room and saw a mixture of shame, embarrassment, and, yes, even a little anger on the aviators' faces. As far as I could tell, working the time line out, Berkshire had been dead about an hour. Plenty of time for most of the story—or at least some version of it—to make the rounds on the ship. Hell, I wouldn't have put it past Doc Benning to call ahead and warn them I was coming.

From the middle of the ready room, I said to the squadron duty officer, "Find your skipper."

The lieutenant nodded, glanced at the other officers, and picked up the telephone. He murmured a few quiet sentences into the receiver, then hung up. He cleared his throat. "The captain will be down immediately, Special Agent Wilson," he said. His voice was formal and polite.

I nodded, looked at the high-backed captain's chairs arrayed in rows over half the room, and decided to remain standing. Adrenaline and anger had carried me that far, but I didn't know if either stimulant was sufficiently powerful to get me up out of a chair once I sat down. I didn't want to find out in front of Jazzman, or these men and women.

Some of them started filtering out of the ready room, shooting embarrassed, anxious looks at me. The door opened and someone else came in. I glanced up. Lieutenant Commander Brian Gerrity, once among my chief suspects.

Gerrity stopped two paces into the room and looked at me. His face was ashen, his voice barely steady as he spoke. "I heard. Oh, Jesus, sir, I couldn't have—"

I cut him off. "You could have. Any of you could have. You only had to be upfront with me about it. Whatever it is—and I don't know the details, yet—you could have stopped it. What I want to know now is why. What is so damned important to you that you all lied to me?"

Gerrity froze, as did the other officers in the room. I shook my head. "So much for honor." Suddenly, I was very, very tired. Tired of the Navy, tired of this case, and already tired of what was going to happen afterward.

I saw the door move again. A figure stood poised in the doorframe, the light from the ready room gleaming on his face. Jazzman, six feet of brilliant, blonde, golden boy. He didn't look much better than Gerrity.

He crossed quickly to me, started to reach out and take me by the arm. I shook him off, as much as I could manage. "I want to talk to you alone. Here." I didn't tell him that it was because I doubted I could make it back down the ladders to my stateroom, to Medical, or to my office.

He nodded and shot a quick glance at the squadron duty officer. The young lieutenant stood and fell in behind his colleagues as they filed out of the ready room. Finally, we were alone.

"You need to sit down, Bud," Jazzman said gently. "You look like you're dead on your feet." He winced at the bad choice of words.

I was too tired to resist. I let him shepherd me over to one of the briefing chairs and sank down into it. I'd solve the problem of getting up later.

Jazzman took a seat on the gray metal table facing me. "What happened?" he asked.

"You tell me." I didn't have the energy to mask the feelings I knew were showing on my face. "It's your squadron."

"There's at least one piece of evidence that supports the theory that Worthington was a spy," I said, keeping my voice detached and neutral. "The photo lab—that's where she was killed. What was she doing there? That was Berkshire's hobby, not hers."

"They were roommates. Maybe Berkshire got her interested in it."

I shook my head. "Not from what I know of them. From all accounts, they didn't like each other much. So they spend off-duty time together? I don't think so."

"There could be other reasons for being down there. I can think of a million right off the top of my head."

"Such as?"

"Such as blackmail. Maybe the MO knew something about her affair with Gerrity—hell, pictures even. I don't know. Or maybe it had something to do with the JAG investigation, pictures she needed for the report. You're the one doing the investigating. You ought to be able to come up with some rationale."

"I thought of those, as well as a couple of others. But there're a couple of problems with all of those theories. First, nobody knew what was going on with Gerrity, not as far as I can tell. There were a couple of suspicions, but this was probably the best-kept squadron secret I've ever seen."

"You're right about that. I didn't even know. Not for sure."

"But you suspected, which was far more than most people did. But as far as the investigation goes, I don't see that theory holding much water. Her report was done—you saw it. The enclosure list looked complete, and there was no mention of photographs on it."

"So maybe it wasn't complete. With computers, even drafts look good."

"The words do, but there's that invariable tinkering with the margins and alignment of the document. I'm not positive, mind you, but the way that report looked, I think she was about done."

"So that means she's a spy? Because neither of us can think of a good reason for her to be in the photo lab?"

His face tightened, and I saw him try to formulate a response. I shook my head wearily. "Don't even try, Jazzman. Sooner or later, someone will talk. Better I hear it from you first. While Berkshire was standing there, trying to kill me, the last thing she said was, 'You'll never get him.' "

Anguish quickly transformed his face into something barely recognizable. Just for a second, he looked worse than I felt. I tried to care about that.

"It's my fault," he said finally.

"Don't start that," I snapped, surprised at the energy I found. "She made her own choices. Not you."

Jazzman lifted his eyes up to mine. "She was my officer. I made her what she was. I can't avoid that anymore. And the rest of this," he continued, gesturing vaguely with his hand, "is probably my fault, too."

"What rest of this?" I demanded. "Quit jerking me off. If anybody's got a right to know, I do."

He shook his head slowly. "No, I don't think so. At least, you're not the only one." He shoved himself off the table, a quick, athletic move, landing lightly on his feet. I remembered the way Berkshire had leaped down off the boiler in front of me.

"I don't want to tell the story twice," Jazzman said, apropos of nothing. "Let's do this right. I'm going to get the Admiral."

31

"MAKE IT quick," Admiral Fairchild snapped. "Those Bears are thirty minutes out right now."

Jazzman nodded. "I know why they're here."

The Admiral glared at him. "You called me out of TFCC for this? We all know why they're here—because they're Russians, and because we're tracking their submarine."

"No. Because Lieutenant Berkshire tried to shoot one of them down last week." Jazzman's voice was calm and level.

"Shoot one—" The Admiral stopped abruptly. I gave him high marks on composure at that time.

"I take full responsibility. She was my wingman, and we were doing a surface surveillance patrol in the assigned area. The Bear showed up, just like when you were up with me," he said, nodding in my direction. "You remember, our orders were to VID—visual identification—only. And escort him, if he made any close approach on the battle group."

"Go on." I could see Jazzman's first sentence was starting to sink in with the Admiral. The political ramifications alone were staggering. He'd spent the last two weeks poised on the verge of an international incident, and now his star fighter CO was telling him it was all his fault.

"It started when we briefed, I guess," Jazzman continued doggedly. A haunted expression was starting to take over his face.

"I wanted to get a closer look at Berkshire. The stories Wilson has heard about her preflighting, about some of her sloppiness—I was a little bit concerned about it. Nothing major, nothing I needed to take to CAG, but something I wanted a firsthand look at. I figured if she was sloppy when I was around, she'd be worse with someone else." He saw the look on the Admiral's face. "She was a good stick, Admiral," he continued. "If I could've saved her, I would have." He paused for a moment, lost in his own memories of the day. Finally, he continued. "We briefed the mission like normal and stopped by CVIC to get an intel update. I made a few jokes about the Russians, about the Cold War, that sort of thing. The usual sort of ragging we do on them."

Jazzman's eyes had drifted off to a point somewhere on the far bulkhead, and now he snapped them back to the Admiral's face, searching for understanding. "You know."

"I know what your rules of engagement were," the Admiral said coldly. "Please continue."

"Well, as I said, they were just jokes. Things like the submarine service never being a family tradition among Russians. Because of the poor shielding on their reactors and the—anyway, a few jokes. That was it.

"She was okay on preflight," he said, trying to get back on track. "We did a little formation flying, and she was as good as I'd been told. A hot stick, the fastest reflexes of any junior pilot on board. I knew she'd be good—I knew it." His expression deepened into bleakness. "Then we split the patrol area into two sectors. I let her take the northern one, and I hung back in the south, watching to see how she'd react. The Bear turned up on schedule, just as he has for the last fourteen days. She made the call and vectored into VID. We both knew who it was, though."

I saw the Admiral glance up at the clock on the wall. Five minutes had passed, that much smaller a margin of safety until he had to make those decisions that Congress entrusted to him based on the stars on his collar. Overhead, I could hear Tomcats turning on deck, their deep basso roar blending with the higher-pitched scream of the Hornets. "Ten minutes," I interjected and saw the Admiral nod. I'd guessed his timetable correctly.

"Then Berkshire called to say he had locked onto her with targeting radar and she was declaring it a hostile act. And before I knew what she was planning, she called a Fox 2. She shot at the bastard." He shook his head, still disbelieving. "I couldn't believe she'd done it. There was no basis for it. My backseater reported no indications of targeting radar, and we were well outside the range of anything those Bears carry. She just took a shot at the poor bastard."

"And missed," I finished.

"Command destruct," he corrected. "That Bear couldn't have gotten away from a Sparrow—no way." The touch of professional pride in his voice was incongruent.

"Do you mean to tell me," the Admiral started softly, his voice slowly growing in volume, "that we're out here with our dicks hanging out in the wind because some junior nugget decided to start World War III on her own?" By the end of the sentence, he was screaming. "You're looking at a court-martial, mister."

I kept my eyes fixed on Jazzman's face. "The rest of it."

"Then I shot one," he said softly. "She was my wingman, Wilson. I had to back her story up."

"And your backseaters fell in line," I finished for him. "Is that about it?"

He nodded. "Gerrity and Franklin. It was such a good day to be flying," he added irrelevantly. "No clouds, perfect air, and the bird was—" His voice trailed off as he realized it had probably been his last flight as well.

The Admiral stood up. His face looked older than it had just a few minutes before. "Instead of starting a war, I have to stop one." He turned and left the ready room.

32

"YOU CAUSED this, you know," the Admiral said. He nodded toward the large screen display.

I'd followed them down the passageway from the ready room to TFCC, not because what they were doing had anything to do with the investigation, but because of some innate reflexive tactical response. Neither Jazzman nor the Admiral appeared to notice. Or if they did, they didn't care.

Four symbols representing hostile aircraft were tracking south, approaching the carrier dead-on. The Admiral finally deigned to notice my presence, followed my gaze to the screen, and said, "Bears. Not hard to shoot down, if I have to. Still, with new standoff weapons ranges, we need to decide. Soon."

"I didn't touch the submarine," Jazzman said, as if that made any difference. "Neither did she."

The Admiral glared at him. "And I suppose that's going to be an easy thing to explain to them? Especially trying to talk to a pilot whose got about zero capacity for independent decision making. You know how they work— everything is controlled by the ground control intercept. They're not like you people." He gazed back at the screen. "More's the pity, sometimes."

The shot hit where it was intended. Jazzman flinched.

"And there's the submarine," the Admiral mused, as though reminding himself. "Three-hundred-mile missiles on that baby." He shook his head appreciatively. "Wouldn't it be nice to have something like that on ours?"

"Admiral?" the TAO said. "I think you'd better hear this." He made a few quick movements with his hand, and the speaker overhead squawked in protest.

At first the words were hard to understand, but your ears get accustomed to accents pretty quickly. By the time the message was repeated for the second time, I was starting to get it.

INCOS-the international compact for the prevention of incidents at sea. In place since the early 1980s, the agreement represented an attempt by the Americans and Russians to avoid starting World War III out of sheer testosterone. It required each nation to avoid provoking the other and set down some rules of conduct that reminded me of a basic lesson in table manners. No shouting, no spitting, no targeting each other with fire-control radar. Just your basic everyday rules to live by.

The Russian pilot was most forcefully invoking provisions of INCOS, requesting that we clear the area to the south and generally citing operational requirements as a reason. I saw the Admiral start to bristle, and I thought I knew what he was thinking. We were in international waters, conducting freedom of navigation operations. Supposedly. In reality, checking out the new Bears and the Oscar submarine had top priority over any assertion of legal maritime rights.

I figured the Russians knew that. In the delicate games of political power, both sides were usually pretty good at sending messages to each other through tactical maneuvers. We park an aircraft carrier here, it means don't interfere. They move troops to the south, we know they're telling us to stay away from the Ukraine. The only time we'd all missed the signals was when the Berlin Wall came tumbling down.

An interpreter appeared in TFCC and stationed himself by the Admiral's right elbow. He looked up at the man with the stars expectantly.

Finally, the Admiral turned to Jazzman. "You know, I don't have many choices. Not after the stunt you pulled." He turned back to the interpreter. "Tell them we will be clearing the area at flank speed, as a courtesy to their military forces. And that we are available should they need any SAR services or other assistance." The Admiral picked up the white ship's phone to call the bridge.

LINCOLN TURNED SOUTH, heading out of the area at thirty-five knots. The Tomcats already in the air followed, snugging up closer to the carrier but still maintaining a CAP position aft. Strung out in a line behind her, the frigate and destroyer accompanying *Lincoln* also beat feet.

Thirty minutes later, the destroyer reported excitedly that the Oscar had surfaced. Only seven miles aft of the destroyer, the huge submarine roiled on the surface, pitching and yawing uncomfortably in the light seas. The destroyer reported seeing people in the conning tower, in the thin stream of black smoke billowing out from the stern escape hatch. Watching the tactical screen, I could see that the Bears had positioned themselves at ten thousand and five thousand feet and were flying hovering orbits above the stricken submarine like a mother hen clicking over chicks. Suddenly, an explanation occurred to me. "Admiral," I said urgently, moving two steps forward to stand next to him and keeping my voice pitched low. "Maybe we've got this backward."

He shot me a weary glance. "I don't have time for this. You're retired."

"But I'm not stupid. For the last two weeks, we've been operating on the assumption that the Russians were in the area to harass us. But everything they've done today, including the spurious electromagnetic signals and the frequent Bear patrols, were because of our presence. But what if they weren't?"

"I'm not following you." Apart from every other run-in we'd had, I gave Admiral Fairchild high marks in tactical savvy. He might be pissed, but he was listening.

"What if the Oscar had problems before we arrived on scene? Maybe they got out a report to Russia, maybe not. If it were a U.S. boat, what would we be doing?"

The Admiral considered the matter. "Probably about what they're doing," he admitted. "Flying patrols in the area, trying to

220

find them. Executing all of the standard sub-missing plans."

"And if Russian forces started hovering around the area where we'd last heard from the submarine?" I pressed.

The Admiral's face cleared slightly as understanding dawned. "Then we'd be damned suspicious. So, we'd probably have the entire Third Fleet out here about now." He looked away from me and back at the screen, assessing the relative positions again. "And I don't imagine we'd take too kindly to a Russian fighter jock taking a pot shot at the Bear–J out looking for our boat. That's what the J-variant does—talks to subs."

"You mean it was already disabled?" Jazzman asked. "We were— oh God."

He turned to the Admiral. "With your permission, Admiral, I'll be in my stateroom," he said stiffly.

The Admiral grunted and waved his hand dismissively. "I think you've done enough."

33

I TRACKED Doc Benning down to Medical, a stunning piece of deductive work that was characteristic of my performance this entire cruise. She was with a patient. I waited.

When she finally emerged from the treatment room, she pointedly ignored me. The corpsman running the administrative desk started to announce my presence and then caught on and shut up. Doc put the medical record she was carrying on the counter, opened it, and made a few notations. I watched. Finally, her point made, she looked at me.

"Do you need medical help, Mr. Wilson?" Her voice was as flatly cold as I'd ever heard it.

"I do. My knee." It didn't take much effort for me to look like I was experiencing that sensation that doctors refer to as "discomfort."

She glanced around, looking for another available doctor, then stepped around to look in the waiting room. No patients waiting and no other docs. She sighed and bowed to the inevitable. "Come on back then."

I followed her down to a curtained treatment room and eased myself up on the examination table, sitting on the edge and letting my feet dangle. A corpsman poked her head in and handed Doc my medical record.

"You've reinjured it," she said briskly, scanning the last report as though she needed to. "Are you taking the ibuprofen that was prescribed for pain?"

"Yes." I cleared my throat, trying to find some way to broach the subject. "But it doesn't do much for something that hurts that much."

She caught the inflection in my voice. "Most of these injuries heal with time, Mr. Wilson. You need to stay off of it for awhile, give it a chance to mend on its own. Unless your symptoms have changed significantly, I'm not inclined to prescribe anything stronger."

"Does time heal most injuries?"

She thought about it for a moment, then nodded. "Most of them. This one, I think most certainly. But don't expect it to feel better immediately."

"Somehow, it hurts more knowing that I reinjured it myself. It would be different if something had just happened, but it was my own fault."

She gave me a stern look. "Your point? The real one, I mean."

"I could use some backup. Those skinheads—that's the only loose end so far."

Her expression softened. "What can I do?"

34

HE DOUBLE-CROSSED you," Carol said, after she'd heard my plan. "It's only fair."

I tried to shrug, made it as far as getting my left shoulder to move. "It's not a question of fair."

"Still. Poetic justice."

"Justice is nice. But not important. Consequences are."

She gave me a wry look. "That's what it is with you, isn't it? This thing about physical evidence, the kind of expectations you have about people."

"Are you in or out?"

"In." She stepped closer, touched the scab on my neck. "As much as you want me to be."

Why was I always having this kind of conversation with her? Never just one meaning but layers and metaphors intertwined so tightly you couldn't cut the meaning from one part without destroying the surface facts. She asked a question to answer one, doing both so seamlessly that sometimes I thought I didn't have a clue where she was going.

Or pretended I didn't. That was the real problem, trying to pretend and simultaneously trying to ignore the sensation of those barely too-long fingernails sliding up along the uninjured skin on my face.

"At the right time," I said finally, knowing she'd understand that for what it was—a plan and a promise for later.

"So explain it to me again," she said, pole-vaulting back to reality. "What my part is in particular. I've got the big picture."

"Back up. You stay out of sight, make sure nothing goes radically wrong. At the right time, you yell for help."

"And the reason you are not asking your MAAs to do it?" She studied me for a moment, and I could tell the answer was important for her.

"A couple of reasons. First, I trust you. They're all good people, but this is going to take a little finesse. Second, some of them might have some qualms about it, and I don't want to find out too late. I need to know who else is in on this, Carol. Before something else happens."

"And I won't have them? These qualms?"

"I don't think so, but tell me if you do."

She sighed. "At least I can make sure you get medical attention if you get hurt. This time."

CAROL WASN'T ON stage until later that evening. I had something I had to take care of first. Alone.

BM1 Fullworth knocked once on my door, then opened it immediately. He ushered Petty Officer Mark Tannin in, then left.

"Sit down." I pointed at the chair.

He took his time, then slouched down into it. His eyes were dark, burning with something I didn't want to recognize, and his hair was clipped close to his skull. He was all long bones covered with hard, tight muscles stretching deep black skin tight. I figured him for maybe 3 percent body fat.

"What's this all about?" Arrogance, and the same you-can't-touch-me I'd heard in the skinhead's voice that night.

"Just want to ask you a couple of questions, that's all. That OK with you?"

"You going to read me my rights?"

I shook my head. "Not necessary. You're not a suspect."

That surprised him a little, but he hid it well. "Ask. I don't know anything you'd be interested in."

I didn't bother to pretend to believe him. As far as I could tell, Petty Officer Tannin was probably a part of some gang on the ship. If he wasn't a Crip, he knew who was. And that was enough.

"I'm investigating some skinheads. Do you know anything about a meeting place they have located on deck 5? 5–102–6–Q?" I reeled off the designation for the skinheads' lair slowly, making sure he heard me.

"No. I don't know anything about skinheads." He looked wary.

I stood. "Thanks for your time, then. That's all I wanted to ask."

It took him a moment, but he finally understood. An appraising look, then he nodded his head. "Glad I can be of help." He started for the door.

"Oh, one other thing. There're a lot of special groups on this ship—groups of good friends, people to hang with. They don't make trouble, they're not my concern."

He stopped just inside the door frame. "Except sometimes."

"Don't misunderstand me, Tannin. I'm not starting trouble. I'm stopping it. And somebody I know has a thing for poetic justice."

CAROL WAS WAITING for me at the access hatch. She'd found a pair of old stained coveralls somewhere, probably borrowed them from an engineer. Her hair was tucked up under a black watch cap. Very tough looking, as long as you didn't notice she was wearing tiny little red Keds, the same sneakers I remembered from childhood. I laughed.

"What?" she asked. I pointed at her shoes. She looked down, then back at me. "So?"

"Never mind. They're cute."

She bristled. "They're very comfortable."

"I guess so. They might get dirty tonight." From the pristine finish on the canvas, that'd be a first. She probably washed them every day.

"They're sneakers, Bud. They can get dirty."

I changed the subject before it got ugly and lost the smile. "Are you ready?"

She brandished her flashlight, the tiny camcorder, and her radio. "They fit in the pockets. I checked."

"Good. Up with you, then." I formed my damaged hands into a stirrup and lofted her up. Carol pulled herself up into the overhead, turned around while balancing on the ceiling retaining strips, and looked back down at me. "You know where you're going?"

"I do. This may take a while?"

"It might, but I don't think so. Get in position as quickly as you can. I'll give you ten minutes."

She started to turn away, then paused. "Bud, do you really think this is going to work?"

I nodded. "Maybe not as fast and certain as I'd like, but it'll work."

She turned and started crawling carefully away, working her way out of sight quickly. I checked my watch, then headed for the brig.

FOR SOMEONE WHO'D been in the brig for two days, Colburne didn't seem all that glad to be getting a visitor. Or maybe it was something I said. The youngster even had the audacity to ask me if I was going to get him off the ship.

Thirty minutes later, he was a free man. I had the Master-at-Arms escort him back to his berthing area and leave him there. I trailed along behind, out of their view, at a discrete distance.

The first scream came two minutes later. I waited until Carol radioed me that it was getting serious.

"JESUS, HE'S A mess," the corpsman said. He knelt down beside Colburne and tried to roll him over onto his back. Colburne was curled up into a position I remembered all too well.

"Bud," a voice said sharply. "Get me down."

The corpsman looked over at me uncertainly. "Would that be you, sir?"

"It would. And if I knew where to stand, I'd do something about these voices we're hearing."

"Over here," the voice insisted. I looked up at the ceiling, saw a piece of acoustic tile jiggling furiously. "Here."

I climbed up on one bunk bed and shoved the tile up. Small hands caught at the free edge and shifted it back. The bottoms of red Keds were staring me in the face a moment later.

Carol dropped lightly onto the top bunk bed, then climbed gracefully down to the deck. She went immediately to Colburne and began her assessment. She could do a better job than the corpsman. After all, she'd watched six skinheads, convinced that their suddenly free buddy had sold them out, just beat the shit out of him.

35

FERNANDEZ AND I finally found something we could agree on—he looked a hell of a lot better out of the brig than in it. Not that he'd admit it. He shrugged the whole detention off with the world weariness of been-there, done-that, got-the-T-shirt. I made sure that word of his role in catching Worthington's killer made the MDI rounds. By the time he was sprung—certainly the fastest out-processing he would ever have experienced—he was a genuine hero.

The assistant Maintenance Officer stepped in to take over Worthington's position as Av/Weaps and Berkshire's as AO Branch Officer while the squadron waited for D.C. to crank out orders for their reliefs. The MO immediately promoted Airman Fernandez out of First Division. Instead of taking care of my office and the surrounding passageways, compartments, and ancillary fitting, Airman Fernandez was now responsible for the care and feeding of Tomcat 301. And, once the MO verified that my late striker had all of his courses and PQS signed off for Jet Mechanic Third Class, he convinced Jazzman to pin a petty officer's crow on the *chollo's* arm. I was invited to quarters that morning to watch the surprise and had the distinct pleasure of seeing newly minted Aviation Jet Mechanic Third Class Sergio Fernandez damn near choke on his own cool.

After Jazzman pinned the collar devices on his coveralls, Fernandez saluted smartly, executed a flawless about-face, and started walking back toward his place in ranks with his division. He stopped dead halfway there, turned, and marched back over to stand in front of me.

I stared at him for a moment, puzzled, then understood what was happening. Petty Officer Fernandez snapped to attention and rendered me a salute. Time seemed to stop for a moment while I examined the latest evidence of what my Navy had become. I'd almost missed it—would have, if it hadn't been for a certain *chollo* airman and one damned fine last flight in a Tomcat.

I returned the salute. Fernandez dropped his arm to his side and finally returned to his place in ranks with his new division.

AFTER QUARTERS, JAZZMAN motioned to me. His Executive Officer tactfully made himself absent. From the expressions I'd seen on the Admiral's face, the XO's chance to fleet up to command of the squadron might come sooner than the Bureau of Naval Personnel had originally planned.

Jazzman had been a silent ghost in the passageways since the Bear confrontation. The sharp lines of his face were blurred, the relaxed self-confidence I'd always associated with him gone. Rumor control had it that he would be putting in a request for early retirement, something that the continually downsizing Navy would probably approve. If he was lucky. The other possibility was a court-martial.

I felt vaguely uneasy around him, almost embarrassed for him. He'd been tested and found wanting. It's always been our way to cut the losers out of the pack, leaving their carcasses lying in the sun along the fast track to promotion and stars. Seeing him now, knowing what he could have been, knowing I'd been a part of stopping it, I felt an irrational sense of anger that he was still onboard the ship. If I'd been the Admiral, I would have—

"It was a good idea," he said. "Promoting Fernandez. I wanted to thank you for suggesting it."

"MO's idea," I said. "I appreciate your inviting me out to watch it."

He looked off at the horizon, staring at something I couldn't see, seeming to struggle for the words he needed to say. I shifted my weight, wanting this awkward encounter to be over but feeling like there was some obligation I had to fulfill.

"Was it like this?" he said finally. "When you were in?"

I shrugged, not really sure what he was asking me. "Flying is always about the same. Faster jets, pilots with tits—that's about the only real differences."

He made a sharp motion with his hand, dismissing the evasions. "Command. The war. Where you were. How did you learn—how did you know? Before you face it, I mean."

I didn't want to answer that question. "You don't know beforehand," I said slowly, trying to find some easy way to say it. "You never know. Not with command, not with—the other. It comes, and you're never ready for it. The pain, getting stripped of everything that makes you human—you can't know, no one should ever have to find out. But you're there, and you find out who you are. You survive, you know what's important. That's all."

"And if you fail?"

I was surprised at how quietly the question came out.

"It happens. Every man has his limits, his critical flaws. You find yours, learn from them, and go on. Because in the end, that's all you can do."

He considered that for a moment. I wondered if he was going to ask me what he should do now, whether he should resign from the Navy, or try to use me as some sort of father confessor and ask for absolution. It would be better for him if he didn't, I knew.

Finally, he nodded. "Thank you." He started to offer his hand, thought better of it, and walked off toward the island. I thought he might have learned something after all.